ANOTHER

FIONA COLE

D1728535

To all the women who have built me up.
You're more than I could have asked for.

PLAYLIST

After the Storm - Mumford & Sons
Elastic Heart - Sia (feat. The Weeknd)
Near to You - A Fine Frenzy
Cool Again - Shoffy
She Loves Control - Camila Cabello
Yours - Ella Henderson
Take on the World - You Me At Six
Someone to You - BANNERS
He Like That - Fifth Harmony
Girl With One Eye - Florence + the Machine
I'll Be There - Jess Glynne
Born to Be Yours - Kygo & Imagine Dragons
Feel Again - OneRepublic
Shut Up and Dance - Walk the Moon
Exactly How I Feel - Lizzo (feat. Gucci Mane)
The Humpty Dance - Digital Underground

1 CARINA

I NEVER USED to spend my weekends in the office. Hell, not too long ago, I was fucking two men.

I'd been engaged.

I'd been happy.

Now, I was scrambling to shut down my computer on a Saturday to go on a blind date my four aunts had arranged as a Christmas gift.

A blind date that was a boudoir photoshoot with a stranger. They'd set it up and wrapped it with a bow in a card. I'd never forget looking up into their giddy faces as my jaw hit the floor. Who the hell got their niece a blind date that required intimate situations with a strange man?

"It will do you some good." Aunt Violet waved away my concern.

"Is this sex?" my dad yelled. *"Did you get my daughter sex?"*

"Stop being such a prude, David," Aunt Vera chimed in.

"Our girl has been down and smiling less than usual," Aunt Vivian defended. *"It will be good for her to have some adventure to take her mind off that dick that abandoned her."*

Aunt Virginia, the quietest, but by no means the calmest, just smirked, letting me know she was the mastermind behind all of it.

I'd put off their gift, but they'd hovered over me for a week until I booked it. They'd promised to ask for all the details once it was over to make sure I went. They'd gushed over the possibilities and finished off more than a couple bottles of wine as I filled out the form.

"Request a big dick in the preference box," Aunt Vivian had demanded. *"No harm in asking."*

All I could hope for was someone hot and not a creeper who wanted me to put the lotion on the skin. Honestly, I just wanted to get it over with, so I could get back to working on my projects—the only thing that sparked my interest these days.

Maybe my doubts would be proven wrong, and I'd actually enjoy myself. Maybe a ridiculously hot man would be waiting to sweep me off my feet and ignite the fire that had almost been extinguished six months ago. Someone to make me have somewhere better to be than the office on a weekend.

I'd made huge strides in my career, but I missed the girl who danced while she cooked, laughed more than not, who bravely slept with two men. I missed the girl who dared her fiancé to fuck her in public. Who owned her body and lacked any inhibitions. Who feared no man and the pain they could cause.

Shutting my car off, I sat outside the building for a few more minutes before heading in. I fluffed my hair that had been pulled up in a bun earlier this morning, practiced my smile that had grown rusty, and took one last cleansing breath, trying to go in with an open mind.

"Hello, welcome to Queen City Photography," a smiling woman greeted from behind her desk. "What can I do for you today?"

"I'm Carina Russo. I'm here for an...appointment."

She dropped her gaze to her computer and typed a few things in. "Ah, yes. The blind date session. Your match is already here. If you want to head through those doors, he's in the waiting room on the other side. Make yourself comfortable, and Sarah, the photographer, will be in to talk with you in a bit."

"Oh...okay. Thank you."

I turned, facing the door like a firing squad was on the other side. When was the last time I'd dated? Six years ago? I'd been with Jake, my fiancé, for so long, it all of a sudden hit me that I didn't remember what dating felt like. Even before Jake, I'd been in college and hadn't *really* dated anyone. It was just parties and fooling around.

What if I sucked? What if I was the worst at dating? What if this was the worst hour of my life and I was scarred from the experience? What if I never dated again. and died surrounded by all the cats I'd eventually buy so that I wouldn't have to be alone?

I was being ridiculous—a coward. My eyes slid closed, and I breathed as deep as possible, stretching my lungs, forcing them to push past the band of panic that had been squeezing them. I was Carina Russo, heir to Wellington and Russo, marketing queen, and a powerful woman. I didn't fail. I pushed on and succeeded.

You failed pretty epically at your engagement, a voice reminded me, faltering my steps.

Shut up, stupid voice.

With my hand on the knob, I reminded myself one more time. I was Carina fucking Russo. Whoever was on the other side of that door was about to have their socks knocked off. Like an engine sputtering to life, my excitement began, a coy smile forming on my lips.

A hallway greeted me on the other side of the door, and I pulled my shoulders back, making my way to the opening a few feet down. My heels clicked with authority, and the first thrill shot through me when I rounded the corner to find a man filling up an entire chair. His legs were spread wide, elbows on his knees as he looked down at his phone. I couldn't see his face, but I could see the dark head of hair attached to ridiculously broad shoulders encased in a gray sweater. I could see his long fingers moving over his screen, his hands elegant but manly.

But everything in me froze when he lifted his gaze to mine, and I was confronted with an unusual set of gray eyes. Gray eyes I'd never been able to forget. Gray eyes that had helped me through the night I'd realized my relationship with Jake was over.

His brow furrowed at the same time his lips tipped up, like he was pleased to see me, but couldn't place why. Maybe he didn't remember me.

I sure remembered him.

"Listen, beautiful. I can be the man that takes you home and finds ways to make you forget who hurt you. I can make you like it. But I'm not sure that's what you want. And I'm not the man to cause regrets." He pressed another soft kiss and I returned it. *"But if I'm wrong, then just tell me. I'll pay for those shots and fuck you before we even make it upstairs. Probably finger you in the cab on the way home."*

"Hi," I greeted, my voice a little breathy.

He stood but didn't rush to introduce himself, still studying me. God, he was tall. I wasn't short by any means, but he had to stand at least six inches above my five-eight.

I reached my hand out when he still stood there. "I'm Carina."

His brows rose, and recognition finally sparked. Sliding his hand in mine, I finally heard the voice that'd been on replay in my dreams. "I remember you."

The combination of his rough fingers encasing mine completely, and the rough tone sliding past smooth, smiling lips sucked the air from my lungs. My body blazed hot from those hands, and I held fast to my veneer of control, so I didn't melt into a puddle at his feet.

"I'm Ian."

My tongue slicked across my dry lips. His eyes tracked the movement, and my confidence grew. He was just as affected as I was.

"Nice to meet you, Ian. Again."

"So, you're my date for today?"

"Looks like I am."

He scanned my body, still holding my hand. "Good."

Unable to handle the intense stare any longer, I dropped my eyes and bit my lip, lightly extracting my hand from his. I was excited to see him, but he didn't need to know how much. The man could work a little for my attention.

"Small world meeting you here."

"I can't say I'm sad about it. But I must admit, I'm shocked to see such a beautiful woman on a blind date. I can only imagine men line up to have a moment with you."

I laughed softly. "Would you believe me if I said this was a surprise Christmas gift?"

He laughed in return, and the deep rumble washed over me, settling heavily in my core. "I actually can since mine was also a Christmas gift."

"Go figure."

A heavy silence filled the small waiting room as we both stood there. The tension expanded like a bubble around us, taking up more and more space, growing so big it could explode at any moment. What would happen when it did? Would we incinerate with the chemistry sizzling between us? I sure hoped so. Excitement thrummed through my blood, scaring me, and thrilling me in equal measures. My skin was like a live wire, the hair on end as I waited at the top of a roller coaster, holding my breath, waiting for it to tip forward and ride the exhilarating rush down.

He took one step closer...and another set of heels came clicking down the hall.

"Good, you met," a petite woman greeted us from the entryway.

Ian and I snapped to attention, blinking out of the daze we'd been in. The woman wore all black, contrasting heavily against her pale skin, blonde hair, and ice-blue eyes appearing wide behind thick lenses.

"I'm Sarah, and I'll be your photographer today. Why don't we take a seat and go over what to expect?"

Ian let me sit first before lowering next to me, letting his strong thighs fall wide, his knee brushing against mine. Just that minor contact had my breath hitching in my chest.

"So, as you know, this is a boudoir shoot. You don't have to do anything you don't feel comfortable with but be sure to communicate with each other about what feels good and what doesn't. I suggest taking advantage of the unique date and stepping outside of your comfort zone, pushing the boundaries."

Reckless ideas flooded me, and I fought to keep my breathing under control. I didn't want to scare him away by panting next to him before we even started.

"This isn't porn, so we don't allow penetration of any kind, but any form of nudity is allowed. We keep it sensual and erotic, but not graphic and gratuitous. Sexuality is such a huge part of a relationship, leaving us bared to the other person. We cultivate this experience for you to get to know each other on another level beyond the typical first date questions."

I shifted in my seat at the image she painted, and my mind flooded with thoughts of fucking him on camera. He resituated himself, and I chanced a glance out the corner of my eyes, unable to miss the bulge growing behind his zipper.

"You'll each have a dressing room with outfits and props to utilize for your shoot. Once we're done, we have a separate room for you to meet and chat, with appetizers and drinks. A place to get to those pesky first date questions. So, I'll leave you each to get ready and meet you on the other side."

We stood, and my knees shook, my heart thumping harder the closer we got to touching.

"Oh, before you go. Would you like to do the photoshoot outdoors or indoors?"

"Inside," I said.

"Outside," Ian said at the same time.

Sarah's eyes flicked between the both of us, and I looked to Ian, feeling a pinprick to the bubble of excitement when he gave me a bit of a condescending smile. I'd been given enough smiles like that over my years of working in a high-demand business consisting mostly of doubtful men.

"Outside," he said again, with a wink this time, like he knew best and expected me to follow along.

Pulling my shoulders back, I gave him my own smile that let him know what I thought about him trying to dictate to me. "Definitely inside. It's too hot outside, and I don't want to be sweaty."

One of his brows slowly rose. "I'd love to be sweaty with you."

I almost caved then and there with the promise in his eyes, but my stubborn pride wasn't backing down. "Inside."

"Ooookay," Sarah said, interrupting the battle of wills. "Inside it is. Lady's choice. You two get ready, and I'll see you in a bit."

I gave him my own wink with a victorious smile before turning and entering the indicated room to change. I'd worn skinny jeans and a sweater, but now that I'd met the man I'd be getting close with, I wanted to push the limits. Thankfully, I'd worn my black, lacy La Perla lingerie. I wasn't sure we'd get that far, but despite his condescending tone, I hoped we did.

Looking through the selection of easy-access dresses, I decided on a black wrap dress I brought myself and kept my pumps on. Looking in the mirror, I tossed my hair again and puckered my lips. "Eat your heart out, Ian."

He'd learn like all the other men that underestimated me.

I tugged the V of the dress open a bit more, exposing my cleavage to its best advantage and stepped out to the studio. Soft jazz played in the background, setting the mood. On one side was all lighting and equipment. The other side was set up like a hotel room; all whites and light colors. A bed, nightstand with a lamp, and a chair that spurred more than a few naughty thoughts. Especially since it held a large man in a black button-up and black slacks.

"You look stunning," Sarah complimented.

Ian's eyes snapped up and immediately dropped to my feet, working their way up my body like I hoped his hands did later. "Gorgeous," he rumbled.

"Let's get started, shall we? The main thing to remember is to communicate with each other. Otherwise, have fun."

"I don't think that will be a problem." Ian stepped up close, forcing me to tip my head back to hold his stare.

The snap of the camera pulled me out of the moment and reminded me that we weren't alone.

"Let's start with an embrace and go from there," Sarah suggested.

I went to move for his hips at the same time he moved for mine and our hands collided.

We both laughed and went to talk at the same time.

"Why don't you move your hands here," I suggested.

"Why don't you let me take the wheel, baby?"

His words were delivered with another schmoozy smile.

"How about I just show you what you need to do since you seem to need help."

He breathed a deep laugh. "I'm sure I can figure it out," he muttered.

The camera kept clicking as we fumbled with the tie around my waist, but not the snap holding it closed. I got his shirt untucked and four buttons opened. All of these done with muttered demands from each of us and fumbling hands. It was a mess, and we were only fifteen minutes in, each one ticking by like a bomb on all my fantasies about to blow up.

"Stop fighting me," he growled when our hands collided again to undo the button on my dress.

"I'm not fighting you."

"Then let me get it."

"It's fine. I've got it."

"You are the most argumentative woman I've ever met."

"Because I don't fall at your feet at your half-ass seduction attempts?"

"Jesus."

"Are you trying?"

"You're crazy, woman." My eyebrows shot to my hairline at the comment muttered under his breath. "Here, tip your head this way," he tried to direct, but I was already moving another way, and we bumped noses.

"If you would just listen to me," I growled my frustration.

Ian took a step back, and my heart sunk at it finally being ended, even if it was a catastrophe. But he didn't walk away like I expected. No. He squatted down enough to grip my thighs and lifted me. My hands shot to his shoulders as he stepped us toward the bed behind me and tossed me back.

I opened my mouth to argue but choked on the words when he followed me to the bed. He situated himself between my thighs and pinned my hands to the pillow. His gray eyes locked me in place, and for the first time since we started, the flame grew more than my stubbornness, forcing back any argument. I was still annoyed at his arrogance but staring up at him and feeling the heat of him over me, it dimmed.

And maybe if he kept his mouth shut, we could make it through this.

2 IAN

For the first time, she was silent. My move had the desired effect and stole her arguments, only leaving behind the attraction lighting up her eyes, making them shine like the sun on the ocean. That attraction mixed with the same look I'd seen from six months earlier: pain and curiosity. Although the pain was much more subtle than the last time.

"Not so bossy now," I taunted inches from her face.

Her wide eyes narrowing should have been my warning. Hell, the first second she put me in my place should have been my warning, because, in the next instant, she flipped me to my back, straddling me. All rational thought vanished as the blood rushed to my cock, now firmly planted under her heat.

With both hands on either side of my head, she leaned over, her long dark hair creating a curtain around us. "Does it worry you that I'm not some easy girl like you seem to be used to."

"What can I say, women tend to flock to me, dropping their panties as fast as they can." Unlike her, I didn't mind being on the bottom. Especially with the way her breasts swayed under her gaping dress. But I liked the way she fought me. It made me harder than some coy smile and easy come-on.

She rolled her eyes, moving to sit up again.

"But," I gripped her hips, loving her gasp. "I'm not worried about you giving in. I have no doubt it will happen eventually."

"Shut up, Ian."

I pulled a move of my own, quickly shifting out from under her, and letting her fall to her stomach. Before she could react, I straddled her legs and pinned her hands above her head again. Holding my weight above her, I brushed her hair to the side and ran my nose up her neck, lightly nipping the soft flesh of her ear. "So, you don't want me to tell you how sexy I think you are?"

If I expected her to melt, I wasn't paying attention.

She huffed a laugh. "I thought I was too argumentative and should let you take the wheel. Crazy was the word you muttered, correct?"

"You are definitely all of those things." She stiffened even more at my confirmation, and I hesitated for only a moment, rethinking my words. Carina didn't want me to woo her with sweet nothings. This was a woman who'd give as good as she got. Just from thirty minutes, I could tell she was ballsy and probably intimidated most men.

Good thing I wasn't most men.

"But you are also, by far, the sexiest woman I've ever met." I let my hips drop and pressed against her ass, wanting her to feel how hard I was.

She sucked in a breath that went straight down my spine to my aching balls. I tried to hold back my moan, but when her ass lifted to rub against my dick, it broke free.

I blocked out the click of the camera but could only imagine the photo she just shot. Carina's arms pinned above her head. Her forehead pressed to the mattress, her body arched perfectly to raise her ass up. Me pressed against her; my lips parted to pant against her bare neck as I grinded against her.

"How far?" I asked, only loud enough for her to hear. We were just getting started, and while I wanted to strip her bare and worship her body, I needed to know her limits.

She thrust back again, rubbing my length. "More."

I turned her, and her legs parted perfectly around my hips, making room for me between her lush thighs. Needing both my hands to feel every inch of her, I let her wrists go. Not wasting another second of mere glimpses of her cleavage, I ripped the button of her dress open not caring if it tore. I'd buy her a thousand more, I just needed to see her. She must have felt the same way about me because I heard fabric tear when she jerked my shirt over my shoulders to get it off my body.

Leaning back on my haunches, I took the shirt off and tossed it away, taking in the sight of her body bared to me.

Holy fuck.

Her breasts were full and spilling from a black lace bra barely holding them in. They sit above a slim waist and the sexiest flare of hips with the smallest amount of fabric covering her pussy. If I looked hard enough, I could make out the darker outline of her nipples under the lace. Heat thrummed through my veins while I tried to guess what color I'd reveal. Pink? Brown? A mix?

"Take your pants off," she ordered.

I wanted to push back at her commanding tone, but why the fuck would I? I think I wanted my pants off more than she did, and I wasn't going to deny myself one less piece of fabric between us. I did as she instructed, and groaned when she stretched her arms overhead, arching her breasts up. She gave me a coy smile that was more of a taunt than anything. I couldn't wait to make those lips part on a gasp—a moan—my name.

I prowled over her, shoving her legs wide to make room for myself, ignoring the click of the camera. The photographer could be telling me the building was on fire, and I wouldn't hear it. Carina and I were in our own bubble, and nothing was penetrating it until I'd finished with this woman.

Pressing kisses along her panty line, I nipped at each hip bone before making my way up her stomach, stopping to tongue her belly button. I may not be able to pull her panties aside and tongue her cunt, but I wanted to, and I wanted her to imagine what it would feel like until she was desperate for it.

Once I made it to her breast, I hovered over her nipple, but not touching her. Slowly, my hand rose past her ribs, and I held my breath waiting for her to tell me to stop before I reached the full curve. But it never came. I palmed her firm breast and strummed the nipple. Her teeth sunk into the flesh to hold back a cry of pleasure. Hooking my finger into the lacy cup, I waited, looking up at her for permission.

Her eyes flashed, and she nodded.

God, this woman was sexy—brave. I bet she had an exhibitionist streak a mile wide, and I was lucky enough to pull it out of her. Not taking my eyes off hers, I tugged the material down, and slowly lowered my mouth until the bud fit between my lips. Her head tipped back as I flicked my tongue back and forth before sucking hard.

"Ian," she whimpered.

My hips jerked at the sound, and I swear, I almost came from the contact. Not daring to stop teasing her, I moved to the other breast, my hand drifting down her body to palm her thigh and ass. I decided to press my luck, with the photographer on the other side of us, unable to see what I was doing, I reached around her thigh until I could finger the lace edge of her panties.

Releasing her nipple, I looked down at the darkened tips, wet from my mouth, hard from the torture I just put them through. I wasn't disappointed with the shade—a darker blush rose. Fuck, I would need more of those.

But first and foremost, I needed to kiss her. It'd been six months since I'd felt her lips on mine, and that night had haunted me. It had been damn near impossible to let her walk away from that bar, but she hadn't been ready. According to the wet heat pressing against my dick, she was more than ready now.

I licked up her neck and bit her chin. I wanted to torture her and make her wait for me to take her mouth, but she beat me to the punch because as soon as I was high enough, she lifted her head from the pillow and kissed me. She sucked on my bottom lip and dominated the kiss. I was a mere passenger to her needs, and I wasn't even sad about it.

But I liked control. Maybe because she pushed back so much, it made the control all the sweeter with her. So, while I let her have her fun thinking she was dominating the situation, I moved my hand further, slipping under her panties and swiping at her slit. She gasped and pulled back from the kiss, not demanding I stop.

"Would you let me fuck you?"

Her eyes bounced between mine, curious, and turned on. "No penetration," she reminded me.

"Let's break the rules."

We both groaned when I pressed my finger further between her lips. Her cunt was wet and slippery, and all I wanted was to coat myself in her.

"Would you like it? Would you try to hold back your moans so she wouldn't know you have a cock stretching this tiny pussy?"

"Ian," she moaned when my finger slid up to glide across her clit.

"We'd have to move slow, so she didn't know I'd tugged your panties aside, and slid inside you."

Her skin flushed, and I wanted to watch her come. Wanted to memorialize it on camera. I couldn't penetrate her, but there were no rules about making someone get off.

15

"You're so wet, Carina," I whispered into her neck.

She was panting now as I worked my thumb in tighter and tighter circles.

"I bet I could slip inside you on the first push. I bet you'd make a mess of me with how wet your cunt is."

Her nails dug into my back and scratched, pulling a moan from me.

"Such a dirty girl. About to come for the camera. Liking someone watching you take your pleasure."

"Please."

"More, baby? Do you need more?" I taunted. Having such a powerful woman beg underneath me had my cock harder than it had ever been before. I began to worry she was going to take me with her when she finally let go.

Needing this to end before that happened, I pressed my thumb directly to her bundle of nerves and roughly shoved two fingers inside her. Her thighs tightened on my hips just as her pussy spasmed around my fingers. I latched on to her parted lips and ate every moan she let free.

When her spasms softened to flutters, I eased my fingers out, and shifted to my side, my back to the camera. Holding her heavy gaze, I sucked every bit of moisture from my fingers, loving the sweet taste.

"I can't wait to bury my tongue inside you."

Her jaw clenched, and the hellcat came back. But this time it wasn't to argue. No, she was ready to make me lose as much control as I'd made her lose.

"Stand up," she ordered.

I thought about arguing but did as she commanded. She followed, standing toe to toe with me. She dragged her fingers down my chest, kissing each mark better as she fell to her knees.

"Now there's a sight," I taunted her. "You on your knees for me."

She narrowed her eyes before nipping at my hip bones, pulling a shocked gasp from me. With a smirk she kissed along the edge of my boxer briefs, making it better. Rationally, I knew she couldn't suck my cock right now, but that didn't shut down the hope the photographer would get an emergency phone call, and I could fuck Carina's mouth real quick before she came back.

My head swam from the lack of blood, and I needed to take back a little control before I passed out. I dug my hand in her hair, and tugged her head back, exposing her long neck straining over a hard swallow.

"Okay, that's a wrap," the photographer interrupted. I reluctantly looked away from Carina to Sarah's beaming smile as she fanned her face. "Whew. That was one of the hottest sessions I've done."

Carina extracted her hair from my fist and stood, grabbing her dress from the bed and slipping it on.

"I'll give you both some time to get changed, and then there's a room down the hall where you can hang out. You're my only session today, so take your time."

As soon as the door shut behind her, Carina looked me up and down, lingering on my cock straining to break free from my underwear. With one last heated glance, she turned and strutted into her changing room. Oh, hell no. I wasn't done with her yet.

The door was almost closed when I lurched forward, slapping my palm to the wood, sending it back open. She jerked around but didn't seem all that surprised to find me behind her. She retreated until her back hit the wall. The wide-eyed look might have been more effective if she hadn't been undoing her dress the whole time.

As soon as I reached her, I gripped the edge of her panties and ripped them from her.

"Those were La Perla."

"I don't give a shit," I growled, lifting her up before pinning her to the wall. "I'll buy you a whole new set. But right now, I need to fuck you."

"Good for you," she taunted but didn't move to get away. Instead, she wrapped her arms around my neck and her legs around my hips.

I held her stare, daring her to stop me as I tugged my boxers down, and freed my dick.

"Are you going to fuck me or just play with yourself?"

With a growl, I poised myself at her entrance and roughly shoved in. She was so wet but tight from her earlier orgasm.

Her moan powered me on. I fucked her like a freight train, lost to the feeling of being buried inside her.

She gasped for air, leaning down to bury her head in my neck, biting at my shoulder.

"Fuck," I growled at the sharp pain.

"Baby," she insulted.

"Hellcat."

She smirked, and I moved to the dresser next to us, needing better leverage. I swiped everything off the table, ignoring the crash. Resting her ass on the edge, I gripped her hips and fucked her, losing myself in the sight of my cock tunneling in and out of her bare cunt.

"Ian. Fuck."

I wanted to say anything to get a rise out of her, but my orgasm was barreling down on me, and I needed every ounce of oxygen I could get to focus on not coming just yet. Moving my thumb to her clit, I pressed down before pinching her pussy lips together and rubbing.

Her mouth opened on a wordless cry. Her back arched, and I took the invitation to bite at her breasts. I lost the battle to not come when her pussy squeezed me like a vice. Burying my face in her cleavage, I groaned my orgasm. Goose bumps broke out across my skin as I emptied everything I had inside her. Her hand was in my hair, playing with the strands while we both caught our breath.

After a moment, I slowly slid out, I enjoyed how docile she was, but also wanted to get her all riled up again. She was fun, and I wanted to play some more.

Brushing her hair back from her damp cheek, I smirked. "Have I fucked you into submission yet?"

Her nostrils flared over her deep inhale before she pushed me away.

"You are such a child," she said, reaching for her shirt.

"C'mon, Carina. Let me try again. I'm sure I can tame that mouth other ways."

She stopped dressing to glare at me but didn't say anything before continuing.

"You're a pig."

"You like it."

She hesitated because she did like it. She just didn't want to like it. It made me wonder which Carina was real. The one who wanted to be pushed into submission, or the one currently glaring at me.

"I do not."

"C'mon, Carina. I could make it fun. All you have to do is admit how much you like the way I rile you up."

"You make it annoying with your immature jokes."

"I make you laugh, and we've already established I can make you come."

"Being with someone isn't just about coming."

"I mean," I gave her my most charming smile, enjoying the banter. "It definitely makes it better."

She shook her head and rolled her eyes, tugging her purse over her shoulder before heading to the door.

"Hey, wait," I said, jerking on my pants.

"Thanks for the orgasms, Ian."

She blew me a kiss and walked out. I managed to get the torn shirt back on, if not buttoned, before I chased after her. She was just getting in her car when I got outside. I jogged to her door and knocked on the window.

She looked me over with narrowed eyes, and I got lost trying to figure them out. There was desire. She liked what happened in there. She liked the banter, and she knew I was only pushing her because I liked her giving it back to me.

But also, behind that, what should have been irritation was fear. She was scared that she liked it. The first time I met her, she told me her fiancé was in love with someone else. She'd been hurting, and it looked like the six months since hadn't done much to ease the pain. So, when she rolled down her window, I softened my tone, letting my sincerity bleed through.

"Can I have your number, Carina?"

She looked me up and down and worked her jaw back and forth before finally answering.

"No."

And then she drove off. Literally, leaving me in the dust.

Again.

3 CARINA

I wasn't sure I was breathing anymore. It was like an out of body experience, and I floated away watching myself staring down at the two pink, double lines in the box. I knew it was me standing there, hands braced on my desk, jaw dropped in shock, but I couldn't feel anything happening to my body. I had no control over it.

Why couldn't it have been food poisoning?

You know shit is bad when you'd rather have food poisoning, the flu, or even Ebola be the reason behind all the vomiting.

But no, it was another virus all together that invaded my body.

A baby.

Tears burned the backs of my eyes, and the plastic stick blurred as I slammed back into all the emotions lighting up every nerve in my body.

I was pregnant.

Taking a deep breath, I tried to calm down. Inhaled slowly in through my nose and out through my trembling lips. I wasn't usually a crier. Stupid hormones.

At least I knew whose baby it was. Thankfully I could make the deduction that Ian was the father since he was the only guy I'd slept with in the past six months.

I'd like to say I was shocked about how it happened like I hadn't been dreaming of it every night for the past six weeks. Like it hadn't had me waking up, sweating in the middle of the night, desperate for relief.

But no matter how much I thought about it, I hadn't considered the consequences. I was on birth control, and they asked for our medical history on the forms, but I hadn't factored in the medication I'd been taking the week before the date. What a naive mistake. I was an idiot.

What the hell was I going to do? I didn't even know who he was or what his last name was. How the hell was I going to find him? Did I *want* to find him?

That had me pulling up straight, my spine stiffening at the slew of issues that bombard my brain.

All of a sudden, my door flew open, and my dad's salt and pepper head popped through. "Meeting in a couple of minutes," he muttered, barely giving me any attention.

When I didn't immediately respond, he stopped and gave me a second glance. His eyes narrowed as he took in the scene.

Move. Stop standing there like an idiot and move. Swipe all evidence from your desk you dumb, hormonal, pregnant woman.

My mind could be a bitch—but a correct bitch.

If I thought he was scowling before at my damp eyes and rigid posture, it had nothing on when he caught sight of the pregnancy test sitting proudly on my desk.

"What the hell is that?" He pushed the door fully open and pointed an accusing finger. Still, I stood there. "Carina!"

I jumped when he barked my name, and I dropped my gaze to where he pointed like I was hoping to find something else—like maybe he hadn't seen the pregnancy test and was asking me about the pen that looked like lipstick. No such luck. Still a white stick with two pink lines.

"Oh, um...I...um—"

"Does Jake know?"

"What?" That brought me out of my stupor. Why the hell would Jake need to know? Then it hit me; my dad thought Jake was the father. Despite Jake being engaged to a man now.

I almost laughed. Almost.

Then I almost choked on that laughter when the man himself appeared beside my father, all playful smile and sparkling blue eyes, unprepared for the category ten disaster happening.

"Does Jake know what?"

"That."

Jake took in my father's glower, stepping into the office to follow the direction of my father's finger. His brows rose to his hairline, and his jaw dropped. "Oh, ummm..."

"How could you do this to her," my father accused.

"Jesus, Dad. No. It's not Jake's." I directed an apologetic look to Jake who was still looking at me like I'd told him I just made a quick trip to Mars and back while he blinked.

"Then who's the hell baby is it?"

"Dad—"

"I didn't even realize you were serious with anyone."

He started pacing, not even willing to hear me anymore, muttering rationalizations on how I could have gotten pregnant, and not have introduced the man to my father. He could be so old-fashioned, completely oblivious to his daughter having a one-night stand.

He froze in the middle of his pacing and faced me, shoulders back. "I want to meet him. I'm not happy that you're not married, but we can fix that."

And back to pacing and muttering about weddings. I looked to Jake for help, because despite our broken engagement, he was still my partner in crime. But even he was at a loss for words, his eyes tracking up and down my body like a baby would pop out at any second.

The amount of ignorant testosterone in the room grated on my already fragile nerves, and I snapped.

Slapping my hands on my desk, I halted my father's pacing. "I'm not dating anyone."

"But that's impossible."

"Are you serious, right now?"

His eyes searched mine almost begging for another answer. I got where he was coming from. I did. My mother was a less than...lady-like woman. They both tried to fit together when they found out she was pregnant with me, but it didn't work. In the end, she left, unable to put anyone above herself.

He didn't want that for me and raised me with structure and discipline. Getting pregnant on a one-night stand was about as far from disciplined as you could get.

"Dad..."

"We have a meeting to get to," he said, cutting me off. "We'll discuss this later." And with that he stormed out, gesturing for Jake to follow.

I stared down at the offending plastic before shoving it in my purse with a disgusted scoff. I'd deal with it later. My father was right, I had a meeting to get to, and work was something I was damn good at, and could control.

At least, I tried to.

My father went over the basics, seeking my opinion on everything, but delegating the biggest tasks to the men in the room. Each job that he passed me over for had my jaw clenching tighter and tighter. My father had groomed me for this position, made me strong enough to stand strong against any man in the business world, letting me know that as a woman I'd be looked down on— doubted and second-guessed.

But his fear of me being disregarded made him into one of the men that doubted me the most. I was his sharpest tool that he never used. Until I forced him to.

"Carina, please make sure you bring Mr. Kent's paperwork to my office before you go," he directed as the rest of the team filed out. "I'll set up a meeting to discuss what steps need to happen next."

"A meeting has already occurred, and plans are already in motion."

"I told you I wanted to be brought in on this."

"No, you said you wanted me to hand it over, and I told you that I've got it. Mr. Kent has made it clear that he is happy with my services."

"But he's not even using the full business team we offer."

"Because he doesn't need it."

"Carina..." he sighed, dragging his hand through his hair. He already knew what I was going to say, but it didn't stop me.

"Wellington and Russo is missing a big profit by not offering an individual marketing plan. Established businesses don't need the analytics and restructuring. They need to expand to different locations that have different markets while still using their tried and true infrastructure. Just like Kent Holdings and his hotel expansions."

He waved his hand, like my idea was a pesky fly that wouldn't go away and stood to leave. "We don't have time for this. Especially in your condition."

"Dad, you're not—" I rarely called him dad at work, but the room was empty besides Jake and me.

"You and Jake make a good team, and right now, it will stay that way."

A low growl vibrated from my chest at his retreating back.

"Are you okay?" Jake asked from beside me.

I took a deep, cleansing breath, trying to expand the tightness restricting my lungs. "Yeah. He just pisses me off so much. He *knows* how good I am, but he still talks down to me."

My muscles eased a fraction more when Jake's hand slid over mine, giving a light squeeze. "You know I'm here for you if you ever need me. As your friend, not just your business partner."

I turned my hand so I could squeeze his in return, giving a grateful smile. "Thank you."

"As your business partner, I support you one-hundred-percent on your choices. If you decide to keep working on the Bergamo and Brandt project without informing your father, I back you." I jerked my wide eyes to his. I may have been taking on clients under the table, so to speak, but I didn't think anyone knew. "It passed my desk a few weeks ago, and I signed whatever needed signing," he said with a smirk. "I believe in your ideas, Carina. And we are the future of Wellington and Russo. But right now, we don't need to convince your father on an individual branch to continue with your plans. We can tackle that when things settle down. Until then, I'm by your side."

A pinch squeezed my chest because the jaded part of me wanted to retort how he wasn't on my side anymore. Instead, I leaned in and pressed a kiss to my friend's cheek. "Thank you, Jake."

He was right. We were the future of this company. Unfortunately, Jake came into his position of power earlier than me when his father died. But when my father retired, I'd take over his position, and I just had to bide my time to get what I knew was for the best.

"Now, get out of here before your father tries to corner you about the pregnancy again."

I groaned. "I just found out myself. I can't deal with him on top of it."

"Are you okay?"

I froze at his serious tone. Slowly, I slid my bag over my

shoulder and looked down at the man who used to be my whole world. It was amazing how much could change in less than a year. Now, I had a small speck of a bean growing inside me, and that deserved all of me—that deserved to be my whole world. As much as I didn't want to admit it, my father was right about the timing. I needed to focus my attention on the task at hand.

"Yeah," I answered with a slow smile. "I think I'm going to be great."

I finished grabbing my belongings and rushed from the office. It was already after five, so today would be a rare day that I left before dinner.

When I got home, I grabbed my mail. A large manila envelope was crammed into my box. I scanned the delivery address as I locked the box up again. Curiosity got the best of me, and I tore into the envelope before the elevator doors closed. As soon as a dark head pressed over a naked breast caught my eyes, I quickly shoved the photos back into the file and clung tight to the package.

The elevator seemed to stop on every floor, and the photos burned hot in my hands. As soon as the doors opened on my floor, I ran down to my apartment and slammed the door behind me, tearing the photos from the folder.

In my haste, they scattered at my feet, like a black and white collage of the day I got pregnant. A CD case fell out last, but I ignored it. Instead, I dropped to my knees and my eyes glued to the top photo I hadn't even realized had been taken. In my memory of the date, the photographer had never been there. It had just been Ian and me in that room. It had just been Ian on top of me, kissing me, touching me, making me hot, making me annoyed.

I forgot when he made me laugh.

But this photo had his smile buried in my neck, my head tossed back, and my mouth open on a laugh. I looked happier than I could remember. He looked happy. I pushed it aside to reveal the next one; my face tilted up to his, with my eyes closed. He stared down at me with a look of reverence and adoration I hadn't felt in almost a year.

Tears burned the backs of my eyes again, and I knew I had to find him. I needed to do this with him.

I scrambled through the photos to find the shipping information. It took me three tries to type in the number for the photographer, hoping she'd give me his information. It rang three more times before someone picked up.

"Hello?"

"Hello, Sarah? You may not remember me. My name is Carina, and I was one of your clients. I'm looking for the name of the date that I had—"

"I'm so sorry," she interrupted. "This keeps happening. Apparently, the person you're trying to reach—Sarah—isn't around anymore. She bailed and totally ghosted on her rent last month. I bought the location a couple weeks ago and ended up with the same number."

My mouth flopped open like a fish out of water. "Ummm...do you know how to reach her?"

"No. But I'm sure the owner of the building sure as hell wished he did. Missing that money."

"Oh. Umm. Okay. Thank you."

"Sorry. Hope you find what you're looking for."

"Me too."

I hung up and sat there, wondering what the hell to do next.

On a whim, I typed *Cincinnati* and *Ian* into Google on an off chance that maybe something familiar would pop up. By the time I had finished scrolling, my feet were numb from where I sat on them.

More tears burned the backs of my eyes, and frustration grew. I shoved the pictures aside and took deep breaths. I wasn't a weak woman, and I wasn't going to sit there crying over being pregnant and alone.

I rested my hand on my stomach. "It's just you and me, peanut."

Nausea hit me, and I frantically crawled to the hall bathroom and emptied the small lunch I'd managed to eat.

Even panting and sweating, I was confident.

I was Carina Russo. I was going to kick pregnancy's ass.

Once I picked myself up off the bathroom floor.

4 CARINA

SIX AND A HALF MONTHS LATER

My stomach bounced under my palm resting there, as the elevator ascended. "It's just an elevator, baby. No need to get riled up."

I did that a lot, talked to the baby. I read that it was good for them to hear your voice, and since it was mostly just Peanut and me, he or she would be coming out very familiar with me. I smiled again when another kick landed against my rubbing hand. I'd just reached eight months, and I'd popped.

Thankfully, the black stretchy dress still fit over my bump, and I was able to dress it up with my mustard jacket, that used to be slouchy. Not so much anymore. The doors opened on the top floor of Bergamo and Brandt, and I winced when I stood upright. I needed to invest in a pair of dressy flats. The stilettos made me feel powerful, but now I just felt like a watermelon balancing on a toothpick with each step.

Another kick and I stopped to soothe Peanut. "Time to calm down now. Mommy has a meeting, and the last thing I need is a swift kick to the lungs in the middle of talking."

In response, more kicks happened in quick succession. I

narrowed my eyes at my stomach like Peanut could see me. "I can already tell you're going to be just as stubborn as me. But we'll blame any bad habits on your father."

I felt no shame since he wouldn't be there to defend himself.

A pinch in my chest still lingered when I thought about Ian, but months of accepting I was doing this alone eased it to a barely there whisper of an ache. I hated that I couldn't find him, but it was like a needle in the proverbial haystack, and in the end, I would make it through, like I always did.

Rolling my shoulders back, I walked deeper into the office, greeting the secretary. "Hello, Laura. I'm here to see Erik."

I'd been visiting Bergamo and Brandt since earlier in the year as a little side project. They wanted to open an office in London and reached out to Wellington and Russo for assistance. Since we'd already helped them set up their current business almost eight years ago, they didn't need a whole team like they had before. No, they needed me and what I wanted to offer. So, without really discussing it with my father, I supplied them with a marketing plan completely created by yours truly. A damn good one, if I said so myself.

Jake helped out a few times when I needed to run numbers and analytics, but he didn't need to waste time away from other projects that needed his full attention. So, he signed when required, and we hadn't brought my father on.

"Look at you." Laura beamed, taking in my belly. "You're radiant, Carina."

"I'm sweating," I deadpanned, making her laugh. "Why the hell is it so hot in September?"

"Because you're pregnant. It's the law that all things to make you uncomfortable will happen in the last trimester."

I rolled my eyes but shared a laugh with the older woman. She'd had three kids of her own, so she was kind enough to listen to me whenever I came in.

"I'll let him know you're here," she said, picking up the phone. A moment later, she let me know to go on in.

I opened the door, and my eyes first locked on Erik rounding his desk. I saw others in my periphery in the seating area around a coffee table and remembered today would be a full team meeting.

"Hey, Carina. Can we get you anything to drink?" Erik asked, placing a gentle kiss on my cheek. We'd become close over the past few months of working together—friends. I'd also become close to his girlfriend, Alexandra, who gave a smile and a wave on her way to the couch. At least, as close as I let people get these days.

I opened my mouth to accept some water when a voice had me choking on my words.

"Carina?" A deep voice croaked my name, pulling my eyes to the others on the couch.

Dark hair pushed back, and the most startling gray eyes I'd never forget, even if I tried.

Holy shit.

"Ian?"

What were the odds? What were the *freaking* odds?

"You two know each other?"

My gaze jerked to the petite brunette sitting pressed to Ian's side. Hanna Brandt, Erik's little sister who worked in another department on the floor below. Her eyes were wide and scanned my body, resting on my stomach. It wasn't anything she hadn't seen before, but as she looked between Ian and me, probably connecting the dots, it took on a hint of worry I'd never seen before.

I looked back to Ian to find his eyes widening as they took me in. My hand rested possessively on my stomach like I could hide the giant belly from his accusing eyes. If he looked shocked before, it was nothing compared to his jaw-dropping gawk now.

"What the hell is that?" he asked like he saw an alien poke out from under my dress.

The silence was deafening as I struggled for words. What did one say in a moment like this? *Surprise? Congratulations? Adios?*

I was saved from saying anything when someone else entered behind me. "What did I miss?" Jared, the lead IT analyst at the company, asked. He froze next to me and took in the sight of everyone frozen and slack-jawed.

Alexandra spoke up for the first time, her tone hinting at restrained humor. "I think Carina was just about to explain to Ian where babies come from."

Jared's face screwed up. "What?"

Ian scooted to the end of the couch, his eyes narrowed, not leaving my stomach like he was struggling to do the hardest math problem of his life.

It must have clicked for Jared because in the next instant he was laughing. "Oh, shit. This is good."

Both Ian and I glared at Jared, who sobered quickly, coughing into his hand. "Sorry. It's just...kind of funny."

"Shut the fuck up," Ian growled.

When Jared went to speak again, I cut him off before this could go any further. "Anyways, we can talk later," I said with a forced jovial voice. I adjusted my jacket and gave my most authoritative tone, not allowing an inch for argument. "Let's get this meeting started."

"Always in control," Ian muttered under his breath.

I was hit with a familiar feeling—annoyance at his constant need to have the last word. There I'd been fantasizing about finding him and sharing the pregnancy with him, romanticizing the looks in the pictures I had, and in less than ten minutes I was reminded of how much he annoyed me. Sure, it made me want to snap back, which kind of got me hot, but lately, my hormones had been swinging into horny territory, so I shoved it down and ignored his comment.

"I guess I should formally introduce you to my partner, Ian Bergamo," Erik spoke up.

"Huh," I breathed a laugh, barely holding back the manic chuckle brewing. I'd been so close to him the whole time, always missing him when he traveled to London for their business. What were the odds?

"Yeah, we didn't quite get to last names when we met," Ian muttered.

Jared choked on another laugh, but quickly pulled it together when Alexandra slapped his shoulder.

"Carina Russo," I stated simply.

"Next time, Erik, let's use first names when talking about the people we're working with." Ian smiled with no humor. "I had no idea you were the Miss Russo he kept mentioning."

"Well, now we know."

Ian and I had a staring duel until a petite hand rested on Ian's shoulder, pulling his attention away. Hanna squeezed his shoulder supportively, and he gave her a real grin that reached his eyes. Jealously pierced my chest, and I almost laughed at how absurd it was. I hadn't seen Ian in eight months. Maybe he was dating Hanna, a petite, demure, beautiful woman who wasn't the size of a whale.

I couldn't blame him. I liked Hanna. She was sweet and had a quirky sense of humor. She also made the most amazing choco-late chip cookies I'd grown to crave in my pregnancy. I'd spoken with her each time I visited the office. We laughed over the men in the room, grabbed lunch on occasion. But now, when I looked at her, all I felt was similar feelings I'd had to Jackson being with Jake: doubt, insecure, hurt.

When fire burned my nose, I quickly looked away from the sweet moment, and pulled out the papers, starting the meeting. I moved quickly and avoided eye contact with Ian as much as possible. Which wasn't easy considering he was the main informant on the London office they were opening. He'd done all the traveling and in-person research.

Thankfully, he was able to keep it professional, and we moved through the meeting quickly. I wasn't sure what the next step was, but the only thing I could think about right now was getting the hell out of that building. Each second it took to shove another folder in my purse, the pressure built more and more.

Go, go, go. Get out of there.

"I looked for you," Ian said under his breath across the table as everyone slowly gathered their things. They were trying not to look curious and failing miserably. It only took so long to grab a pamphlet and phone.

"Not right now, Ian. We're working." We technically weren't anymore, but anything to hold him off.

"Tough shit, Carina," he growled loud enough for everyone to hear and stop.

I didn't have the ability to form words out of the frustrated chaos swirling through my mind, so I settled on a glare.

"That's my baby," he said even louder, his finger pointing at my stomach. "I think that takes a little precedence over work."

"Maybe for you, but my work is important to me. Have a little patience and wait ten fucking minutes until we leave this office."

Ian's jaw clenched before snapping open with his own reply, but Erik cut him off.

"Well, as much as I'd love to stay and watch, I have another meeting to get to. Lovely to see you, Carina."

"We done?" Ian asked Erik.

Erik gave me a cursory glance for approval, and I nodded. "Yes."

"Good." Ian latched on to my arm and dragged me behind

him. Everyone stared with wide eyes, mostly filled with humor and excitement.

Except Hanna who watched with hurt lingering in her green depths, and I couldn't help but wonder if he pulled me out with him, leaving a girlfriend behind.

If Ian had a girlfriend, then where did that leave the baby and me? Would he try to take the baby for shared custody? My steps faltered at the thought.

Seven months—for seven months, I'd accepted that I was on my own. I made plans on my own. I prepared for a future that held just Peanut and me. Now, Ian clutched my hand, dragging me to where we would talk about a future that included him and whatever his life looked like.

The endless possibilities of what that could be swarmed and crashed through all my plans, rocking my foundation, and making me want to tug free and run.

Some nights, I'd lain in bed and concocted scenarios where I'd run into Ian, and I'd picture the man in the photos, laughing with me. We'd meet for coffee, realize we were in love, and all would work out. I knew they were just fantasies to help cope with being alone, but never in a million years had I imagined this scenario of possibly having it all taken away.

As we crossed the threshold into his office, I made a promise to myself and Peanut—I wasn't going to crumble under my fear, and I wasn't going to let him barrel through my well-constructed plans.

I knew I'd have to let him in our lives, but I would say how much.

5 IAN

HOLY FUCK. Holy fuck. Oh. Holy. Fuck.

With every step closer to my office, my chant rang louder.

That, and thinking about how soft her hand was. Somehow my mind tore in two. One side was panicking about the pregnant woman behind me, and the other was wondering how fast I could feel those soft hands on the rest of my body. Although, that thought shriveled up and died when I finally closed us in my office and turned to find her harsh scowl. I even took a step back from her until I bumped against my desk.

Rather than letting her know how shaky my legs felt, I leaned against the edge and crossed my arms, lifting my chin like that had been the plan the whole time.

"It is mine, right?"

"Maybe it's not."

"Carina," I growled.

Her hands moved to her hips, pulling the jacket she wore open and exposing more of her belly. The belly that had my baby inside it. A baby. *My* baby.

She didn't have to say it, because I may not have spent much time with her, but I knew enough to know she wouldn't screw around about this if it wasn't mine.

My throat threatened to close up on me, but I swallowed hard, blotting that out for now. Carina stood before me, her chin high and proud, her eyes hard and scared.

Carina, the woman who haunted me at night—and during the day. The woman who had me jerking off more than I'd like to admit over the past eight months was standing in my office, looking gorgeous...and scared.

I'd had an hour to deal with the fact that she was pregnant, and, in that time, the fear was crushing me under its weight. I'd barely taken anything in during the meeting, focusing on controlling the increasing pressure on my chest—trying to create a plan of action in my head. Questions had bombarded me, fears of being a father—of being responsible for another life created chaos, images of how my life would change, making it hard to breathe.

But she'd been dealing with that pressure for months. And she'd been alone.

She didn't have to be alone. "Why didn't you find me?"

One eyebrow slowly rose. "Well, Ian," she began, her tone dripping with condescension. "Without a last name, you're hard to find."

"You've been working with us for seven months. How could you *not* know?"

Her arms flung out to the side. "I don't know, Ian. How could *you* not know? Could it be I've only been here six times, and you weren't here for any of the meetings? Could it be that I was working directly with Erik? Maybe *that's* it."

She stepped away from the door, prowling further into the room with each reason for not making the connection. I had to admit, with each sarcastic remark, I recalled how much I missed her sass. No other woman had compared since her. All of them too easy. There'd been no challenge like Carina.

"You know, none of this would have happened if you'd just have given me your number."

"I'm pretty sure none of this would have happened if you could have kept it in your pants. And maybe I didn't want you to find me, thinking I wanted a repeat."

"You didn't seem to mind my company when I had my fingers between your legs or when I fucked you against a wall. In fact, I seem to remember you crying for more."

Color rose high on her cheeks, but she didn't look away. "Momentary lapse in judgment."

I shook my head and laughed. "You're still such a pain."

She didn't respond. Instead the seconds ticked by as we continued to stare, a world of tension swimming in the small two feet between us. As much as I could've stared at her for hours, we had bigger issues to deal with.

"So, what are we going to do?"

"Nothing," she answered easily, but I could hear the hitch in her voice. She was nervous. "I'm doing fine on my own. And now you know."

My heart thundered in my chest, picking up the pace until I was worried it would break free. She expected me to do nothing?

Of course, she did, Ian. No one expected anything serious from you. I shook that voice off, not liking how close it sounded to my parents. "Are you shitting me, Carina? That's my baby."

"I'm aware."

I almost laughed at how she could appear so haughty at a time like this, while my mind ran rampant.

I was going to be a father. And I had to tell my parents they would be grandparents. That thought filled me with a mixture of fear and excitement. They never thought I was capable of being more than a flippant playboy. Being a father would force them to see me. Of course, I'd have to admit that it was a one-night stand with a woman whose last name I hadn't known, and that was where the fear came in.

They'd probably shake their heads and share a look of disappointment, but I had to hope maybe I'd also see a spark of excitement at becoming grandparents.

They were both successful doctors and had spent their lives traveling abroad while they pawned me off on nannies. The world had always been more important than their son.

Maybe if they had a grandchild, they would stay for more than one holiday a year.

Maybe if I had a wife.

The idea lit like a light bulb, flooding me until it came pouring out.

"Marry me."

Her head jerked back like I'd slapped her. "What? No. God, no."

I tried not to be too offended and ignore the squeezing in my chest at the disgust twisting her face. "Why?"

"Because we've been around each other for less than an hour and we're already arguing." She held up her fingers as she listed reasons off. "All we do is argue. Because I don't know you. Because I could continue for another hour about all the reasons that's a bad idea."

"Then get to know me." I offered what I thought was the easiest solution. Softening my tone, I stepped away from the desk and closer to her. "Like it or not, Carina, that's my baby, and that means something to me. I can't brush it off like you seem to want me to. So, we might as well try."

The fear was winning over her stubborn pride, and I fought from pulling her to me and holding her close to comfort her. She swallowed hard, and I gave her space to think over what I said. I'd give her as long as she needed in here because no matter what, she wasn't walking out that door without me knowing exactly how to reach her, and a plan for what was next.

"Do you have a girlfriend or...someone in your life?"

I blinked at her question, trying to keep up with the subject change. "What? No."

"Are you lying?"

My head jerked back like she'd slapped me. "No, I'm not lying. Your faith in me is awe-inspiring."

"I don't know you."

"Again..." I tried to control the irritation her doubt arose. "Then get to know me."

She swallowed, searching my face, the moment stretching on endlessly.

"Fine. We can get to know each other." The breath I hadn't realized I'd been holding rushed out. "For the baby," she clarified.

She pushed past me, and snatched a pen and paper from the desk, bending over to write.

"What is it?" I asked, watching her hair fall over her shoulder, aching to run my fingers through it.

"What?"

"The baby? Do you have a name?"

She stood upright and rested her hand on her belly. I struggled not to do the same. "I don't know yet. I wanted to be surprised at the birth."

That didn't sound like her at all, and I liked the little tidbit that maybe Carina wasn't as strait-laced as she portrayed. Although, I kind of already knew that when she let me make her come in front of a photographer.

"I want it to stay that way. So, no finding out," she rushed out. "I've been preparing for this, and I have a plan that works."

"Don't worry. I don't plan on storming in and making demands."

Her shoulders sagged, and it hit me that that was what she

thought I'd do. Come in and take away her control of the situation.

"We need to get together and work this out."

She nodded, and I ached with the need to touch her—to feel where my baby lay. Unable to fight it anymore, I rested my hand over her belly, letting my fingers feel the soft fabric over her hard stomach. I half expected her to pull away and was pleased when she didn't.

"You look beautiful, Carina. Radiant."

Again, she blushed, and I struggled not to step closer and press my lips to her cheek to feel the warmth. Instead, I settled on using my other hand to stroke her skin, just to feel if it was as soft as I remembered. The blush deepened, and when she caught my smirk, she stepped back, pressing the paper to my hand.

"Send me your number, and I'll let you know when I'm free to meet up."

"This week," I inserted, demanding at least one thing.

"This week," she agreed and then she was gone.

I smiled going over her reaction to me touching her. She may not want to be, but she was still attracted to me, and I planned on using it as much as I could.

The thought of Carina and the baby was still terrifying. But now, picturing the family I wasn't sure I'd ever have, it actually started to sound pretty damn good too.

6 CARINA

Dad: I need to see you in my office.
Dad: Now.

LIKE A PETULANT CHILD, I repeated his message in a snarky voice, mocking his command despite him not being able to hear it.

Rolling my eyes, I pushed my phone away and finished responding to Kent's email. He asked me to travel to New York at the end of the year to get started on the hotel. Since my due date was in October, I agreed. I wasn't one-hundred-percent sure how being a working mom would go, but I'd prepared for every contingency with a list of highly recommended nannies and preschools. Not that I was sure I'd need them since our company had a great childcare program, and I had fabulous aunts already fighting to watch Peanut. But a woman could never be too prepared.

My father, of course, encouraged me to take a year-long maternity leave, which I chose to ignore. My aunts had not-so-kind words to say about his idea, knowing it wasn't what I would want, and since they were his older sisters, they had no issue saying them to his face.

I guess I also had Ian now.

I would probably know for sure if I'd returned his message from yesterday, but I just wasn't ready. Would I ever be ready?

Groaning, I dropped my head into my hands. Just when I thought I had a grip on this pregnancy thing—accepting doing it on my own—along came Ian.

He put all my plans back to an unknown balance, setting my emotions on a spiral with it. Every time I tried to nail down how I felt about him being a part of our lives, things just churned harder. The one that haunted me the most was fear. I was terri-fied of how much he would take from me—how much of Peanut I'd have to share with him. Would Peanut love him more? Would I become second-best?

My phone pulled me out of that train of thought to nowhere with a reminding buzz of my father's message. I needed to get up there before he came to get me.

I grabbed some papers I needed him to look at and covered my yawn. Each day, exhaustion wore on me a little more, but I was determined to squeeze in as much work before maternity leave as possible.

Walking the halls, I wondered what had my father issuing such harsh commands. He was brusque, but this sounded differ-ent, like he was mad. Maybe he was just eager to micromanage me a little bit more. I scoffed at the thought.

I knew he loved me—that he was proud of me, he just had a very old-school way of thinking, and I did my best to understand and continue to prove him wrong.

"You rang?" I said, popping my head through the crack in his door.

He looked up from his desk; his brows pulled low. The dark expression made even darker from the sun shining through the wall of glass behind him.

"What the hell is this?" he demanded.

I stepped closer to his desk and looked down at the stack of papers he tossed to the edge for me to see. Underneath our letterhead was the beginning of a contract with Bergamo and Brandt. But not one that worked directly with our company, but rather one that worked with me and a small team I'd assembled.

I'd tried to bring it up to him over the past few months, but he was so damn stubborn and never wanted to hear it. So, I did it anyway. Not necessarily behind his back—hence how he found it so easily. Just without taking it up with him directly.

"Where is the rest of the team on this? Why haven't I seen it before now?"

Pulling my shoulders back, I rested my palms on the top of my stomach and stood proud, not letting him steamroll me. "Because I'm handling it on my own."

"Carina..." The muscles in his jaw ticked. "Did Jake at least help you settle on the contract?"

Meaning did Jake make sure the big men didn't talk little ole me into a lower cost than what we deserved. Obviously, he hadn't looked past the first page. Otherwise, he'd be eating his words.

"No, he didn't because I can handle it myself. I *did* handle it myself."

His shoulders dropped, and his hand rubbed at his mouth, trying to hide his exasperated sigh. "I'll have to re-read it. See if we got the most out of this contract."

"What?" I breathed the word, barely able to speak past the frustration his doubt incurred.

"I've met Mr. Bergamo before. He's a hell of a shark and knows what he's doing."

"So do I."

He kept talking like he didn't even hear me. "I'm sure he worked a better deal on his behalf. I'll look it over."

Oh, fuck this. Maybe my father never saw me as a shark in the boardroom because I let him take the lead, but I was done listening to him ramble about how I failed.

"He didn't get a better deal," I spoke loudly, so there was no doubt that it was time for him to hear me. "I know because I talked Mr. Brandt up ten percent. And no changes are needed because it's *my* contract. End of story."

Jake took that moment to walk in, stealing my father's attention.

"Did you know about this?" My father asked not bothering to greet Jake.

Jake looked to me, and I continued to stand tall, I would not cower. This was my chance to force my father to hear me, and I wasn't letting it go another second without him acknowledging what an asset I was for this company.

He moved to look over the paper still lying at the edge of the desk and didn't allow any emotion to show.

"Yes, sir," he answered easily. "Carina brought it to me."

"Did you check it?"

Two things make Jake the go-to guy for my father: he's fifty-percent owner since his father died, and he has a penis, making him supreme. Which he laughed about constantly because he claimed I was the more supreme worker any day of the week.

"I didn't find a need to. She ran it through the proper legal channels before bringing it to me. I trust Carina and the work she does."

Stupid hormones. That was the only excuse for the lump of emotion currently working its way up my throat. Jake was on my side at work, but I was missing it in my personal life, and having my father continuously question me didn't help the despairing doubt. Before, I'd had Jake in both personal and business, but since our breakup, there'd been no one.

"Jesus," my father's head fell back. "We're probably losing money."

It's like he didn't hear a word me or Jake said.

Time to slap him with facts he couldn't ignore.

"This is one of three projects I've taken on this past year." He opened his mouth to interject, but I spoke over him. "Just this month, I've increased our revenue by thirty-two percent. All by myself, by offering only marketing projects."

"Carina, you can't just use our company's name to take on solo projects without consulting the team."

"I can, and I will." My tone dropped into dangerous territory. He knew me well enough to know the signs of my patience thinning. "I didn't consult the team because I didn't need to. I utilized the correct resources to make smart decisions because I'm damn good at them." Peanut chose that moment to kick, and I took a deep breath, trying to calm my racing heart. This past year, I'd lost part of myself. I did these projects behind my father's back where before I'd have been strong and stood my ground, but here in his office, I was reclaiming a bit of myself. "I've tried talking to you about this, but you always shut me down."

"Because it's silly."

My blood pressure spiked. *Sorry, Peanut.* "It's not. We're missing out on a whole market that has already established business techniques and just needs marketing. I want to create a branch for that."

"Now isn't the time." He gestured to my stomach like that justified everything. "Give it a couple of months. Maybe Jake and I can sit down with Owen and figure out if it's worth it."

"Of course it's worth it," I shouted, throwing my arms wide. "Look at the numbers."

"Carina," his soft, pleading tone was the only warning I needed, to know I wasn't going to like what I heard. "You know how the business world works."

"That it's a man's world," I repeated his words back to him that I'd heard since high school. "But you raised me to hold my own in it, and it's about damn time you realized I can. It's time you realized that they should be scared of *me*."

It was time I reminded myself of it. It was time I remembered I wasn't just being a strong woman for myself, but for my child too.

"Carina..."

I looked back to Jake, and he remained stoic at my side, only giving me a minute nod of support. It was all I needed.

"I will not negotiate. I can submit my already-made business plan or my resignation, but I'm done with this."

His jaw clenched tight, and his eyes sparked with hurt, but I ignored it. He pushed me here, and I was done waiting for him to come to my side.

"I need time to think about it."

"Be fast, because I'm a hell of an adversary, and I don't think you want me on the opposite side."

I didn't wait for a response. Instead, I stormed out and didn't stop until I'd made it to my office.

"You okay?" Jake asked. I hadn't realized he'd followed.

"Yeah, yeah." I dragged trembling hands through my hair, the energy of the fight, leaving me weak. "Thank you for that."

"Any time. You know I trust you and agree with moving the business forward. He just doesn't want people walking all over his daughter."

"Then he can come to meetings and watch me crush them like the tiny men they are."

He laughed at my passion. "I always said you're the real shark on this team."

I laughed with him.

"Hey, I wanted to give you this," he said, reaching into his suit pocket. "I know it's soon, but I'd love to have you there."

I opened the thick cream envelope and pulled out a beautiful, simple wedding invitation. And my heart dropped.

I didn't want my heart to drop. I knew it wasn't a rational reaction or one that even matched up with my thoughts. But when you're with someone for as long as we were, your body reacts despite your mind, and mine just dropped my heart to my stomach seeing the two names boldly engraved on the card.

Jackson Fields and Jake Wellington.

Not Carina Russo and Jake Wellington.

Any confidence I'd gained earlier dimmed. Two names on a piece of paper and I shrank back into the woman I was after the breakup. I forced my most confident smile even though I knew it didn't reach my eyes.

"I wouldn't miss it."

And I wouldn't. Jake was my friend—my partner, even if he wasn't my life partner anymore. I wouldn't miss him getting married for anything.

He leaned down to press a gentle kiss to my forehead and left.

I dropped the envelope and pushed the feelings aside. I was just lonely, and maybe a little jealous.

But maybe I didn't have to be alone right now. Not taking time to consider my fears, I picked up my phone and quickly sent out a message.

Me: Dinner at Nada tomorrow at seven?
Ian: I knew you couldn't resist. ;*
Ian: Meet you there.

I rolled my eyes at his response.
But I also smiled.

7 IAN

SILVERWARE CHIMED amongst the quiet hum of talking. The restaurant was too posh to be noisy.

But it all translated to white noise as I waited for my parents to arrive for lunch. Nothing was loud enough to break through the nervous chaos running rampant in my mind. I almost laughed at the situation I found myself in. A thirty-three-year-old man shaking in his boots, about to tell his parents he knocked a woman up, hoping they didn't think too lowly of him. Jesus, could I be any more of a little boy hoping for their approval.

I knew one thing; they'd love Carina. She was strong and put together.

My father's salt and pepper hair stood tall above the other patrons entering the restaurant. My mother towed behind him as he broke through the waiting guests. When he approached the table, I stood, wiping my sweaty palms on my slacks before shaking his hand.

"Dad."

"Son."

My mother moved around him, and I still had to lean over for her to kiss my cheek, even when she wore her stilettos. How she balanced in them, I'd never know, but she vowed to wear them every chance she got, claiming she wore tennis shoes and scrubs enough that she had to dress up when she could.

"Hey, Mom."

"Ian," she held my face in her palms and looked me over, seeming to approve of what she saw because she released me and sat in the chair my dad pulled out for her. "How are you?"

I had to take a deep breath and put the reins on my nerves, demanding I shout it out. I didn't want the first thing out of my mouth to ruin the meal before the appetizer. "I'm good. Staying busy. Nothing to complain about."

Before we could continue the riveting conversation, our waitress came over, and we ordered.

"So, how was your trip?" I asked, getting the conversation going again. Sometimes, conversation between my parents and me could be stilted.

"It was good. Africa is always beautiful this time of year," my father answered.

"We're sorry we missed your birthday."

Not only had they been gone—which was nothing new, they'd missed over half my birthdays—but they also hadn't called until the following week. "It's okay, Mom," I answered on rote.

"Time just goes by so fast, and the dates blur together," she explained.

"I understand." I didn't understand, but it was easier to just say I did.

"How's Erik?" my dad asked, changing the subject.

"Good. He's been happier with Alexandra."

"It's good he's finally settling down."

Somehow, I was always surprised they never asked if I was settling down. Was I so disinteresting to them to not even inquire?

I ground my jaw and took my opening, knowing it wouldn't come from them. "Speaking of settling down, I called you here for a reason."

Our waitress took that moment to bring us our food. After everything was situated, I began again.

"So..." With a deep breath, I laid it all out there the only way I knew how, with a little bit of light humor. "How do you feel about being grandparents? Because I'm nervous as hell about being a dad."

I used my best business meeting smile and held my breath as two sets of wide eyes meet mine, their silverware dropping to their plates.

My mother was the first to recover. "I had no idea you were seeing anyone seriously."

My dad cleared his throat. "That's great. It's about time you settled down. I'm assuming we didn't miss the wedding?" he asked, his brows lowering, forming the deep grooves of disapproval.

I opened my mouth to correct him, but my parents were on a conversation roll, which meant I wouldn't get many words in edgewise.

My mom slapped my dad's arm, playfully. "Of course not."

"Obviously, that will be remedied," my dad said to my mom like I wasn't even there, and they were so sure of my future. "So, when's the big day?"

I thought about it and realized I didn't even know when Carina was due. I did the math quickly in my head and figured she must be close to eight months along. "She's due next month sometime."

Again, my mom was the first one to see the missing connection. "Next month? Why are we just now hearing about this if she's eight months pregnant?"

My dad might as well have not even heard her. "No, Ian.

When's the wedding? If you haven't already set the date, maybe you can do it soon or closer to Christmas so we can be there without having to book an extra flight home.

Did he really just ask me to plan my future around their trip next month. I laughed softly, trying to hold on to my patience, but it was hard when he always managed to push my buttons. I didn't even know why I was shocked by his comment. Their lives—their trips—always came first. I looked across the table at their expectant eyes, and my blood pressure rose.

"There's no wedding, and we're not together. The reason you're just now hearing about it is because I found out about it not too long ago."

"What?" My mother lifted a trembling hand to her lips like I'd announced I murdered puppies.

"It was a single date—"

"Another one of your one-night stands," my dad sighed, and I struggled not to react to his disapproval.

"It was a single date, and she didn't have a way to get a hold of me. We happened to run into each other yesterday, and to say I was shocked was an understatement."

Just reliving the moment now had my head spinning, and my heart thumping harder. The image of her tall body, round belly, and wide blue eyes stole my breath all over again.

"Well, I'm not surprised. I've been waiting for something like this to happen eventually from you. You never take things seriously."

"Except my business," I defended with my jaw clamped.

My dad leaned across the table, leveling the same gray eyes as mine at me, letting me feel the full weight of his disappointment. "Life is more than one-night stands and work, Ian."

"Seriously?" I asked, gesturing to the two people who left me alone most of the time to work.

"We're a family," he proclaimed, stabbing the table like he was making his point.

"No, you and Mom are a family. I'm just some trophy you leave on the shelf at home."

"Boys," my mom admonished. "Not here. Please."

My father leaned back in his chair, but nothing in his stare changed.

"When do we get to meet her?" My mother's overly chipper tone tried to break the tension, and it barely put a crack in it.

"I don't know. I'm meeting her for dinner tonight to discuss where we go from here."

"You marry her," my father decreed. "That's where you go. I didn't raise you to abandon your kid. For once, Ian, try to be dependable to someone other than yourself."

"You didn't raise me." It was a petulant comment, but he was pushing me hard.

"Ian, please," my mom pleaded quietly. She knew she was just as guilty as my father for leaving me alone.

I dragged a hand down my face and blew out a hard breath. I tried to get my irritation under control, but when I looked across the table and saw the contempt on my father's face, I knew this lunch was over. Neither of us was backing down, and he wouldn't hear anything I had to say past this. We both needed to cool down before any more talking happened.

"I have to get back to work," I said, tossing money on the table for more than my meal. "I'll keep you updated on what I can."

Without bothering to meet their eyes or stay for hugs from my mom, I bolted. I needed to get back to work, something I couldn't be questioned on.

Back at the office, I sank into my chair, grateful to not have run into anyone. I wasn't in the mood to chat or explain my sour attitude. I looked at the clock and saw it was just past two. That gave me plenty of time to get through my crowded inbox and tackle a few phone calls. I needed to be done before seven, so I could meet Carina for dinner.

God, my heart thundered in my chest, sending an electric current of excitement through my veins. I'd thought about her more than I wanted to admit over the past eight months. Hell, even before then, when I'd only spoken to her briefly in the bar last year. She'd been beautiful and hurting, and I'd wanted to be the man to make her feel better, but she'd turned me down, which had probably been the right choice. I'd been drinking my woes away too, after another argument with my parents.

But after having her, tasting her, touching her, knowing what her cries of pleasure felt like, what her heat felt like wrapped around my cock, there was no coming back from that. I'd fucked a few women since then, but it'd been hard to concentrate on them, and Carina had always been there in the back of my mind. Now, I'd get to sit across from her for dinner and discuss our future.

The idea had a smile stretching my lips like a love-sick fool. Not that I loved her, but I loved that baby. I'd only rested my hand on her stomach, but the connection was there—the want and need were there. My dad could say all he wanted about me not being dependable, but that baby would know nothing other than devout devotion from me. It'd be the family I never had, and I couldn't help but see Carina by my side in that image.

Maybe I'd leave work early and grab some flowers. The restaurant was just around the block, so I'd have plenty of time.

I HUNG UP THE PHONE, and dropped my head back on the leather seat, running my hand over my face. The phone call had gone on longer than I'd expected. Between the excruciatingly long conversation and my parents at lunch, my brain was fried. I was ready to power down my computer and go home, maybe drink and watch baseball until I passed out.

Just as my computer shut off, a woman came barreling in. She smiled as she prowled across the room, ocean blue eyes locked on me like I was fresh meat and she hadn't eaten in years.

"Rebecca."

One of the few women I'd had a repeat with over the past six months.

"Miss me?" she asked, rounding my desk.

Not really, but instead of answering, I gave her an easy smile. It wasn't her fault; I just didn't miss any of the women I fucked.

"Because I missed you." She gripped the fabric of her pencil skirt at her hips when she stood before me and began bunching it up. "I happened to be in the area and thought, why not stop by for a quickie. You've always been up for that."

She bared her creamy thighs exposed above her black lacy garters before she wedged her legs on either side of mine and straddled me. Immediately my hands moved to her hips to hold her steady, and she took the invitation to latch on to my neck, humming her approval.

I leaned back to give her room but hesitated when I thought of Carina. Would she care that I had a woman on my lap? It wasn't like we were together, and I could really do with blowing off some steam for the day.

Just as I began to let myself give in to the woman on top of me, my eyes snagged on the clock on my desk. Seven-thirteen.

Alarm bells clanged in my head, and it hit me like a train—fucking dinner with Carina.

"Shit. Fuck. Fuck."

"Yeah," Rebecca moaned when I gripped her hips hard. But it quickly shifted to a gasp when I shoved her off and tugged her skirt down.

"I can't do this right now—or ever. Sorry, Rebecca, but I have to go."

I ushered her out of my office and to the elevator, opting for the stairs so I could sprint down and save time. Before I left the building, I sent a quick message, praying she didn't send my ass to the curb forever.

But knowing I deserved it if she did.

8   CARINA

Ian: On my way.

On his way? *On. His. Way?*

I re-read the message at least seventeen more times, very quickly losing my mind until I was screaming it in my head.

I sat my phone down on the wood tabletop before I chucked it against the wall in a fit of rage. I'd been sitting at the table for twenty minutes because I was a responsible person and showed up early. And now it was fifteen minutes after he was supposed to be here, and he messaged me with on. His. Way.

This must have been what it felt like before people went on a massive killing spree because I think I could kill him, and everyone that got in my way of that task.

I snatched the last chip from the basket and almost crushed it when I shoved it in the salsa, barely paying attention to what I was doing. I probably looked like a rabid animal as I chomped a bite off, my lips snarled, my eyes trying to set fire to the empty seat across from me. Not only was I sick and tired of waiting for some incompetent asshole, but I was also hungry—no, I was hangry. The chips and three glasses of water weren't cutting it.

I'd been thinking about this dinner for the last twenty-four hours, and my nerves were frayed. I'd run through all the possible outcomes of what we'd decide, but one thing had been paramount; I'd been hopeful because I wasn't alone in this anymore.

Hope was stupid, and Ian was even more stupid for making it enter my mind.

Stuffing the last bite in my mouth, I made a decision. Fuck Ian. Fuck this fancy-pants restaurant with their delicious, unfulfilling chips.

Ian could show up to an empty table for all I cared. I was done waiting, and I wasn't going to sit there for another second. No, I was going to McDonald's because a Big Mac sounded epic right now. And a large fry. And a coke, god their coke was the best.

I let the waiter know with the best smile I could muster and a big tip for wasting his time.

Just as I'd made my way through the door, Ian damn near crashed into me.

"Oh, thank god. I thought I'd miss you. But I'm here."

My nostrils flared, and I ground my jaw, taking him in. His chest heaved over panting breaths like he'd run here. "Really, Ian?"

He held up his hands like he was holding me off from an attack. "I had a phone call that ran overtime. It fried my brain, and I'm sorry."

I didn't give an inch, instead, taking my time to look him up and down and glare like I found him less than. Anger flooded my veins and nothing else. At least, until I saw the orange-ish smear of lipstick on the collar of his shirt. Then the anger was diminished when another emotion poked through. Hurt. So much hurt.

Like the last remaining bit of hope was obliterated and the sharp edges from the explosion pierced my lungs.

How dare he make me feel like this? I was Carina Russo. I didn't get stood up by men so they could fuck around with someone else. Not anymore. His eyes widened when I took my time stepping in his personal space. I did my best to make myself as intimidating as possible even when I had to look up to meet his eyes.

"You wanted this," I said through my clenched jaw. "*You* wanted to meet me for a chance to talk this over. And you show up late with some lame excuse about a phone call? Like I can't see the disgusting lipstick on your shirt? Reeking of someone else's perfume."

If possible, his eyes widened more, and he jerked back and pulled his collar out to find the offending mark. His mouth fell open, and he looked to me with panicked eyes, taking a breath in to issue his defense. But I didn't want to hear it.

"This was a mistake." My shoulders dropped in defeat, and I turned to go. Before I'd even turned the other way, he grabbed my arm and pulled me back, the panic still covering his face.

"No, it's not, just let me explain."

"I'm eight months pregnant, Ian." I cut him off, this time with a lot less fire and a lot more exhaustion. I didn't have time or energy to fight. "I'm tired, and I need to focus on what's to come. I can't depend on someone who can't even make a fucking dinner."

He dug both hands into his dark locks, and it almost sparked the urge for me to do the same. I remembered how soft they felt under my grip that day I'd had the pleasure of touching him— when things had been so much easier.

"Goddammit," he grunted to no one but himself. He took a breath and held his hands up again, pleading with me to hear him. "Okay, Carina. I fucked up. Honestly, I did have a phone call that ran late, and I did forget the time. An old hookup surprised me at work just as I was ending the call, and you know what, I'd had a shitty enough day that I let myself go for a bit. At least until you popped into my mind, and I immediately remembered dinner."

I fought my cringe as he admitted the woman coming to him and him liking it. I wanted to turn away from it, but he wasn't done. He dropped his hands to his side and took another deep breath, his tone pleading.

"I'm sorry. I fucked up, but it wasn't because I was fucking someone else. So, please—*please*—give me a chance here. Just to eat. Just to talk. Because, Carina, that's my baby and that..." His voice cracked, and he swallowed before continuing. "That means something to me. You don't know me, but that *means* something to me. So, please, just talk to me."

Watching the emotions mar his face hit me harder than his words. It wasn't so much the words, but the way he said them that had me giving in.

"Fine." I lifted my chin and stood tall, doing my best to look down my nose at him. "But you better feed me because I'm hangry and I'll snap your head off if you breathe wrong."

He laughed but sobered quickly when I didn't join him. "Okay. Let's go back inside."

Reaching out, he tried to direct me back inside with a hand to my back, but I stepped away. "No." He turned to me with wide eyes, probably expecting another argument. "I want a Big Mac now. So that's where we're going."

"McDonald's?" He looked at me like I said I wanted to dine in Timbuktu, and I glared harder. "Okay. McD's it is."

We ended up driving separately, and it didn't take long before I decided not to kill Ian when he set a Big Mac meal in front of me. He stared with a mixture of amusement and awe as he watched me suck down a small coke and sigh in satisfaction.

"So, any other cravings?"

"Not right now," I said around a bite of French fries. I quickly moved on to my Big Mac and giggled a little at how happy I felt when that tangy sauce hit my tongue. We ate in silence--well, him in silence and me moaning around every bite.

"Thank you." I sighed and wiped my mouth, slouching back in the hard, plastic chair, rubbing my belly. Ian watched every movement of my hands, choosing not to comment on my complete mood swing now that I'd eaten.

"How has the pregnancy been?"

My hands paused, and I looked up, losing myself a little in his gray eyes. They always fascinated me, the color so unique and sharp. I shook my head out of my trance and remembered his question.

"It's been okay. Nothing monumental. I had morning sickness, but nothing too extreme. I'm uncomfortable most of the time, especially now, but nothing is wrong. So, I'm grateful for that."

"Good. I'm glad everything is okay. Are there any other cravings I should know about?"

I laughed when he looked down at the meal that no longer existed with raised eyebrows. "Not really. Nothing consistent. Except fruit. Which makes me think it's a boy. It's one of those old-wives-tales that you crave more sour things when it's a boy. Sweets if it's a girl."

His head cocked to the side. "I'm surprised you don't want to know the sex. You are always so in control of everything; I figured you'd want to be with this too."

"Nope. I want to be surprised when he or she arrives."

"You're not curious? How are you buying things?"

"I just buy everything in gray and yellow. And I'm not finding out the sex, so don't bother trying to change my mind," I defended.

He held up his hands in surrender. "Wouldn't think of it. I'm excited to be surprised with you."

"Good."

"When is the due date?"

"October eighth."

Ian blinked a few times and sat back in his seat like the date made it more real and knocked him back. "Wow. So soon."

"Yup." I didn't know what else to say.

"Do you need anything? Anything I can buy for the baby —for you?"

A lump formed in my throat and I forced it back down. *Jesus, Carina, he offered to buy you some diapers, not sweep you off your feet.*

"No, I have everything. I've had quite a few baby showers, so I'm pretty stocked up. The rest I'll get as I go. Although I still need to get one of those fancy glider chairs for the room. I've read they're essential."

"Okay. Good. If you need anything else, let me know. I'll get it."

I offered a small smile that he returned, and we settled into silence, because the easy stuff was covered, and the bigger topics were looming.

"What do we do next?" he asked.

I helpfully offered a shrug.

"Do you want me in the room? To hold your hand?"

That lump rose again at the eagerness in his voice. He wanted to be there for the delivery, and his words from earlier in the night finally hit me with some truth. This meant something to him, no matter how he screwed up, it did mean something.

But I didn't know what I wanted next. All of a sudden, this pregnancy—that had been racing at me a second ago—seemed so far away. Like a lifetime could happen between us in the next four weeks.

"We have a month. Can we just...take some time? Get to know each other?"

"Yeah," he gave an easy nod and swallowed. "Yeah. Whatever you need."

"Thank you."

"Will you let me know if anything happens—if you go into labor?"

"Of course. I'll keep you updated."

"Thank you."

Silence settled again, but it lacked the stress and tension. It was lighter like we had cleared some fog and we could see more of the path in front of us, even if everything beyond was still hazy. At least we had somewhere to start.

"Well, I should get going," I said, clearing up my trash.

At my car, I went to open the door when his hand grabbed mine, stopping me in my tracks and bringing my eyes to his. "Carina, I am sorry. I want to be there for you both, and I'll prove to you that I can be. We'll figure this out, and I'll be there to do it."

I wanted to give in to his words, but I remembered the twenty minutes I sat in a restaurant eating chips while he made out with some woman, and doubt held me back. I tried to give him some affirmations, but nothing was holding the doubt back from coloring my voice. "Okay, Ian. Night."

His eyes slid closed as if he was in pain, but it wasn't my job to make him feel better. He did this. When he opened them again, he tried for a smile, but it didn't reach far. "Goodnight, Carina."

He stepped closer and placed his hands on my stomach

between us, leaning to press a soft kiss to my cheek. All the air sucked from my lungs at his touch, but he pulled back before I could do anything but barely register the heat that spread from his touch.

Just a single touch and my body burned for him.

Stupid hormones.

9 IAN

Ian: Craving anything??
Ian: I can have it here waiting for you.
Carina: I'm good. Thank you.
Ian: Sure?
Carina: Yes.
Ian: What about me? Are you craving me? ;*
Carina: *rolls eyes*
Ian: Ha! I don't hear a no.

"Look at you, smiling like a fool," Erik said as I strode into his office.

I flipped him off, but he wasn't wrong. The past week Carina and I had been exchanging text messages. Well, I'd been sending them, and she'd been giving brief responses in return. But I was hopeful I'd break her down. I knew she had a wild side—I'd seen glimpses of it—but I knew she'd been hurt. It would take time to bring it out, and I was willing to be a patient man.

"Hey, Little Brandt," I greeted Hanna, who was already sitting on the couch. "How's life down in accounting?"

Bergamo and Brandt took up two floors of the sky rise, and Hanna was a floor below. Erik and I had claimed the two biggest offices, even though he won the better one. I tried to demand a rematch in Rock, Paper, Scissors every year but he never took the bait.

"It's *accrual* world down there," she responded with a smirk, standing to meet me halfway across the room. "But we do our best to be *audit* we can be."

I laughed at her jokes, pulling her in for a hug. "Someone is full of puns this morning."

"Better than dirty jokes like *someone* I know."

"Whatever, you love it." Pinning my arm tight around her, I held her close and gently rubbed my knuckles atop her head. She squealed in laughter at my soft noogie.

She broke free and brushed the dark strands out of her face, her green eyes sparkling with happiness, bringing forth my own smile. I did all I could to make Hanna happy. After what she'd been through, she deserved more.

Once her hair was clear, she leaned in for another hug. "I do love it," she said softly.

A throat cleared behind me and I turned to find Carina standing proud, her chin lifted high, Jared next to her. He was rubbing the back of his head like he was uncomfortable with mine and Hanna's affection. She was like a sister to me, and he was used to how we interacted over the years, which made me question his reaction until he glanced toward Carina.

Did Carina see it differently? Was she jealous?

She wasn't even looking at me anymore. Instead, making her way over to shake Erik's hand. She didn't even care I was in the room—I highly doubted she was jealous of the noogie I just gave Hanna.

"Where's Alexandra?" Carina asked.

"She had a study group she had to be at. So, we can go ahead and get started."

The meeting moved quickly. Or it seemed quickly. Probably because I was stuck in a trance watching Carina move around her trifold posters. Her hands moved animatedly as she talked, taking moments to rest on her round stomach. I even caught her looking my way a time or two. She quickly looked away, but not before I gave her a knowing smile.

Before I knew it, we were all packing up, getting ready to go back to our own work.

"Hey, Ian. Do you want to grab some lunch?" Hanna asked, pulling my attention away from staring at Carina.

"No can do, Little Brandt. I'm going to try and talk Carina into having lunch with me. Maybe tomorrow?"

She looked down before returning with a smile that looked a little forced. "Yeah. Totally." She hesitated, looking past me to Carina. "So...she's really pregnant with your baby?"

My heart thundered like it did every time I thought about it. "Yeah," I breathed, turning my attention back to Hanna. "Can you believe I'm going to be a dad?"

"It's hard to imagine," she admitted. Her eyes lifted, shining like melted emeralds, so much like Erik's, except filled with more warmth than I'd ever seen from my best friend. "You're going to be amazing, Ian. You always are."

Hanna was family. She'd known me since we were kids. Having her approval eased a knot in my chest. I pulled her in for a side hug and pressed a kiss to the top of her head. "Thank you, Hanna."

"Any time."

Before Carina could bolt, I gave Hanna a wave and ran to my baby-mama. "Hey," I called when we stepped out of the office.

She turned, her nose still raised high. How someone shorter than me could look down at me so efficiently amazed me. It had to be a special talent of hers because no one had done it quite like she did. "You want to get some lunch?"

"I can't. I have an OB appointment."

"Is everything okay?" Alarm bells rang in my head, and she must have seen the panic because her face softened.

"Yeah. It's just a check-up. Listen to the heartbeat and that kind of stuff."

"Whew." I lifted my hand to my forehead. I may have been more relieved when she even cracked a smile at my reaction. "Can I—Would you mind if I came?" She hesitated, and I rushed to plead my case. "I'd love to hear the baby."

Another soft smile let me know my answer before she did. "Sure."

When I pumped my arm and hissed "Yess," I even got a laugh from her.

Her laugh choked off when I leaned down to press a quick peck to her cheek, her eyes widening like saucers. I thought about apologizing for possibly crossing a line, but I wasn't. So, instead, I smiled down at her and whispered, "Thank you for letting me come."

I smiled the whole way to the doctor's office and even while we waited. When we got called back, I put on my best mature, I'm-the-baby-daddy face. The nurse did all the regular things, checking Carina over. When the boxes were all checked, she asked Carina to strip from the waist down and let us know that the doctor would be in.

"Will we be able to see the baby?" I asked before she could leave the room.

"Ian..." Carina admonished quietly, but I ignored her and kept my eyes on the nurse.

"Oh, umm, we've already done a twenty-week ultrasound. We don't usually do another unless we need to see something specific."

My heart sank, and I'd never been so devastated by such a small piece of information. I felt like a toddler, not getting his way.

"Is there anything we can do?" I asked, not ready to give up. "I kind of missed the beginning, and I was hoping to catch up."

She must have felt the desperation pouring off me because she gave a smile and narrowed her eyes like she was considering my request. "Sure. I'm not sure if we can do the 4D ultrasound, though. It's not always covered by insurance."

"I'll pay whatever extra it costs."

The nurse laughed at me. "Okay. We'll make it work."

When she left, Carina moved to sit on the edge of the table, the paper crinkling with every adjustment. I lounged back and frowned when she just stared at me. "What?"

"Leave, Ian."

"It's not like I haven't seen it all." Her lip curled, and I knew that was the only warning I'd get. "Okay, okay. I'm going. Call me back in when you're ready."

I'd only been outside for five minutes before she called me back in, a thin pink sheet thing covering her lower half, her flowy black shirt covering the top.

"So, is all this normal? Stripping down with your butt bare back there?"

"Ian." She tried to sound irritated, but the laugh she couldn't hold back ruined it.

"Don't act like if I walked around this table, I wouldn't find your beautiful ass there. That sheet thing is only so big."

Carina shook her head, biting her lip to hold back more laughter. "Yes, this is all normal," she answered. "I'll have them once a week in this last month."

"Can I come?"

Her blue eyes shined, reminding me of the sea I saw when my parents took me on a trip one time to the Amalfi Coast. They were wide and surprised by my request. "You—you don't have to," she stuttered, shaking her head. "I can just message you updates."

I reached across the space between us, resting my hand atop hers that clung to the edge of the padded table. "I want to. I want to be here for you both."

Swallowing hard, she finally gave in. "Okay."

There was no holding back my smile. It felt like a small step was taken in the direction of me winning her over. Winning her over to what, I wasn't sure yet. But I knew I needed to be closer and maybe this concession narrowed the gap.

The door opened, and a woman with short dark hair and glasses came in with a warm smile. "How are we doing today?" she asked Carina before her gaze turned to me. "And who is this? Dad?"

"Yeah."

"I'm Ian. Nice to meet you."

"Nice to meet you, Dad." She shook my hand and looked me up and down before returning to her iPad. "Okay, your stats look normal. I'm going to do a quick exam, and then the tech will be in with the ultrasound. I hear we're getting to see baby today."

"Yeah," I breathed.

"Then let's get started. Is it okay that Dad stays in the room?"

I gave Carina my most pleading eyes, mouthing *please* as I scooted my chair back to be up by her head.

She rolled her eyes. "Fine."

"Yes," I hissed victoriously.

"Just stay up here."

"Yes, ma'am," I agreed with a salute. Before the doctor disappeared between Carina's spread legs, hidden under the sheet, she looked at me. "She's always bossing me around."

The doctor just shook her head and was gone.

"Shut up, Ian."

"Remember what happened the last time you told me to shut up?" I asked, a slow grin spreading. I wish I could have filmed her reaction so I could watch it forever. Red bloomed on her cheeks even though she tried to hide it with a laser stare. *You do,* I mouthed, bobbing my eyebrows.

The doctor must have hit a spot or something—I really had no idea what happened down there—because Carina winced and hissed, reaching out to grasp something. Thankfully, my hand was there at the ready and damn did she have a firm grip.

"Almost done, Carina," the doctor explained.

Carina nodded and bit her lip, her eyes scrunched closed. I covered our clasped hands with my free one and gently stroked back and forth, doing my best to soothe her.

"All done." Carina exhaled a huge sigh and finally relaxed. "Now, I just need to examine your abdomen, and it'll be over. Can I lift your top?"

Carina nodded and pointedly didn't look my way as her round stomach was bared. I stared in awe at the firm skin pulled tight around my baby. Her belly button protruded a little, and it was adorable. She winced and squeezed my hand again when the doctor pushed on a tender spot.

"Okay. We're all done. Everything looks great. The tech should be in in a bit, and I'll see you next week."

"Thank you, Dr. Sawyer."

When the doctor left, I couldn't keep my awe inside anymore. "Look at you," I breathed.

"I look like a whale." Carina went to cover her stomach, but I held her hands in place.

"You look like a goddess." I smiled in wonder up at her and

then back to her stomach. "That's our baby you're carrying. You're amazing, Carina."

She held my stare as her eyes glazed over. I didn't comment on her reaction because a muscle jumped in her jaw, and I knew she was clenching her teeth like she could will the emotion away. This woman didn't show emotion lightly.

Her hand jerked over her stomach, and she winced. "I guess Peanut didn't like being pushed on. He's kicking."

"He?"

"I call the baby by different pronouns to avoid calling it 'it' but I change it up."

"It's good to be fair. Wouldn't want to convince it one way or another."

Carina laughed. "I don't think that's the way it works."

I looked down just in time to catch another thump pushing against the skin. "Wow. Jesus, that's amazing. Can I...can I feel it?"

"Sure."

We were making progress; she didn't even hesitate before giving in. I held my hand against the spot where the last kick happened and waited. When I felt it, a burst of laughter erupted from me. "Holy shit!"

Carina was laughing with me with each kick I felt.

Not thinking about it, just acting on instinct, I leaned forward and kissed her warm skin. She gasped, but I didn't pull back. Especially when she didn't protest, she smelled so good, like coconuts and sunshine.

"Hey, baby," I said right against her skin. "It's Daddy. I hope everything is going well in there. I know it's getting tight, but soon you'll be able to roll around in all the space you want."

I peeked up at Carina to find her eyes glazed over again, and her lip firmly clasped under her teeth.

Another kick brought my attention back to her stomach.

"That's a hell of a kick. Are you going to be a soccer player? Or maybe that's your arm, and you'll play baseball just like Daddy." Another kick and I was so excited; I just got lost in the moment. The next thing I knew, Carina was laughing—her whole body shaking—as I started doing baby-talk. "Who's gonna be the best baseball player ever? You will. Yeah. You will. You're gonna kick all their asses. Yes, you will."

"Ian," Carina reprimanded around her laughs. "Stop swearing at the baby."

I smiled up at her, and I could have stayed there forever, but I didn't want to press my luck. Pressing my lips one last time to her skin, I stayed close and whispered, "I love you." Because I did. So much, I ached in every bone in my body for this baby I hadn't even met yet. But I knew I'd die loving he or she more than anything I'd ever loved.

After a moment of silence, Carina asked, "You played baseball?"

"Yeah. All through college."

"Why didn't you go pro?"

I shrugged. "Lots of reasons. Honestly, I just wanted a scholarship so I could get through college without asking my parents for a thing."

Carina's brow furrowed and her lips parted. I knew a question was coming because even I could hear the bitterness coloring my tone. But before she could get a word out, the door opened again with a plump woman backing in, dragging a machine behind her.

"All right. Let's get this party started," she said.

She was efficient, and before I knew it, the screen filled with the profile of my son or daughter, a thumb firmly planted in their mouth. The tech used her mouse to point out different body parts and did plenty of screenshots of tiny feet and tiny fists and tiny everything for us to take home.

Fire burned at the back of my throat, but I was holding it together. At least, until she switched it over to the 4D ultrasound. The grainy black and white image shifted to a sepia color of blurs. She moved it this way and that, trying to avoid showing us the gender, until finally, the tiniest, most beautiful face appeared.

Tears slipped down my cheeks, and I didn't even care to wipe them away. Carina's soft hand slipped in mine, holding me tight. I looked to her with my jaw dropped and didn't have to say anything. She just nodded and squeezed tighter. Not wanting to miss a moment, I turned back to the screen to take in the little nose and tiny mouth.

When the monitor was shut off, and a handful of pictures were given to me, I'd finally pulled myself together.

I waited outside, flipping through the printouts, unable to believe it. I'd been telling myself I was going to be a father over and over again but seeing is believing.

Along with the beautiful reality came a wave of panic. My chest squeezed, and my head swam. Oh, shit. I was going to be a father. I was going to be in charge of this tiny perfect thing. Me.

I was going to fuck it up—ruin it all.

I struggled to pull deep breaths in through my nose, but I did it because Carina was about to step outside, and I didn't want her to find me in a full-blown panic attack.

We made it all the way past check out before she finally asked. "You okay?"

"More than okay." It was true because the love I had for our baby far outweighed the fear, and I decided to focus on that. "You want to get some lunch?"

"Sure."

"How about Mexican?"

"Blech. I want a burger."

"How many burgers have you had this week?" I asked playfully only to get a glare in return.

"Listen to me, Ian. We're getting burgers, and that's that."

I shook my head and laughed. "You're still a crazy woman."

She swatted me but laughed too, and the last of the panic slipped away because, for the first time since meeting Carina again, I felt like we were officially in this together.

10 CARINA

Friday.

Ian: Show me our baby.
Carina: What?
Ian: Show me that beautiful belly.
Carina: OMG! Ian!
Ian: ... waiting.

Ian: Damn, woman. Our baby is lookin' good.

Saturday.

Ian: Can we talk so I can talk to Peanut?
Carina: In a minute. I'm eating.
Ian: It's a cheeseburger, isn't it?
Carina: Shut up.

Sunday.

Carina: Do you know that Big Burgers won't deliver a burger to me! What is Uber Eats even good for?

Ian: Gasp.

Ian: Those bastards.

Carina: Right?!

Ian: Want me to bring you one?

Carina: No. I'm a mess today, and I want to continue being a mess.

Ian: Okaaaay.

Carina: Don't judge me, Bergamo.

Carina: OMG! You brought me a burger. AND FRIES! I'm so happy!

Ian: It wasn't me. Must have been the burger fairy.

Carina: Well, I'm eternally grateful. So is Peanut.

Ian: Eternity is a long time. I could come up with a lot of stuff for you to show your gratitude for an eternity.

Carina: I'm not even going to respond to that. I'm going to eat my burger.

Monday.

Ian: Cheeseburger for lunch?

Carina: No. :(

Carina: I'm having a salad from home. I need to cleanse my body from the grease.

Ian: Let me know if you change your mind.

Wednesday.

Carina: I just got to work, and I already want a burger. It's been a long two days.

Ian: Your abstinence is admirable.
Carina: It is. I deserve a reward.
Carina: I'll add a chocolate shake today.
Ian: Well deserved.

I scanned over the message again, unable to stop my smile. I'd been doing a lot of that lately, staring down at my phone smiling, waiting for it to ding with another message. Hoping to hear from Ian. It probably wasn't a healthy addiction, but maybe it was good we were building a slow connection through messages rather than face-to-face.

We tended to bicker when we were around each other, so the messages were a good barrier to get to know each other.

"What are you smiling at?" Jake asked, pushing through my cracked office door.

I shoved the phone to the side and sat up straight with my most innocent face like I'd been caught looking at porn.

"Nothing."

His brows scrunched, but he smiled and shook his head, letting it go. "It's good to see you smile more."

"I smile," I defended.

"Yeah, but you're more serious."

"Well, that tends to happen when you're dumped."

I regretted the words as soon as they popped out. I was feeling cornered and judged, and I snapped. I hated seeing his downcast eyes and clenched jaw. I hated seeing the guilt. If for no other reason than it reminded me of the demise of our engagement. But we still had our friendship, and I decided to let the past go so I could hang on to my friend. I didn't have many.

"I'm sorry. I'm just hungry."

His lips quirked up on one side. "You mean, hangry?"

"Maybe," I said innocently.

79

"We ready to go over these numbers?" my father said, striding into the room, his eyes glued to a stack of papers.

"I thought we were meeting in your office in ten?"

"We figured we'd meet here, so you didn't have to waddle across the floor," Jake joked.

I gave him the middle finger at the same time as sticking out my tongue. I liked to mix petulant with adult hand gestures.

"Hey, now," my father admonished. "That's my little girl you're talking about."

Jake and I laughed because my father had put up with us play fighting since we were teens. At the same time, my chest warmed a little at his defense. It wasn't always so hard to be around him, and it was moments like this that I remembered he really did love me, just in his own way.

"Before we get started, I wanted to give you this," my father said, sliding a file folder across my desk.

I flipped it open and froze. My lungs worked overtime, and stupid tears burned the backs of my eyes as my mouth spread into the biggest grin. "You signed it."

"Not that you left me much choice," my father grumbled. "I looked it over, and not surprisingly, it's a good plan. You are my daughter, after all." I beamed with pride under his compliment. "There are stipulations with the timeline. Like it or not, Carina, you *are* pregnant and about to have a life-changing event. You'll need time to adjust, and I don't want you adjusting with too much on your plate. So, yes, it will happen. But we will talk time-lines after your maternity leave."

I pretended to think it over, but he was right, and I didn't want to argue. "Okay." He flopped down in the chair opposite my desk and sighed. "Thank you, Dad."

He didn't say anything, just gave me a wink and started the meeting.

We were finishing up the last page of the report when my

secretary, Anne, poked her head through the door. "Carina, someone is here to see you."

Her wide eyes and flushed cheeks sparked a bit of alarm. Was someone angry? Someone that shouldn't be there? "Tell them I'll be with them soon. I'll be free in a few minutes."

"Umm..." She held on to the door jam and turned to look down the hall before whipping her head back in. "I don't thin—"

"Burger fairy, coming through."

My eyes nearly bulged out of their sockets at the voice coming closer to my door. Anne stepped back and in walked Ian. I mean the burger fairy.

A rush of heat washed over me at seeing this tall man in a charcoal tailored suit, stretched around his broad shoulders, fill my doorway. My heart thundered, and I couldn't tell if it was excitement at seeing him in my space, panic at having him in my space with my ex and my father, or sheer joy at the aroma of juicy burger wafting across the room.

He stepped all the way in, and I almost jumped out of my seat when I saw a cup with white cream on top.

"My milkshake," I whispered, bringing all eyes to me.

Feeling heat rise in my cheeks, I cleared my throat and looked down until I could school my expression into something other than awe.

"Thank you, Anne."

Anne took one more long look at Ian's backside before finally walking away.

"You're Ian Bergamo, right?" my father asked. "From Bergamo and Brandt."

"Yes, sir," Ian answered, setting the bag and drinks down on my coffee table, way too far from me. "Nice to see you again."

"Again?" Jake asked, looking Ian up and down with shrewd eyes.

"Your father and I helped set up his company almost nine years ago," Dad explained to Jake.

"Yes, sir," Ian said, giving his most charming smile. "Still going strong. I was sorry to hear about Mr. Wellington."

"He was a good man." There was a moment of silence for the other half of our company before Dad spoke again. "This is his son, Jake. He's been filling in perfectly the past few years."

Jake stood and shook Ian's hand, and it was a bit surreal to see the man I was supposed to marry right next to the man whose baby I was having.

"Are you here to talk to Carina about the London project? She usually meets you there, right?" Jake asked.

And all at once it hit me.

I hadn't told my father or Jake that Ian was the father. I'd been so busy with work I honestly hadn't even thought about it. My skin prickled with panic at the scenario about to unfold. Like a train wreck, I could only stand by and watch.

Ian's gray eyes lifted to mine, and I knew it was coming. My pulse thundered in my ears, and I couldn't hear anything but saw his lips move. Saw their heads jerk my way.

"When the mother of your child wants a cheeseburger, you bring her a cheeseburger."

"The what?" Jake and my dad said in unison.

I think I started laughing, but it was dangerously close to a cry. "Yeah, didn't I tell you?"

"You sure didn't," my father growled.

Ian's brows dropped low, and something like hurt flashed behind them. The baby chose that moment to kick hard up into my ribs. I gasped and placed a hand on my stomach, bringing Ian to my side. "You okay?"

"Yeah, yeah." The heat from his hand on my back wasn't helping the light-headed feeling. "Just a kick to the ribs."

Ian's hand dropped to my stomach, and he leaned low. "We

talked about this, Peanut. Only kick out and avoid all vital organs."

Forgetting everyone in the room, I smiled at the dark head hovering over my belly. I think I swooned a little when said head shifted and the beautiful lips I'd been thinking of too much lately, smiled up at me.

"Carina." Dad barked my name, bringing me out of the trance. "What the hell is going on?"

I quickly recapped the story of how Ian and I ran into each other, and by the end, Jake looked a mixture of contemplative and concerned, while my dad's chest puffed up more and more.

"You going to make an honest woman of her?"

"Dad," I gasped.

Ian laughed softly. "She won't let me, sir."

My father's shoulders dropped, and he laughed too, shaking his head. "Sounds about right from my daughter."

I felt like I was in an alternate dimension when my father stretched out his hand, and Ian grabbed it.

"Don't let her walk all over you. I raised a real ball-buster over there." He winked my way, and it might have been one of the best compliments he ever gave me. "I'm glad to hear the business is doing well. I guess I'll be seeing you around."

"It helps that we had a solid foundation to build on, thanks to your work."

My father stuffed his hands in his pockets. "Don't be a kiss-ass."

"Dad," I gasped again. Jake laughed beside me, and I slapped his arm. "It's kind of funny," he defended.

"Traitor," I muttered.

"Well, I won't stand between my daughter and her cheese-burgers. We made it through with barely any cravings, and this one came at us hard. Thankfully, we're all here to support her addiction."

"Oh, my god. Just go," I pleaded.

Jake pulled me in for a hug and kissed the top of my head. "Let me know if you need anything."

When they stepped out, Ian closed the door behind them.

"Who was that?" he asked far too lightly.

"What do you mean? My dad and Jake?"

"Who's Jake to you?" he asked, his eyes sharp like a knife.

I thought about playing dumb, but it wasn't like I had any reason to lie other than to avoid an uncomfortable conversation.

"My ex-fiancé."

"The guy who left you upset at a bar doing shots that night?"

Sometimes I forgot how I'd met Ian initially. I forgot that he'd seen me at one of my lowest points. "The one and only."

"Dick," he muttered.

I huffed a laugh. "He's really not. It'd probably be easier if he were." Ian hummed and looked at me, but I was over this conversation. "Now bring me my burger."

"Yes, ma'am."

Silence descended in the office other than my hums of happiness with each bite.

"Oh, my god. This shake is giving me life."

Ian laughed, polishing off the last of the fries before tossing the box in the trash. "Yeah? You want to share so I can know how good it is."

I scowled, holding the cup close to my chest. "No."

He held up his hands in surrender. "All right then."

I took another long drink and looked him over. He made the loveseat in my office look minuscule under his big body. A body I could remember every inch of. A body I wanted to be under again.

Suddenly, I was hot, and having a hard time prying my eyes from his crotch. The way he lounged back with his legs spread invited my eyes there perfectly. God, he'd been big. Like a tripod. And he'd known how to use it.

I missed sex. I missed sex with Ian. Once wasn't enough.

"Carina?" His soft voice called my name like a siren, but also snapped me back to attention. Needing to form words before I asked him to try and have sex with me, I said the first thing I could think of.

"I have a doctor's appointment tomorrow." The words were aggressive like I'd shot them out of a gun. His brows rose high, and I rushed to follow it up in a softer, I'm-not-imagining-your-big-dick, way. "If you wanted to come."

He smirked like he knew what I'd been thinking, but thankfully he let me off the hook. "I'm there."

"We won't get to see the baby," I warned.

"Carina," he sat up, resting his elbows on his knees, focusing his laser attention on me. "I'll be there, no matter what."

"Okay."

The silence stretched as I considered how serious he was. Ian was a smooth talker, and I was a little off my game right now, with my hormones hijacking my body, so I was easily misled. But he didn't give the slightest indication that he wasn't in this all the way.

"I have a favor to ask you," he began, breaking the silence.

My eyes narrowed. "Okay."

"I'd like you to meet my parents."

"Oh…" That wasn't what I expected. "Umm…okay."

"Are you sure?"

Was I sure I wanted to meet my baby-daddy's parents? No. "Yeah," I answered instead. "I guess I'll meet them soon anyway. When were you thinking?"

"Tonight?"

"Umm…okay."

"Good, because I told them we'd be there."

"What if I was busy?" I asked, pursing my lips.

He gave an arrogant smile just to get a rise out of me. "You'd make it work for me."

I rolled my eyes—a typical move around him. "You're so presumptive."

"I like to get my way." He shrugged unapologetically.

"Good luck with that."

"I don't need luck. I'm getting skilled in the ways of Carina."

"Please. I could crush you."

"And I'd like the fight." The words were low and almost a growl reminding me of all the other things he'd growled in my ear that night.

I tried to lift my chin and give him a regal ice stare, but my body was on fire.

He slapped his hand on the side of the couch, making my heart try to jump out of my chest. "Okay, I have to go. I've got a meeting I can't miss. Erik would throw a fit if I made him meet this client on his own." He rolled his eyes but smiled. "Can I pick you up?"

"I guess."

"Good. See you at 6:30."

Maybe by then, I'd be less of an over-heated, lust-filled mess.

A girl could hope.

11 IAN

"Thanks for doing this."

Carina turned her head and smiled from the passenger seat, the descending sun shining through the windows, lighting her up. God, she was gorgeous.

"Of course. Family is important to me. So, it's good for me to know Peanut's grandparents."

"They're excited about the baby. Not so thrilled with the way it's playing out," I muttered. "But thrilled nonetheless."

"What do you mean?"

"I guess..." I took a deep breath, considering my words to explain my parents without the bitterness seeping out. "I guess they're more traditional about family. Their first question when I told them was when the wedding was."

I tried not to let Carina's snort from beside me sting, but something about her complete denial of me as a husband pinched a nerve.

"It wouldn't be *that* terrible."

One eyebrow slowly rose above her doubtful eyes. "Ian. Come on."

"We've been good lately," I defended.

"When? The few handful of times we've been around each other? Of course, our track record is good if we don't actually see each other to bicker."

I gave her my best charming smile. "I'll just keep plying you with cheeseburgers, and it will all be fine."

The small giggle she let free at my joke sank deep in my bones and settled, filling me until I thought I'd float away. All from a single laugh.

I'd felt heat and desire and passion. I'd felt need. Need to fuck, to touch, to taste. But this warmth building in my chest was new, and it scared me enough to change the subject.

"So, I've met your dad. What about your mom? Is she a mogul of another company somewhere?"

The smile died from her face before she looked out the window, hiding her reaction. "I don't know. She left shortly after having me." Another laugh, but this one was full of resentment that mirrored my own. "She tried for a while. But you could say my dad's traditional views were a lot for her free spirit."

"I'm sorry, Carina."

She shrugged. "Meh. It happened a long time ago. Plus, my dad has four older sisters. Peanut will have plenty of female love."

"That is a lot of women." I shook my head, trying to imagine four sisters. Hell, one was hard to imagine. "Will I get to meet them then?"

"Oh yeah, and they will eat you up."

I pulled to a stop and turned off the car before facing her. "Then it's a good thing I'm delicious."

I left her laughing in the car and ran around to open her door, enjoying the electricity that shot up my arm when she placed her hand in mine to get out.

As we walked up the steps to my parents' ostentatious house,

I muttered out the side of my mouth. "Wink three times if you want to get out of here."

"Will do. Eye twitch it is for escape."

I mimicked the move, over exaggerating, as I opened the door. She had to rest a hand to her stomach as she laughed, and I wanted to slam the door, pretend we were never there, and take her somewhere to be alone. But it was too late because my mom pulled the door open the rest of the way and tugged me down for a hug.

"Ian," my father greeted from the other side of the foyer, a glass of scotch in his hand.

"And you must be, Carina." My mother's eyes flicked between Carina's bump and back up to her face. "Look at you. You're gorgeous."

"Oh, thank you. You're too kind."

"Way too beautiful for my son," my father said, stepping up to shake Carina's hand. I fought not to roll my eyes. He delivered it as a joke, but I heard the undertones of truth.

Carina blushed a little but didn't drop her stare from my father's, and it was the same bold look she gave Erik and me in meetings. I bet she was a total shark when it came to business. I knew she drove a hard bargain when Bergamo and Brandt hired her.

"I'm Santo, and this is my wife, Mirabella."

My mother skipped the handshake and pulled Carina down for a hug. My mother was barely above five-foot, and Carina towered over her, especially in her heels, which I had no idea how she was still walking in.

"Thank you for having me. Dinner smells delicious."

"Well, I sure didn't make it. I'm not much of a cook, much to my Italian mother-in-law's distaste." She waved us toward the dining room. "Now, come sit. Would you like water, tea? We have just about anything."

"Water would be great."

I made sure to pull her chair out and perform all the perfect gentlemanly duties.

It didn't stop my dad from making little digs here and there, all under the veil of joking. I somehow made it through most of dinner without drinking glass after glass of bourbon. Looking at Carina through the meal helped immensely. She was gorgeous and calm and polite. Not that I expected anything else, but she knocked each conversation topic out of the park.

"So, do you have any family traditions around the holidays?" Carina asked.

"We don't really *do* holidays," I answered before my parents could. "Mom and Dad are usually gone."

Carina's smile slipped for the first time the whole meal when she looked to me with concern. Apparently, I hadn't done a very good job of masking the resentment.

My mother rushed to smooth it over. "I'm sure we can be here for a few holidays for the baby."

"Of course. For the baby," I raised my glass, saluting my mom before taking a drink.

My dad hid his scowl behind his own drink, forming a smile by the time he set it back on the table. "So, Carina. Have either of you discussed what you will do next? Marriage," he suggested like he was asking if she wanted cake after dinner. "Maybe move in together?"

"Oh...umm." Carina fidgeted with her fork as she thought over her words, looking to me for help. I responded with as many winks as I could muster, bringing forth a sigh of relief.

"Ian, what's wrong with your eye?" Mom asked.

I rubbed at my eye. "I feel like something is in there."

Carina hopped in without missing a beat. "That was bothering you before. Maybe you should rest it."

"Yeah, it's been slowly getting worse as the day goes on." I gave the most sympathetic look I could manage to my parents. "Sorry, but I think we should be heading home."

"Are you sure? We could move to the sitting room for drinks and coffee," my mom suggested.

"I appreciate the offer, but I also have to work tomorrow. Early meetings."

"Of course, of course. Let us walk you out."

We all made our way to the front door and handshakes, hugs, and promises for future gatherings happened before we were finally set free. I made sure to rub at my eye a sufficient amount to keep up the ruse until we got in the car.

By the time we made it to the end of the driveway, we were both laughing.

"Wow, you really went for it," Carina said.

"Had to make it convincing. And what about you? I almost felt real concern from you for my poor eye."

"Yeah, right."

"Come on. Admit it; I even had you going. The poor father of your child would have to wear an eye-patch. Our baby would have to grow up believing I was a pirate."

"The horrors. We'd probably have to lie and hide you away. We lost him at sea," she said with an exaggerated frown.

"Don't let her convince you, Peanut," I said in the direction of Carina's belly like if I leaned over a couple inches, the baby would be able to understand me. "Daddy would be the coolest pirate you've ever known. I'd make eye-patches a new fad."

When I parked in front of her building, her head was thrown back, her smooth neck exposed. Her hands resting atop our child as she laughed. She was beautiful.

"Thank you for coming tonight."

"Any time, Bergamo."

She got out and was surprised to find me on the sidewalk waiting for her. "You don't have to walk me in."

"Of course, I do. I'm worried for your health in those heels."

"I should stop wearing them, but they make me feel powerful."

"Trust me, Carina," I said, holding the door open for her. "You are more than powerful, heels, or not."

I rested my hand against her back, walking her to the elevator. She didn't press the button, instead, turning to me with pinched brows. "So, you and your parents don't get along so well?"

I looked away, a little embarrassed she picked up on the tension. Did she agree with them? Did she think I was unreliable and wasting my time too? "Yeah, I'm a poor little rich boy," I said, brushing it off as a joke. "They just weren't there often, and I missed out on having a family for the family holidays. Mostly it was my nanny and me, or I was with Erik's family."

She reached out to hold my hand, bringing my eyes to hers. "I can see why being here for the baby means so much to you."

Her wide, blue eyes pulled me in like a magnet. Her understanding had me stepping close, brushing her dark hair behind her ear. "Just trying to keep up with Wonder Woman," I breathed the words, hoping she could feel them on her mouth since we stood so close.

"Ian," she whispered.

I licked my lips and knew it was all over when she stared down at my mouth and did the same. Closing the small gap between us, I kissed her. We both moaned, and I wondered if she remembered how good it was the last time we kissed. There was no hesitation—we went at each other like it was what we'd been waiting for since we first saw each other again.

Her lips welcomed mine like pillows, so soft and eager. Her

hands moved under my arms to my back. I dug one hand into her hair, desperate to hold her to me. Her stomach bumped into me, and I gently held her close as my mouth ravaged hers.

Her nails scoured my back like she wanted to claw through my clothes, and I pressed my tongue between her lips, groaning when hers met mine halfway like she was as eager to remember my taste as I was hers.

Time meant nothing as we stood in the foyer of the apartment building, losing control one second at a time. I needed to get her upstairs. I needed to feel more of her. I just needed her.

The elevator dinged, and Carina pulled back, her hand covering her mouth like she couldn't believe what we'd just done, and she needed to feel her swollen lips to prove it.

She stepped back as the doors slid open and looked up at me with wide eyes. A guy I wanted to curse at for breaking the moment stepped out, his eyes glued to his phone as he left.

"That was a mistake," Carina breathed, shaking her head. "I'm sorry. It's—it's the hormones."

"Well, your hormones can take advantage of me any time."

My joke broke the tension, and she laughed. But the color was still high in her cheeks, and her lips were still swollen from mine. Even if she wanted to pretend it didn't happen, the evidence was all there.

"Goodnight, Ian."

I wanted to push her to talk about it, but even under the desire, I could see her exhaustion. Working all day and then dinner with my parents was a task for anyone, let alone a pregnant woman. So, I let it pass. For now.

"Goodnight, Carina." Before she could step away, I leaned down and placed both hands on her belly, pressing my mouth close. "Goodnight, baby."

Then I released her and stepped away, loving her wide eyes

and heavy swallow. She stepped into the elevator and continued to stare as I backed away.

"Oh, and Carina...that wasn't a mistake."

The doors slid closed, giving me one last glimpse of a flushed and stunned Carina.

12 CARINA

FIGURING I had a few minutes before Ian arrived with lunch, I stepped out of my office to do a lap around the floor. My back ached, and I'd had Braxton Hicks all morning. The first time I'd had them, I'd panicked and thought I was going into labor at seven months. I ran to the ER all alone at midnight just to find out I was overreacting. So, now when they came, I just counted the time between them and walked it off.

If they were random, it was just false contractions. If I noticed them regularly, then it could be labor. These had been happening all morning, but they were all over the place but hurt more than normal.

But it wasn't a fake contraction that stole my breath when I stepped out of my office.

No, it was Ian smiling down at that slut Nina from accounting.

Okay, maybe she wasn't a slut, and I barely knew her. But I hated her and the way she was smiling up at Ian like he was the best thing since sliced bread. She must have been the funniest person ever because he threw his head back and laughed, and she took the moment to step closer. What pissed me off more, he didn't back away.

How many other women was he flirting with? Was he still dating? Maybe screwing all these other women in between bringing me lunch? Maybe he thought he could have a quickie and check the box of taking care of his baby-mama in one go.

Fire burned up my throat and squeezed my chest.

He rested his hand on the half-wall, almost like he was going to lean in and kiss her. Just like he'd kissed me last week. I'd avoided the subject, but I wouldn't have if I'd known he was going around fucking all the women in the city. Next to his hand was *my* bag of lunch.

Well, I wasn't going to wait for him to get done doing her on the copy machine to eat.

I stomped over and didn't say anything when I reached between them and snatched the paper sack. I didn't even look at him before turning and storming back to my office. I didn't even get the satisfaction of slamming the door because he slapped it with his palm, pushing it open and closing it gently behind him.

Everything felt close to boiling, and I wanted to go over and slam it anyway, just for the satisfaction of hearing the bang.

"What the hell was that?" he asked, pointing at the door.

"Nothing." I sat down, and dug in for my food, shrugging and clearing all rage from my voice. "I'm just hungry and didn't feel like waiting for you to finish eye-fucking Nina to eat."

"I wasn't—" He halted and paced two steps before turning back. "Jesus. I asked her if you were in a meeting and got caught up for a minute when she asked me about a software program. Sorry it took so long."

His tone let me know he wasn't really all that sorry. Or if he was, he was more irritated than anything.

Annoyed at his annoyance and shitty apology, I slapped my burger down on the table. "God, you can't even admit when you're flirting on your way to bringing the mother of your child lunch." I stood and faced him head-on, letting the emotion bursting from me come out. "I don't know why I'm surprised. You probably have women in a line to be with the great Ian Bergamo."

An incredulous laugh broke free. "Are you kidding me?" He shook his head before leveling narrowed, steel eyes at me. They were no longer confused. No, they were taunting and angry. "What? Is the ice-queen Carina Russo jealous?" he sneered.

I stumbled back like his accusation was a physical force and scoffed. "No."

His lip curled, and he took a step closer. "Come on, Carina. Admit it."

Pulling my shoulders back, I channeled the same power I used in a boardroom. "Don't turn this around on me. You're the one screwing around."

"I'm not," he said with a hard edge. "We've promised each other nothing, so we don't owe each other anything." He took a few more steps, the lines between his brows softening and a dark glint entering his eyes. He didn't stop until he stood right in front of me almost brushing my stomach, forcing my head back to meet his eyes. I swallowed when his lips tipped up in a devious smirk. "Unless you want to."

"I want nothing from you." I tried to hold on to my anger and infuse my voice, but when he stood so close, it was like he stole my oxygen, and it all came out breathy.

He brushed my hair back, and a shiver ran down my back. "You sure about that? Didn't seem so sure last week."

I licked my dry lips, struggling to hold it together. It was so hot in here, my head swam. "It was a mistake."

It was his turn to scoff as he ran his fingers across my cheek. I struggled not to sink into it. His hand slid around the back of my neck, and the shock ran down my back again, wrapping around to form an ache in my stomach. I was almost panting for him, and I was almost past caring.

How did he do this to me?

"Are you sure you don't miss my kiss?" he asked just before his lips pressed to the corner of my mouth. "Tell me you don't dream about our date, about being together. Tell me you don't remember how good it felt."

"Ian." Was that breathy moan from me? My body sizzled like a live wire, all of it moving to my lower belly, pulling tight like an aching need.

He leaned down, pushing my hair aside so he could whisper in my ear. "Because I do. All the time. Sometimes..." Warm lips sucked on the lobe of my ear, coming off with a pop. "I wake up with my hand on my cock, stroking myself to the memory of your heat, your moans, until I come, your name falling from my lips." He pulled back to meet my eyes again, his lids heavy over dark charcoal eyes. "Just say it, Carina."

My lips parted, and another wave of need hit me.

Wait.

No.

My stomach pulled tight, my back ached, and I gripped his shoulder for support as the pain racked through me and liquid began trickling down my leg. My face flushed even more because all I could think was that it felt like I was peeing myself.

"Are you okay?"

Ian looked down with concern more than desire now.

"My water just broke."

Any desire that had been there had vanished, and he stepped away, his hands pulled back like I just told him I had the plague. "What the fuck?"

"My water just broke."

"What do you mean your water just broke?"

I clenched my jaw as the feeling I'd thought was desire

coiling through me hit again, only harder with no doubt that it was a contraction. A real one. "I mean, my water. Just. Fucking. Broke."

He stared on with wide eyes and swallowed. I realized he had no idea what to do. We'd gone to all the appointments, but we never talked about when the baby came. I'd never talked about the birthing classes I'd taken and what to expect.

"I need you to take me to the hospital."

His brows lowered, and he hesitated. "Will it ruin my seats?"

If I could have lit him on fire with a look alone, he'd have been ash. "Are you fucking kidding me right now?" I almost shouted.

It did the trick because, in the next instant, his hands dropped, and he blinked the shock away. "Right. Doesn't matter. Okay," he said, stepping back up to me to take my hand. "Just... just tell me what to do."

I took a deep breath because now that I didn't have his dirty mouth distracting me, all I could think about was every feeling in my body. "I have a bag in my car. We need to grab that and head to University Hospital."

"K. On it." He actually walked in a circle, looking around the office like he was lost, before coming back to me. It was almost enough to make me laugh. "Should I carry you?"

I did laugh at that. "No. I can walk. I just need my phone to time my contractions."

"Got it." He snatched it off my desk and handed it to me. "What about the food."

"No food." He took my hand, and we were almost out the door when I stopped.

"You okay?"

"Maybe just the French fries."

He smiled, nodded, and grabbed me my fries, holding my hand the whole way to the parking lot.

While I chomped down on the fries, getting more nervous as the miles passed, Ian looked like a Zen monk in the driver's seat. I wanted to slap him as he helped me from the car with a comforting smile. I really wanted to smack him when he looked back at the passenger seat to check I hadn't ruined it with my broken water. He'd breathed a sigh of relief when I'd told him I had a spare towel in my car just for this situation.

"Hi," I greeted the front desk attendant of the hospital. "My water broke, sooo yeah." He looked up with one eyebrow raised and didn't say anything for a minute, and in my nervousness, I rushed to fill the silence. "I'm probably overreacting and should just go home..."

I faded off as a contraction hit me hard, stealing my breath. This one lasted longer than the others, and Ian's hands held me up even when I kind of wanted to sit down on the ground.

"We just need to check-in," Ian stepped in.

The attendant's concerned gaze scanned me over and passed a clipboard to Ian. He filled out all the paperwork, and we had someone waiting with a wristband and a wheelchair to take me up to the delivery floor.

"Hey, Mom and Dad," the nurse greeted. "I'm Mary, and I'll be your nurse for the next few hours. Dr. Abrahms is on call right now. Why don't you get changed out of your clothes and I'll be back with him to check you out."

"Okay, thank you."

Ian sat my bag on the bed and turned to face me. "I'll just step out so you can get changed. Let me know when you're ready."

"Ian, you don't have to—" my words were cut off by a small contraction that barely lasted ten seconds. "You don't have to stay."

He stood before me, looking more dominating than I could

ever recall him being, like an immovable wall. "Do you have someone coming?"

I looked away because, no, I didn't have anyone coming. I didn't really have anyone, and I figured, like any job, I could crush this on my own with the nurse's help. I'd read as many books as I could get my hands on, preparing for this very moment. My aunts had offered, but I'd turned them down, not wanting to be overwhelmed by the four of them. Aunt Virginia had let me know that if I ever changed my mind, she'd be there for me, but I was confident I could do it on my own. I was Carina Russo, I prepared and conquered, not needing anyone's help.

I didn't have to say anything for Ian to read my answer from my reaction. "I'm staying."

"Ian," I breathed his name, my shoulders dropping. I didn't want him doing something he really didn't want to, but I was already too tired to fight him.

"You don't get to argue with me on this...I mean, you can, but I really want to be here for you. Please."

I looked him over. This solid man, standing before me like a wet dream in a suit, offering to hold my hand while I rode the struggle bus. Who was I to stop him?

"Okay."

"Good." He gave a victorious smile that almost had me taking it back, just to argue, but he was already on his way out the door before I could. "Holler when you're ready."

Shaking my head, I smiled at his retreating back and quickly changed. When I called Ian back in, he brought the doctor with him.

"Hello, Carina. I'm Dr. Abrahms," he greeted me as he looked over my chart. "I'll be with you for a few more hours, but then Dr. Sawyer will be in later." He set the clipboard aside and gave me a quick smile. "So, how far apart are your contractions?"

I leaned back with Ian by my head and got in position.

"Umm...They're pretty erratic, but always less than twenty minutes apart. Sometimes as little as seven minutes apart."

He hummed and checked me out quickly. Looking up to Ian, I almost laughed at the scowl he delivered to the doctor between my legs. "You're almost to four centimeters. We'll get you all hooked up and keep an eye on everything. For now, we just wait." He checked some more boxes on the chart. "Are we getting an epidural."

"God, yes." He laughed and checked another box. "I'd like to wait a while before I get one, but don't want to miss my window to get it either."

"We can do our best to make that happen."

With one last smile, he left, and I was alone with Ian.

"So, what does one do when waiting for a baby to appear from their vagina?"

"Oh, my god, Ian." Despite my nerves, he made me laugh, and I realized maybe he was a better asset to have by my side than I originally thought.

We made it a little over two hours before I broke down and asked for the epidural. In that time, we played card games with the deck Ian ran down to the gift store to buy. He'd rubbed my back through the harder contractions and winced like a baby when I squeezed his hand.

"Damn, woman," he said as the anesthesiologist left. "That needle was huge."

"Thanks, Ian," I deadpanned.

"But I wasn't worried." He winked and slid his hand over mine. "You've taken much bigger than that."

I snatched my hand away and smacked his arm, laughing hard. "You are disgusting."

He grabbed my hand back and sat in the chair he'd moved close to my bed. "Why don't I turn out the lights and you get some rest. The nurse said you should get some sleep if you can, now that you've had the epidural."

"Okay," I agreed readily. The pain was minimal now, and the beep of the baby's heartbeat was soothing me to sleep. It may have also been the drugs but hearing Peanut's heartbeat helped. "Why don't you get something to eat."

"Nah. If you don't get to eat, then neither do I. Solidarity and all that."

"Okay, but when this is all over, bring us both cheeseburgers."

"Deal."

He dimmed the lights, and I was soon passed out. I wasn't sure for how long, but I woke up when a contraction wracked my body. It wasn't as painful as before I got my epidural, but I was still very aware of it.

"Good, you're awake," a new nurse said. "I'm Angie. I'll be taking Mary's place. And I might be the nurse to help deliver your baby. Your contractions are pretty close. I'm going to examine you and see how far along you are."

Scanning the room, I found Ian passed out on the tiny chair, his head falling forward over his arms, crossed on his chest. He looked ridiculously uncomfortable.

But I would have given anything to be uncomfortable like that a few hours later when I was hunched over my bent legs, pushing for all I was worth.

"You're doing great," Ian kept saying. He had one arm over my shoulders and a hand in mine, cringing when I squeezed. "You're a goddess, Carina. Isn't she a goddess?" he asked the doctors and nurses in the room.

They all eagerly nodded, half mooning over the sexy Ian Bergamo. I didn't blame them. I was a sweaty mess, my makeup all gone, and hair in a messy bun, while he looked devastating in his white button-up with the tie gone and the sleeves rolled up.

I went to go push again, the nurse counting down for me. When she said one, I fell back on the bed, breathing hard.

Ian took a cold washcloth and wiped my forehead. I'd only been pushing for a little while, but it'd been a long day, and I was so tired.

"Come on, Carina. You can push harder than that," he joked.

"I will murder you," I growled out through clenched teeth.

"Totally kidding. That was sufficient pushing." When I continued to glare, he rushed to correct again. "It was the best pushing I've ever seen. You're the pushing queen."

The nurse told me it was time to push again, and the doctor announced the baby was crowning. Only a few more pushes. In the middle of a push, I saw Ian trying to look past my legs, and I released a hand to slap it over his eyes.

"Don't you dare look down there," I almost shouted.

His eyes shot to the ceiling, but a smile stretched his lips, distracting me from the pain. The epidural dulled the pain but didn't make it magically disappear.

After one more push—Ian's head pressed to mine, both our eyes squeezed shut—the most beautiful sound in the world filled the room.

Our baby's first cry.

"It's a girl!" Dr. Sawyer proudly announced.

A sob broke free, and I relaxed back against the pillows.

"You did it. Damn, woman. You fucking did it." Ian brushed my hair back and kissed my forehead.

He stood tall when Angie stepped forward with our baby girl, laying her to rest on my chest. She screamed for all she was worth, and I shushed her and held her close, taking in her scrunched up tiny nose, and tiny mouth stretched wide.

Holy shit.

I was sure in my twenty-five years I could have said I'd felt every emotion possible, but *nothing* prepared me for this. No book, no class, no *anything* could prepare me for the overwhelming flood of love consuming me. Tears burned the backs of my eyes as I looked down at my baby girl. *Mine.*

My whole world shifted like it clicked perfectly into place and if I thought I'd been grateful before for having Ian there, nothing compared to how perfect it was to have him by my side, watching him experience the same emotion.

"Dad? You want to cut the cord?"

Ian blinked a few times, brushing his watery eyes. "Yeah. Definitely." The nurse passed the scissors and directed him what to do. Before he cut, he looked to our little girl. "Sorry, if this hurts, Peanut."

The nurse laughed and assured him Peanut couldn't feel that. It was kind of adorable that he thought it would and cared so much.

"Okay, let me take her and get her cleaned up and checked out. We'll be right here the whole time," the nurse explained, pointing over to a baby station across from me.

My heavy lids slid closed, and I took a deep breath, letting myself relax a moment. One of Ian's large hands wrapped around mine while the other brushed strands back from my face. I couldn't have imagined this moment alone—without him by my side. Opening my eyes to find his silver ones looking back at me, grounded me, and let me know I wasn't alone.

"Thank you for being here, Ian."

"I wouldn't have missed this for the world."

The nurse came back and placed our tiny bundle back in my arms. "Hey, Peanut."

Ian brushed her soft cheek with his thumb. "We should probably come up with a name. If you don't have one already picked out," he quickly backtracked.

I appreciated him trying to not step on my toes, but he was part of this, and I wanted his input. "I have a few in mind."

"Hit me."

"Serena, Elizabeth, or Emery, but none of them feel right."

"Audrey," he whispered. "What about Audrey?"

"Is that some ex-love I should know about?"

"Hardly. It was my grandma's name. When I was with her, it was the closest I felt to a real family."

He watched Peanut while I watched him. Ian was a complex man. He was light-hearted and always the life of the party. But he also had more depth than maybe I'd given him credit for. Watching him reveal the layers that made him was fascinating and alluring and created an energy that pulled me into his orbit. The thing was, the more time I spent with him, the more I didn't mind giving in.

"Audrey it is."

He flashed me a beautiful smile that had my heart skipping a beat before leaning in slowly to press a soft kiss to my lips.

"Audrey it is," he whispered against my lips.

It was the next day before I started letting people know they could visit. Surprisingly, my aunts weren't the first people to push through the door. Ian had just stepped out to grab some lunch for us when my dad came in.

"Hey, baby girl."

"Dad," I breathed.

My aunts had filled the place for my missing mother, but my dad had always been my rock. He'd been hard on me, knowing I wouldn't be satisfied with being anything but the best—all while protecting me as much as he could. So, seeing him walk in, his eyes wide with wonder taking in Audrey, filled me with pride. I was strong because of this man.

"Look at her," he breathed. "May I?"

"Of course."

I passed Audrey off to her grandpa, and he cuddled the sleeping baby close to his chest.

"She's got your nose," he said, smiling.

"You think?"

"I know. I remember holding you in the hospital thinking how perfect your nose was." He bounced a little, using his thumb to stroke her plump cheek. "How are you feeling?" he asked, as I laid back and let my eyes slide closed.

"Tired."

"It's just the beginning, baby girl."

"Don't I know it."

"But if anyone can do it, it's you."

His easy compliment had my eyes sliding open to find him staring at me now.

"You are the strongest woman I've ever known, Carina. I'm so damn proud of you. I don't say it enough. I know I'm hard on you and shelter you, but it's because I love you and I want to keep you from any pain or disappointment."

"I know, Dad." I barely choked the words out. "It's okay."

"It's not. I never wanted you to doubt yourself, and I know I've been the one to make you do it more than anyone. Sometimes I get caught up and still see you as my little girl."

I swallowed the lump climbing its way up my throat. "I'll always be your little girl."

"I know, but it's time I see you as the strong woman you are too. I mean, look at you—my baby having a baby. I'm so proud of you."

A few tears managed to break free, but I quickly swiped them away. "Thank you, Daddy."

"Everything okay?" Ian asked, walking through the door.

"Yeah, yeah. Just my hormones being crazy."

His eyes flicked between my dad and me before finally greeting my dad. "Hello, David."

"Ian. Good to see you. Congratulations on this beautiful little girl."

"She's pretty perfect, isn't she?"

"Absolute perfection," my dad answered, his eyes on me.

My dad stayed for a little while longer, holding Audrey while Ian and I ate.

"I'll leave you two to it," Dad said when the nurse came in to examine me. He leaned over the bed and pressed a kiss to Audrey's head before repeating the process with mine. "Take care of you and my grandbaby, but when you're ready, we'll talk about your business plan and get the ball rolling."

He always told me that actions speak louder than words and while his words meant everything to me, the fact that he was taking my idea for our company seriously was the greatest gift he could've ever given me.

"Thank you, Dad."

13 IAN

ONLY THE DIM light peeking around the curtains shined in Carina's room when I walked in. We'd been in the hospital for a total of three days, and I knew she was ready to head home.

I gently set the car seat in the corner of the room, doing my best not to wake her and Audrey. Carina was curled up on her side with one arm reaching out to our beautiful baby girl resting in her hospital cot. I didn't know who to look at first, both girls capturing my attention. Audrey made a small grunt and shifted, making her little cap fall off, baring that ridiculous amount of dark hair. She took after her daddy with all those luscious locks.

God, just thinking I had someone taking after me, referring to myself as daddy, filled me with the most terrifying joy I'd ever felt. I stroked my finger across her plump cheek and looked on a little longer before moving my gaze to Carina. Her hair splayed across the pillow and around her shoulders like a halo. She'd demanded a shower last night but refused to let me help. She'd even gasped like I'd offended her morals just by offering.

She could hide all she wanted. But what she didn't know was that I was going to make this work—make *us* work. I wasn't sure what that looked like right now, but if it happened to include touching her and helping her shower when needed, then I was on board. I was willing to accept damn near anything to be with my girls, even if that meant roommates that raised a child together. But what I really wanted—what I was going to go for—was us together.

I wanted more.

I wanted our baby all the time.

I wanted this family.

She'd been hurt before and had trust issues, but I was Ian Bergamo, and I could be very persuasive to the female population.

More grunts pulled my attention back to Audrey. Her little face screwed up and she wriggled inside her cocoon. It looked uncomfortable, but then I remembered Carina's reprimand when I undid it last night. Apparently, she liked to be wrapped up like a burrito.

I didn't know. She looked awfully pissed right now.

Then the loudest grunt followed by a fart I hadn't even heard from college guys came from my angel. It was the only warning I had before the foul smell assaulted my senses. I gagged and almost backed away when two blue eyes cracked open and just stared.

Immediately, I stepped back up and leaned lower to the stink grenade. "Hey, baby girl."

She blinked and wriggled some more before her face started scrunching again, except this time it was to cry. I quickly picked her up, balancing her in my palms and bounced, making a continuous shushing sound, hoping to calm her. It didn't work. Not that I could blame her. Based on the smell that continued to get worse, she probably needed changing and would continue to increase in volume until it happened.

Not wanting to wake Carina up, I got all the supplies out and unwrapped the baby burrito. Her legs kicked free, and arms shot out like she was cheering for freedom, Mel Gibson style.

"You are adorable, but that smell is foul. I may need a gas mask for this task."

Holding my breath and gagging repeatedly, I managed to get her clean.

Just as I was fumbling with her burrito blanket, Carina woke up. "Hey."

I gave her a brief smile and struggled with the wrap. "Hey. I didn't want to wake you."

"It's okay. Looks like it was just in time. Bring her here, and I'll wrap her up."

"Sounds like a plan. Doesn't it, baby girl." I picked Audrey up and continued to talk baby-talk, wondering if she remembered me from all the times I spoke to Carina's belly. "Yes, it does. Mommy knows best. Yes, she does."

Carina was smiling and shaking her head by the time I passed Audrey off. She efficiently wrapped the baby burrito up like maybe she'd secretly worked at Chipotle in a past life. She pulled Audrey close and bounced and hummed until she passed out again. Unable to keep my hands off her, I reached out until Carina put our baby in my arms.

I'd been in the hospital as much as I could over the past three days, but it was never enough. I needed more of this tiny human. I'd had to leave for a few work meetings I couldn't miss. Thankfully, Carina's aunts had stepped in when I couldn't be there.

"Look at you, baby-daddy," Carina said, smiling at us both.

"We look good together, don't we?" I said with a wink, holding Audrey close to my face.

She rolled her eyes at my antics but still laughed.

"You always look good," Carina's Aunt Vivian said, stepping into the room.

She boldly looked me up and down, which no longer

surprised me. I'd met all four women over the past few days, and they were an interesting bunch. I felt a little sorry for Carina's dad, but they were all pretty awesome in their own way. Vivian was brash and constantly treated me like man-meat. I think she did it to make Carina laugh.

"Hey, Aunt Vivian."

"How are my girls?"

"Good. We get to go home today."

"I heard. Are you ready?"

Carina heaved a sigh and shrugged. "As ready as I can be."

"I'm taking her home," I stated, staying strong for Carina's impending argument. "She won't be alone tonight."

"Ian..." Carina half-heartedly protested. I knew she wouldn't ask for help, but she didn't need to. These two girls were my responsibility, and I was stepping up.

"No arguments."

She pursed her lips but thankfully listened. "Fine."

The nurse came in after that, running over everything before she gave us the go-ahead to leave. I helped pack and tucked Audrey into her car seat. She was a real champ and didn't wake up at all. Hell, she didn't wake up the whole drive or when we got to Carina's apartment.

I set her on the floor in the entryway and just stared. "Can we leave her in there?"

Carina stood next to me and stared too. "Umm...I don't know."

We both looked to each other with wide eyes, except Carina's began filling with tears. "Hey, hey. Come here." I pulled her to me, and she buried her head against my shoulder and sniffed.

"I don't know, Ian. How am I supposed to do this when we've been home for a minute, and I'm already stumped? Oh, my god." Her breathing increased, and I palmed her cheeks and pulled her head up to face me.

"Stop. Look. Breathe with me."

She nodded, but tears still tracked down her cheeks.

"I'm going to let you in on a secret. But you can't tell anyone because it's mainly how I get through every day coming off like the genius I am."

She nodded again, but this time, it came with a laugh.

"We Google. Google knows all."

"O—okay. Let me get my phone."

I walked the rest of the bags inside while she googled. Her apartment was neat, clean, and perfectly decorated with muted grays and a few splashes of color. By the time I came back, she was reading her phone and chewing on a nail.

"Find anything."

"Yeah. Looks like we can't."

"Okay, then out we go."

"Hang on, I need to get her sleeper set up."

"I already saw it set up by the couch."

She stopped moving and stared at me, confused, before moving past and walking into the living room. She bent over the coffee table and picked up a piece of paper. "Oh, my god."

I unclasped Audrey, pulling her out, and walked to Carina. "What's up?"

"I had a few baby items still in boxes and Jake came in to get it all organized and set up. He knew I was finishing up as much client work before maternity leave and planned on getting it done later."

"Cool." I was surprised how calm that came out. Rationally, I knew Jake was just a friend, but he was also a close friend who had slept with this woman and broken her heart. I kind of also hated him and the pinch of jealousy he created within me.

"Oh, wow. He also got me my rocking chair I wanted. Oh, my goodness." Her hand was covering her mouth as tears formed again. "I can't believe he did this."

"Probably his guilt."

That earned me a hard side-eye, but I just shrugged and kissed my baby. Anything to take my mind off the rocking chair I currently had sitting in my apartment that I'd bought a few days ago. It was the one thing she hadn't got herself, and I was so excited to surprise her with it, but it looked like I wouldn't get the chance.

Carina took Audrey and gently placed her in the rocking sleeper. "Are you leaving?"

The question was soft and probably meant to come off as indifferent, but I heard the fear that I'd just take off now that she had settled. "No, Carina. I told you, I'm staying."

She stood upright and faced me; her arms crossed against her chest. "You don't have to. I'm sure you have things to get done."

"Carina." I waited until she looked up before continuing. "I know we need to talk and figure things out. But for right now, let's get settled and know that I'm here. As long as you want me to be. Maybe even longer."

She smiled. "Thank you."

"You don't have to thank me. We're in this together."

Her eyes dropped to the floor, and her hair fell forward like a curtain, blocking her face. "I'm sorry about crying. It's just these stupid hormones."

"Would it make you feel better if I cried too? I could work up a few tears."

Another smile and I wished she could just keep those coming for the rest of forever. She was stressed and emotional, and if my sole purpose was to hold Audrey and make Carina laugh when shit got hard, then I was there for it.

"Now, let's order in and pass out while we can."

"Okay."

We ended up ordering Italian and watching the news on

mute because we didn't want to risk waking Audrey. When we finished, I offered to clean up while Carina took care of the baby.

I worked my way around her kitchen, finding where things went, it didn't take me long. I picked up in the living room before deciding to go check on my girls. Soft humming was coming from down the hall, and I walked into a sight that stole my breath.

Carina rocked back and forth on a cushy chair with a half-circle pillow around her waist, supporting Audrey as she ate. Carina's shirt was pulled up just enough for Audrey to reach her breast. I could see the full curves covered in soft pale skin. But in that moment, my thoughts were the furthest thing from sexual.

Fire burned its way up my throat, and I stepped into the room, halting Carina's humming and bringing her eyes to mine. She kept staring as I came closer not taking my eyes off my little girl feeding, her little fist balled up against Carina's breast. Without thinking, I dropped to my knees in front of her and stroked Audrey's full head of hair.

"Thank you, Carina. Thank yo—" I had to swallow past the lump in my throat and try again. "Thank you for this beautiful gift."

When I looked up, she had tears in her eyes too, and I offered a smile, getting one in return. "Thank you," she whispered.

I kissed Audrey's head and pulled back to my haunches. "Do you need anything?"

"No. I've already changed her, so when she's ready, we're going to head to bed to get some sleep."

"Okay. I'll be on the couch if you need me."

"Are you sure?"

"I've never been so sure of anything in my life."

14 CARINA

For the first time all week, I woke up on my own and not to the cries of a baby. Audrey was still passed out in her sleeper, her thumb firmly planted between her rosebud lips. I could've sat there and watched her sleep, but I heard noise coming from out in the living room. I turned on the baby monitor and headed out. Ian sat on the couch, a slew of papers spread out on the coffee table and the television on some news channel with the sound off.

"How'd you sleep?" I asked, stepping into the room. His head jerked up not having heard me come in. He'd stayed at my place every night since we got home from the hospital and still, finding him there in the morning, those gray eyes taking me in first thing, shot a spark of excitement through me.

"I think I'm going to buy you a new couch," he joked.

Wincing, I made myself comfortable on the armchair catty-corner to said couch, pulling my feet up on the cushion. My couch was more for design rather than sleeping comfort, and Ian was a big man.

"You don't have to stay," I offered, even though I kind of— okay *really*—liked not being alone.

"I want to be here. Neck cramp and all."

I tried not to smile too much at his little jokes here and there, I was worried it would give him a big head, and I didn't want him to get the wrong idea that I liked him—even though I kind of did. Kind of. But I remembered our conversation right before my water broke and I didn't want to encourage him to push for more.

Because you wouldn't be able to stop yourself from caving.

I ignored the thought and thankfully didn't have to dwell on it because Ian was talking again.

"You know, we could always stay at my apartment," he suggested slowly like he was dipping a toe in the water.

My first instinct was to laugh, but his face lacked any amusement. The idea had come so far out of left field, and I didn't know what to think.

"What?"

"Just something to think about. Your place is smaller, and I have a huge apartment not far from here, so it wouldn't change the commute."

My eyes widened as each word sunk in. "Oh, you're serious."

"Yes, I'm serious. I can take you there to check it out."

"Ian, that's kind of ridiculous. I mean, this is my home. I can't just leave. I can't just move in with you."

The more I thought about it, the crazier it seemed. How did he not think this was the most insane idea ever?

"It'd be no different than me sleeping here."

The more he spoke, the tighter my chest got. Bringing Audrey home was crazier than I expected and leaving the comfort of my home right now, scared the shit out of me. Leaving the comfort of my home on a chance with the man across from me, had my heart pounding like a jackhammer.

I hadn't even lived with Jake, and we'd been engaged. And when everything fell apart, my apartment had been my sanctuary. I couldn't imagine giving that up or putting that much on the line.

No, I needed steady, and he was Ian being Ian, not thinking through all the complications of his idea.

"Like I said, you don't have to."

"And like I said, I want to. I want to be with you and Audrey. Preferably with more space."

"And I appreciate that, but I can't just pick up and move." His shoulders dropped, and he sighed. "Listen, I can look into getting a new couch, but I can't even think of moving."

"Okay."

I was surprised by how quickly he let the conversation go. Then again, I'd been surprised by how serious he was—by this whole conversation. It was like we'd entered an alternate dimension.

But just as soon as we entered, we were back out when Ian gave me his signature playful smirk.

"I was going to grab some breakfast, but I didn't want to get myself something wrong to eat," he deadpanned, making a joke about how I always tell him he picked the wrong thing to eat. "So, no pancakes for you."

Biting back my smile, I rolled my eyes, letting the conversation go. "Ugh. I'd want eggs anyway."

"Do you do it on purpose?" he asked, not even bothering to hide his disarming smile.

I did do it on purpose, sometimes. Ian and I bickered, and I knew he intentionally provoked me more often than not. I didn't know why we continued, but it seemed natural. At first, we would argue about food or where to eat, both of us having been on our own for so long. But then it came with hidden smiles and mischievous looks, like some weird form of foreplay.

Or it felt like foreplay to me. Maybe he just liked to see me irritated. Maybe I was the only one who got heated and wanted to shut his mouth with my own.

"No," I answered, shoving my thoughts down. "You're just really bad at making decisions."

His grin went from playful to victorious. "Then it's a good thing I got eggs too."

I shot him a glare, and he returned it with a wink before shuffling papers around. "What are you working on?" I asked to keep myself from running over to the kitchen and devouring the pancakes I'd never tell him sounded like heaven.

"Applications. I let Erik know there was no way I could take over the London office once it was complete."

"Oh..." I'd been curious about that, but in all our meetings, we'd never addressed how they'd run the London office at the end of it. Ian was the main contact there and had spent a majority of the last six months overseas, but there had never been a decision made.

"Don't act so shocked."

"I'm not," I fibbed. "I just know how much this project means to the both of you."

"It still does. So, we need to find someone to train. I'll have to travel frequently at first for set-up, but I won't ever be there for long."

He held my stare, letting me feel the sincerity of his words sink deep. It was his way of letting me know he wasn't leaving me —that he didn't want to. Warmth flooded my chest at his sacrifice. I knew how much his work meant to him, and he was choosing us over a project he'd been working almost a year on. When was the last time someone had given so much up for me?

The loud cry of our baby from the other room broke the moment, and I blinked out of my trance.

Before I could stand, Ian was already up. "I got her. Here," he said, handing me a stack of applications. "Look these over and let me know what you think."

Shocked, I blinked at his retreating back. Maybe because I always had to prove myself, it stunned me that he handed me these applications like he genuinely wanted my opinion on who to hire. A slow smile stretched my lips, and I ignored the way pride filled my heart and instead focused on the papers in front of me.

"Who's the stinkiest baby in the whole wide world?" Ian said, coming back in the room. "You. Yes, you are. The prettiest, stinkiest baby there ever was. Mommy's not allowed to have any more Chinese. No, she's not."

"Yeah, right," I muttered.

He smiled and settled himself back on the couch, resting Audrey on his chest. My body froze as I took them in, just like it did every single time it happened. When would my body adjust to seeing this big playboy cradling our daughter? Probably never. Some ingrained gene that made me salivate at him being a protector to her. His big hands patted her back as he kissed her head, and I literally had to bite my lip to hold back the moan.

Jesus, Carina. Get a grip.

It had to be the hormones. My emotions had been all over the place, and Ian had taken each one in stride. The only one I'd managed to hide from him had been my deep arousal around him. I was like an animal in heat when he was near.

"How did you sleep?" he asked.

I swallowed the saliva building in my mouth and forced an answer past my tight throat. "Uh, pretty horrible actually. She was up for a couple hours between feedings last night."

"Why didn't you come get me?" he asked, genuinely shocked.

I waved him off. "It's fine, Ian. I'm used to doing things on my own."

It wasn't like he'd be here forever anyway, and I'd need to be okay doing it all on my own. Yes, I enjoyed knowing he was here, but rarely did I ask for anything.

"How come?"

It was weird having to explain my past to someone. I'd been with Jake since college and hadn't dated much before him, so he knew my past, and he knew the ins and outs of who I was. But Ian was a whole new beast.

"I don't know. I guess growing up with just my father, who was so successful, drove me to want to be good enough for him. He taught me well but still sees the business world in an old-fashioned way, thinking men won't take me seriously in the boardroom. So, I worked hard and did a lot of it alone to prove to him I was just as good as any man—that I was better."

"Well, I'd much rather have you in our meetings over anyone else," he said with a scan down to my chest and back again, waggling his eyebrows for good measure. "But I've also seen what you're charging us and frankly, I think anyone else wouldn't have driven such a hard bargain."

He raised a brow at my proud smile. I did a damn good job negotiating their contract and brought in a hefty amount for Wellington and Russo. I sat up a little straighter with Ian's confirmation.

"But I get it," he said, kissing Audrey's head again. "I did the same with my parents until I kind of just lived for me. Nothing I did seemed to keep their attention, so I said fuck it. In the end, nothing changed, except maybe I pissed them off more with my choices. I just cared less about their opinion of me." He finally met my eyes and shrugged. "Kind of."

"I get wanting to impress them, even if you don't want to want to."

We shared a rueful smile of commiseration about trying to prove ourselves to our parents.

"Your dad is proud of you," he said, surprising me. "I can see the way he talks about you."

"I know. He's just protective of me, and it comes out like he doubts my ability." I huffed a small laugh and shrugged, changing the subject. "When do your parents get back?"

"Next week," Ian groaned.

"Maybe we can do dinner. They can meet Audrey."

His face scrunched up. "Do we have to?"

"Yes. Now give me our baby. She needs to eat."

Ian passed me Audrey, who had been stirring on his chest. She stared up with wide eyes, her mouth already open before I even had my shirt up. Ian didn't stare uncomfortably, but he did watch. It wasn't in a sexual way—more like he was fascinated by the sight of us together. Like he was in awe of it. So, I didn't shy away because I was comfortable and frankly, if he was staying here as much as he was, then I just had to get used to whipping a boob out with him around. I sure as hell wasn't going to hide under a cover in my own home.

"You're good at this," Ian complimented.

I sat tall and gave him a smirk. "I know."

"So modest."

"Wow," I deadpanned. "Coming from you."

"I'm the most modest man you'll ever meet."

"Oh, God," I laughed, rolling my eyes. "Lord, help us, Audrey."

Ian sat back on the couch and just watching him lounge made me realize how little sleep I got, and I yawned.

"Why don't you use that contraption thingy," he said gesturing to my chest. "I can take her to work with me, and you can get some uninterrupted sleep."

"The pump?"

"Yeah. It looks like a torture device for your poor breasts. I hate that you'd have to use it," his scrunched face softened to a flirtatious smirk. "But whenever you do need to use it, I can always kiss them better. Give them a little TLC."

Audrey grunted in displeasure when my chest shook with laughter. "You're horrible," I tried to admonish him, but really, color stained my cheeks at the thought, and my chest filled with happiness that he still found me attractive enough to even make sexual comments about. "Well, they were made to withstand the *torture* to feed her."

"But later, when she's done with them next year, they're all mine, right?"

I didn't answer and instead rolled my eyes. I did that a lot around him, but it usually came with a smile too.

Ian got up and headed to the bathroom to get ready for work, and I was left smiling, thinking about his words.

Later. Next year.

I didn't want to dwell on him being around that long. We hadn't even talked about next week. There was a part of me that still held him at arm's length, fearful of relying on someone like I had with Jake—a part of me that still saw Ian as the playboy when we first met. But that part grew smaller each day, and the more time I spent around him, the more the thought of him being around filled me with excitement and had me repeating the words in my head.

Later.

Yeah, I liked the sound of later.

Not that he needed to know that I liked anything that came out of his mouth. I had to make sure his head could still fit through the door.

15 IAN

It took two weeks before she finally let me take Audrey to work.

And, holy shit, I regretted it almost instantly, rethinking keeping her there. It was like she could sense my weakness and cried unless I held her. Then, I remembered how tired Carina looked this morning when she finally caved and agreed to rest for a few hours. She told me she'd come get Audrey at lunch and then her eyes closed before I even walked out.

That left me with a tiny human strapped to my chest as I bounced my way through a phone conference. Hell, I bounced all the time, even when I wasn't holding her. Erik caught me bouncing the other day while I looked over spreadsheets. He'd quirked a brow, shaking his head with a laugh as he walked away.

Both guys gave me shit. Jared spent the morning laughing at me as I struggled to move without waking Audrey. I didn't think he'd ever stop laughing when he caught me baby-talking. I'd flipped him off and continued talking to my girl. Ain't no shame in baby-talking to the most beautiful girl ever.

By the time lunch rolled around, I almost collapsed in relief when Erik held up a bag from our favorite sub place. "Lunch in your office? You've got that baby bouncer in there, right?"

My face lit up, remembering the chair Carina promised was magic. I pulled Audrey off me with a groan, my front a little sweaty from where she'd been resting all morning. Gently placing her in the seat, I sent up a tiny prayer to the heavens that she didn't wake up. Her face screwed up, and she grunted a little, but when I began bouncing the seat, she settled again.

Just like magic.

"Damn, I don't know how Carina did this for the last few months," I complained, stretching my back before plopping down in my chair.

"Because she's a hell of a lot stronger than you."

I scowled, but then shrugged. "You're not wrong."

"I rarely am."

Scoffing, I threw my sandwich wrapper at his head, which he easily dodged. "God," I groaned. "This sub tastes like heaven after all the calories I burned bouncing her. My quads are gonna be feeling it tomorrow. No wonder Carina has such phenomenal legs."

"Can't say I've looked since I stare at Alex all the time."

"Alexandra's got some great legs too. I've looked at hers plenty of times."

I was barely holding back my laugh before the wrapper hit me in the head. Erik was so easy and protective of Alex. I liked getting a rise out of him.

"So, how has the last month been?"

"Good. Exhausting, but good. Every time I feel like I might face plant from lack of sleep, I look at her tiny face, and it's all worth it."

"She's pretty damn cute."

"Of course she is. She's my kid. How could she not be the best-looking baby there ever was."

"How does Carina put up with you?"

"I think she's secretly in love with me," I said with a wink. "She at least likes to look at my body and who could blame her."

Erik groaned and rolled his eyes. I had that effect on a lot of people. "How are things going with you two? You stay there, don't you? Are you guys...together?"

"No, we're not together-together. But things are going well. We're a team." I thought of how to explain it and realized I wasn't sure because we never talked about it. "A team that never talked about how to be a team, but we're making it work."

"So, you've never sat down and talked to her?" Erik said, slowly. His scrunched face was a mix of confusion, and doubt and it kind of pissed me off.

"No."

"Ian, how the hell have you been with this woman for two months—basically living on her couch for three weeks as you raise your child with her—and you haven't talked about what's next?"

I scowled at his logic and ran a hand through my hair. "I don't know. Jesus. Things have been crazy, and we've just...fuck, I don't know."

He laughed, and I thought of lobbing something sharper at his head. "What do you want?"

"I don't know." I sounded like a broken record.

He gave me a doubtful stare. Erik knew me better than anyone; he'd been my best friend since we were kids. "Yes, you do."

I tried to hold his stare, but Erik was better at being a hard-ass than I was. "Fine. I want her," I almost shouted, throwing my hands up. Audrey stirred in her seat, and I quickly bounced her again until she quieted down.

"Was that so hard?"

"Yes. Happy?"

"A little," he admitted with a smirk.

"Don't gloat. It looks bad on you."

"Nothing looks bad on me, and you know it." He laughed at my scowl but sobered. "Talk to her, Ian."

"I know, it's just been crazy, and I'm just trying to be as helpful as I can without getting in her way."

"She isn't your parents, Ian," Erik said, nailing the issue on the head. "She's your partner in this and if you want more from her, then talk to her. Let her know."

I tried to swallow past the knot of nerves strangling my throat. Carina laughed when I made jokes, but she also glared a lot. It was fifty-fifty on the reaction I'd get from her. What would her reaction be when I told her I wanted more from her? And what kind of more *did* I want?

"Yeah, I'll think on it."

"Good. And on that note, I have a phone call to make."

Erik stood and headed out, opening the door to Hanna about to knock on the other side, her fist raised in the air. He gave her a quick hug and explained his meeting before walking away.

"Hey, Ian."

"Hey, Hanna. Come on in. What can I help you with?"

"Can't a girl just come say hi to a friend?"

"Any time you want," I answered, smiling. Her dark, shoulder-length hair swayed when she sat back in the seat Erik had just vacated.

Hanna was like a sister to me, and I loved her like family. I always made time for her, giving her the attention she deserved. She was a bit of a recluse after what she'd gone through, so I always tried to be there for her, but it went both ways. We were friends, and she was there for me as much as I was there for her.

"How you hanging in there?" she asked with a warm smile.

"Well, I'm currently stuffing a sub in my face as fast as I can while I bounce a baby with my foot. So, things are going well."

She laughed and looked down at Audrey who had woken up at some point and now had a thumb in her mouth. My heart melted a little more each time I watched her little lips work around that tiny thumb. God, I loved her.

Her big eyes looked around as she kicked her legs and remained quiet for the first time all morning while I wasn't holding her. That chair really was magic.

Hanna wasn't immune to her baby magic either because she was out of her seat and crouched over Audrey in a second. "Oh, my god. I'll hold her. She's begging me with those gorgeous eyes."

Hanna picked her up and cradled her, burrowing her face close to Audrey and taking in her baby scent.

"So, how's life, Hanna?"

"I can't complain." She took a moment to look up and smiled. She was beautiful—she looked a lot like Erik—but still beautiful.

"Dating anyone?" I asked, using a stern, deep voice.

That made her laugh. "Hardly." She shrugged. "I'm kind of caught on someone else anyway."

"Oh, really?" I waggled my brows, but then sobered. "Best to not pursue that and stay single. Erik and I would have to beat up whoever lusted after his baby sister."

"Ian, I'm twenty-three years old."

"So, you're still Erik's little sister."

"I'm hardly a little girl."

"Whatever you say, Little Brandt," I said with a wink. "We'll always protect you, even when you're fifty."

"There's a vision," she deadpanned but laughed.

"We'll beat him up with our old-man canes."

She dropped her head back and laughed just as Carina came strolling around the corner into my office.

I couldn't stop my smile from growing even more. She looked radiant in her flowy dress and boots, a section of those legs I'd told Erik about, displayed perfectly. Her hair was down and curled, and for the first time since we came home, exhaustion didn't cling to her.

I waited for her to smile back, but her face was blank. It was almost like she was frozen with her hand on the door jam, taking in Hanna with Audrey. For a second, I saw an emotion similar to the one I saw in the bar that night she was drinking over Jake, but it was gone before I could blink.

"Hey, Carina," Hanna greeted her.

"Hey," she responded, giving Hanna a cordial smile. "How was she?" she asked me.

"Perfect. How could she not be? She takes after Daddy."

That same reaction she always had—the Carina-responding-to-Ian reaction—relaxed shoulders, reluctant smile, and eye roll. This time there was even a little laugh and a shake of her head. Like she knew laughing would encourage me, but she couldn't stop it if she tried.

"I was just holding her while he ate," Hanna explained, handing Audrey over after Carina had lost her jacket.

"Thanks for helping out."

"Anytime. She's beautiful."

"Thank you," Carina answered politely.

"Well, I've got to head back. See ya, Ian."

"Bye, Hanna. Stop by to say hi anytime."

She bit her lip and nodded, tucking hair behind her ear before giving one last smile and leaving.

My attention moved back to Carina, who looked like she was scowling at the open doorway.

"You okay?"

She blinked like coming out of a trance and smiled. "Yeah, I'm great. It's amazing what a two-hour nap and a shower can do. I curled my hair for the first time since being home from the hospital, and I feel almost human again."

"You look great."

She blushed, and it was nice to watch her eyes drop away like my compliment made her shy. Carina wasn't shy, but I liked that my words could make her submissive to me. She was a dominant personality, but I think that was just a shell to protect her from what she'd gone through. I think once I cracked through, she'd bend to me—at least in the bedroom.

Erik's words came to mind, and he was right, I needed to talk to her about what I wanted. I needed her to know that I wanted more.

"Do you mind if I close the door?"

"Not at all. I don't want anyone else seeing the goods."

"I'm just feeding, Ian. There's nothing sexual about it," she explained, unbuttoning her dress and bringing a hungry Audrey to her breast.

I watched in awe, warmth moving through me, down to my cock. "I've seen you do this tons of times and I'm in awe—not necessarily turned on by your boobs—although they're spectacular. I mean they're really freaking great—but it kind of turns me on watching you feed her. Watching you take care of her."

More color rose high on her cheekbones, and she swallowed. "I get it. It's just a parent thing," she explained with a shrug even though she looked anything other than nonchalant. "It's kind of like when I find you with our girl against your broad chest."

A slow smile formed as realization of what she was admitting spread through me. She struggled to meet my eyes as I rounded the desk and squatted at her feet. "I turn you on?" I asked, my voice deep and filled with desire.

"What?" she asked, breathless and with too much innocence to be real.

"I mean, I get it. You being a mother completely does it for me. You're beautiful taking care of our baby. A goddess." I looked down at Audrey latched onto Carina's breast, and a growl worked its way up from my chest. I was a caveman, possessive of his woman and offspring.

"Ian..." Carina was almost panting from just my claim, and I wanted to make it worth it. I wanted to make her breathless and gasping.

I rested my hand on her knees, her skin soft and warm under my rough palms. Holding her heavy-lidded stare, I slowly slid up her thighs, past the edge of her skirt.

"This is a bad idea," she breathed.

I smiled and adjusted my legs so she could see the hard-on pressing against my slacks. "I don't think it is." She gave the gasp I wanted when my thumbs brushed down between her thighs. Nowhere near where I wanted but getting closer. "You know, we never talked about what happened before Audrey arrived."

Carina swallowed and tried to lift her chin in the air, but her parted lips and burning gaze gave her away. "There's nothing to talk about."

"I disagree." I didn't pull my hands away, but I didn't push for more. She knew what I wanted, and that had to be enough for now. I had my foot in the door. "It's up to you, Carina. I just want to let you know; I'm here for any lusty desires you may have."

She gave me that typical look I associated with her—the laugh and shake of her head, but this time, it was mixed with her heavy breathing, and it was everything I wanted.

Before she could respond, a knock on the door broke the moment.

"One moment," I called out. "It's feeding time."

"Okay. Be back later," Jared called from the other side. He had two kids of his own, so he knew the drill.

I stood and took Audrey to burp her as Carina fixed her dress back up. My girl gave a completely unladylike belch and then went back to sucking her thumb.

"We should get going," Carina said once she was all put together again.

"Okay," I strapped Audrey into her seat before facing Carina who was trying to give me the proud, I'm-not-effected-by-you look. I shook my head, knowing she was trying to hide behind it, but I wasn't going to let her anymore. "Let's talk tonight. I'll bring home some dinner," I suggested as I opened the door.

Surprisingly, she nodded as she stepped outside. Jared and Hanna were standing by Laura's desk, discreetly watching our goodbye. Nosy bastards.

Carina noticed but ignored them and faced me. "I'll see you at home," she said with a smile. "Thanks for this morning."

I froze when she stepped closer, but naturally moved my hands to her waist when she raised on her toes to press a kiss to the corner of my mouth. I was so shocked or else I would have held her to me and taken more than that tiny peck. She stepped back and gave a shy smile, looking behind her to see Jared and Hanna gawking. She brushed them off, gave me one last smile and left.

I looked over to the two still staring. Hanna's eyes were downcast, and Jared had a brow raised in question.

I adjusted my suit jacket and pulled my shoulders back, feeling about ten feet tall. I smiled like getting a kiss goodbye from Carina was the most natural thing in the world and headed back into my office where I could relive her lips pressed to mine for the rest of the day.

At least until I could get home and get a hell of a lot more than just a peck.

16 CARINA

A FEW DAYS LATER, I still couldn't stop reliving every millisecond of my lips pressed to Ian's. It wasn't even his full lips, just the corner of his mouth and I was an overheated mess each time the memory slammed into me.

Somehow, I'd been able to avoid him and that conversation he'd wanted to have. I'd been pacing back and forth across my apartment that day waiting for him to come home and instead my phone had buzzed on the coffee table, letting me know he had a meeting he couldn't miss and would be back late. Then we became ships passing in the night, or at least passing around Audrey's sleep schedule, which had been extra rough the past couple of days. She'd been pissed about something and kept me up.

So, instead of talking about how I'd almost dissolved into a puddle of lust when he touched me or how I kissed him, he let me sleep while he took some baby shifts.

I knew it had been wrong to kiss him, but I'd seen Hanna watching, and I remembered the fiery burn of jealousy that had consumed me when I'd walked into his office to find them laughing and her holding my baby. I'd needed to make a point.

A laugh tried to bubble up as I realized how damaged I was from Jake leaving me for another person—his friend. Hanna was Ian's friend. Did he like her more than me?

This time, I did laugh. Could I have sounded any more like an immature girl in high school?

"Carina, what's so funny?" my Aunt Virginia asked.

I blinked, snapping out of a daze and looked at her tilted head across the table. My aunts had called and suggested we get some lunch out so they could see Audrey and have mimosas.

"She's probably thinking about the delicious man-meat waiting for her at home," Aunt Vivian muttered.

"Oh, my goodness, Vivian," Violet scolded. I gave her a smile of thanks, but she made me want to take it back immediately. "Don't call her out on her dirty daydreams we all know she's having. She's blushing now. If she wants to fantasize in the middle of a restaurant, let the girl have a moment."

"Nah," Vivian responded, resting her chin on her hand. "Carina, why don't you tell us all about your daydreams about Mr. tall, dark, and sexy."

Virginia shook her head, smiling down at the table, not stopping them, but thankfully, not joining.

"Hell, we know how committed I am to Gloria, and even I find myself wanting to daydream about him," Vera chimed in.

"Come on, details," Vivian pleaded. "Just one. How big is he?"

I coughed and did my best to glare at her. She shrugged and finished off her second mimosa.

"All right, you old hags. That's enough," Virginia finally stepped in.

"Thank you, Aunt Virginia." I could always count on her to save me.

However, I could also count on her to call me out on the serious topics. "All jokes aside, what's going on with you two?" she asked.

Keeping my eyes glued to my plate, I went for innocence. "Nothing." It wasn't a lie. Nothing was going on between us. We were surviving together, but the more accustomed we became to our situation, the more opportunities arose.

"Okay," she said slowly. "What do you *want* going on between you two?"

I peeked up from under my lashes at four sets of blue eyes staring back at me, and I knew I wasn't getting out of this.

"I don't know. Honestly. Audrey's all I can focus on right now."

"Do you want more than the partner you have now?" Violet asked. "Do you care for him?"

"Of course, he's Audrey's father."

"Listen," Vivian cut in. "You can have a kid with someone, and not care about them, trust me." Vivian had a son from her first marriage, and he was kind of a douche—like his dad, Vivian's ex-husband.

I took a deep breath, letting my frustration bubble up. If I could admit my feelings anywhere, it was with these women who helped raise me. "Yes," I confessed, and once I started, it all boiled out. "We bicker all the time, but it's like a weird version of foreplay. He provokes me because he likes my bossiness. And he's so caring and, oh my god, he's so hot," I groaned, my hands fisting on the table. "And the further I get from this pregnancy, the more I remember how amazing it was between us, and I swear to god it's all I can think about some nights."

Silence met the end of my verbal vomit, and I hesitantly lifted my eyes to find some smirks and smiles.

"Yeah, that's what I thought," Vivian gloated.

My shoulders dropped in defeat. Saying it out loud didn't make it any better than when it was floating around in my head.

"You need to talk to him," the always sensible Virginia said.

They all nodded, and I wanted to take back the last five minutes so I could keep avoiding the talk Ian and I were barreling toward.

Audrey took that moment to make her presence known from the car seat propped on a highchair, and there was no build-up. She was pissed and wasn't giving any warning about it. I lifted her out and tried to bounce her. I checked her pants, and nothing was there. We tried to eat, and she wasn't having it.

"I'm sorry, guys. I think I should take her home."

They all agreed, and we decided to meet up again soon. After hugs and kisses—done at super speed because Audrey was still wailing—we left. I'd just started the car when the most horrendous sound from the tiniest human came from the back. The silver lining was that she stopped crying, but the drive was long and smelly.

"Your daddy is right; you are the smelliest baby in the world."

I almost dropped Audrey's car seat when I opened my apartment door, and Ian came around the corner from the kitchen. I'd given him a key a while ago since he pretty much stayed here every night, but it was still early in the day. I assumed he was at work.

"Where were you?"

His accusing tone had me pulling up short and slowly setting the car seat down. I took in his tense shoulders, hands on hips, and clenched jaw.

"At lunch," I answered slowly, still unsure of his mood and what caused it.

"With who?" he barked.

His third-degree questions and irritation had my tone shifting from cautious to bitchy. "Not that it's any of your business, but my aunts."

It was as if my answer poked a hole in his balloon of anger. His shoulders sagged, and one hand ran across his face as he blew out a hard sigh. He looked across the space as I got Audrey from her seat, and I saw the apology before he even opened his lips.

"Listen, I'm sorry. I just got home, and you weren't here, and I basically reacted like a teenage girl, working myself up. I realized you could be out doing anything, and I have no right to know otherwise, and it killed me. And then I started thinking about what you could be out doing and I just...kind of lost it in my own head. I overreacted. I just..." He stopped, and his face screwed up. "My god, is that her?" he asked, pointing an accusing finger at the tiny baby smiling in my arms.

"Yup. Our little angel."

Ian made gagging noises as I passed, heading to her room to get rid of the offending diaper.

I scrambled to understand Ian's reaction when I'd walked in. He thought I was out with someone else? A guy? Was he jealous? The thought of Ian being jealous of me with someone else sparked a light in me that I wasn't sure I wanted to look too closely at. But it felt a lot like happiness.

When I came back out to the living room, Ian still had a guarded look, and I realized the conversation I'd been avoiding was about to happen. I swallowed down the nerves and tried to stand tall—look more confident than I felt—and waited for him to start.

"Listen, I get that we aren't officially together, but I think it's best that we don't bring anyone else into this."

My muscles pulled tight, his suggestion wrapping around my chest and squeezing. I knew it wasn't rational—this anger that flooded my veins. Maybe it was because I felt attacked as soon as

I walked through the door. Maybe it was already frazzled nerves at having this conversation at all.

But, really, I knew it was because of that spark of happiness I'd felt at his jealousy. I knew it was another way to open myself up for hurt—and that terrified me. I wanted to believe it'd only be Audrey and me but hoping for that left an opportunity for him to let me down if he didn't follow through—if he lied.

Despite knowing how irrational I was being, it didn't stop me from reacting.

"That's rich coming from you," I scoffed.

It was such a bitchy thing to say, and I regretted it, but now that I'd said it, I wondered how true it was. He wasn't with me all the time. He could have been having quickies all over town, and I'd never know. Hell, Hanna spent all day with him, and they were close. Maybe they'd already slept together.

"What the hell, Carina?"

"Ian, how long do you usually go without someone? You're a woman magnet and flirt with anything that has legs. You're telling me you won't or haven't been with anyone?"

His nostrils flared, and his eyes blazed with a mix of frustration and hurt. "That's not fair," he said around a clenched jaw. "Who I was before Audrey doesn't come into play. I've given all my time to both of you."

Not able to hold his gaze anymore, I dropped my eyes to the floor, knowing I was in the wrong. The happiness from earlier no longer flickered with hope in my chest. Instead, I felt a jealousy of my own. He wasn't doing this for me; he was doing this for Audrey.

The realization that I was jealous of my own baby had me choking back a laugh at what a mess I was. I closed my eyes and breathed as deep as my lungs would allow. I needed to reset and calm down before I opened my stupid, hormonal mouth again.

"I know." I forced my eyes back to his, letting him see my

regret. "I'm sorry. The lack of sleep and my own issues are getting to me."

He nodded, and the tension and irritation faded, leaving us both tired after the sway of emotions.

"You never told me what happened that night," he said surprising me with the change of topic.

That night I saw Ian for the first time.

The night he found me drowning my sorrows in alcohol.

The night I kissed him.

I huffed a laugh and shook my head. Where did I begin?

He closed the gap between us and tugged me down on the couch next to him where my knee brushed his thigh. Even that small connection eased the pinch that always accompanied thinking about Jake.

"I'd just realized my fiancé was in love with someone else that night."

"How did you find out?"

I laughed outright at that, not wanting to tell Ian about the threesome I'd had with Jake and Jackson. That was a can of worms for another night. So, I stuck to the lighter side of the truth.

"We were working on a new project, and the manager of the company was one of his old college friends. I liked Jackson." I ignored the sharp pain from that over-simplified statement. I'd loved Jackson too. In a different way, but I'd trusted him, and we'd grown so close. "He was a fun guy, and when Jake hesitated on closing the gap between them, I pushed for it. It was my fault Jackson was back in his life because I wanted him there. I had no idea that Jake had had feelings for him before or that they'd come roaring back. So, yeah," I said with a shrug. "That night at the bar was when I finally saw what had been there all along."

"What a dick."

I laughed at his easy insult. "Yeah, I guess I just haven't been the same since."

Another understatement. I'd closed so much of myself off.

I thought back to the girl who frequented sex shops and sex clubs and danced in the kitchen. I remembered the girl who laughed easily and took on adventures with excitement and no doubts. Now, I took on business deals with a precise, no risk mindset and stopped having sex before Ian.

I wasn't sure who I was or if I'd ever get the first girl back.

Fingers stroking my hair back behind my ear brought me back to the man beside me on the couch. His touch was soft, and the look in his eyes was the same as when he touched me in his office—full of desire and want.

"I think you're pretty great."

His words caressed my skin and brought goosebumps in their wake. I may not know who I was anymore, but every moment I was with Ian like this, the old Carina came out from behind the curtain and urged me to throw caution to the wind.

"There's no one else, Ian. You and Audrey take up all my time." The words were breathy, and I couldn't stop myself from staring at his lips as they stretched into a gorgeous smile. It lulled me into a trance, pulling me forward.

"Good," he growled, his fingers moving to my hair.

When he leaned forward to meet me halfway, a baby toy fell from the couch, the rattle loud like a warning bell. I jerked back and looked anywhere but at him.

"Dinner," I almost shouted to break the tense silence. "What do you want to do for dinner?"

He didn't respond right away, and I took the risk to look up. One eyebrow raised high, and he didn't have to say a word. He knew what had almost happened and knew he could push to make me admit it. But I pleaded with my eyes for him to let it go.

He shook his head, and I knew he would give me this, just

once, but my time was running out before we confronted the attraction between us. "Italian?"

"Ugh," I answered easily, falling into our safe banter. "Mexican."

"Tough shit, woman. We're doing Italian."

I rolled my eyes but let him have it. He'd let me have more reprieve than I deserved today. Italian was the least I could do.

But I couldn't lie to myself and shut the door on my growing desire.

Old Carina had popped out, and I wasn't sure she wanted to go back in.

17 IAN

"Son of a bitch." Carina gave me a dark warning look about my language, but the throbbing moved from my stubbed toe up to my ankle. "Mother effing-piece of shii..." I faded off and finished with a growl of frustration.

If I stumbled over one more baby item, I was bound to break something or fall and crash and burn.

"Sorry." She gave an apologetic smile now that I'd word vomited my pain. "I was bouncing her as I looked over some work."

Audrey sucked her thumb with her eyes closed from her rocking crib next to the couch. Carina rocked her with her foot as she flipped through the papers spread out on the coffee table. I looked to the right at the empty swing wedged in the corner between the chair and the tv stand.

"What about the swing?"

"She wasn't happy there."

"Of course not. That girl is a diva," I said, pointing at the sleeping baby who probably got her diva-ness from me.

Carina shrugged and kept rocking.

"Can I put it back in her room?"

"Umm, yeah," she agreed, looking around the cramped room like a spot would magically appear. "Just kind of stick it between the chair and her crib."

Flipping on the light to the baby room, I took in the tastefully decorated—but overly full—space. There was baby shit piled on top of more baby shit. The closet was tiny for storage and overflowed into the dresser, jam-packed with clothes and diapers. This room was designed to be more of an office than an actual room.

I thought about my empty apartment that had too many rooms and had been empty for the better part of a month. Dropping my eyes to my poor abused feet, I thought back to when I first suggested we move into my place. She'd looked at me like I'd lost my mind and immediately shut me down.

But that was then, and I'd approached it cautiously, letting her back away from the topic too easily. She probably never expected me to stay on her couch as long as I have, but I meant what I said when I told her I didn't want to be away from them.

I was ready to broach the topic again, and this time, I was going to smother her with good reasons and not let her back down. The plan sounded fantastic in my head. It sounded even better when I tripped over a rattle as I made my way out to the living room.

It sounded less good barreling out of my mouth, and Carina looked at me like I had grown a second head.

"Let's move in together."

"What?" she almost shrieked. "Ian, we already discussed this."

I ignored her scrunched frown and pushed on. "Come on," I urged, moving to sit beside her on the couch. "We're basically doing it anyway, and my place is so much bigger. It makes sense.

Things have settled, and we've created a good rhythm. Let's keep it going with more space."

"You want me to give up my apartment?" she asked like I'd suggested she get rid of a limb. "We're not even a couple, Ian."

"We sure aren't," I answered quickly, a victorious smile forming. She raised her brows, shocked at how happy I was she'd pointed it out. Carina was practical, and I was only winning this battle by not trying to seduce her. "We're partners in this, and that means more than anything else."

I held back my fist pump when I saw the first crack in her resolve—practicality for the win.

"Yes, it does mean a lot," she agreed slowly. "But how long can this last? What about a year from now when you want to start seeing someone? Or I want to start seeing someone?"

Clenching my jaw, I barely held back the jealous growl at imagining her with someone other than me. My inner caveman was shoving practical aside, but I managed to keep him at bay with a deep breath. "I know we haven't talked about us, but I don't see myself having anything to give when I give it all to Audrey."

And her, I added mentally. Carina wasn't ready to hear that...yet.

"But we bicker all the time..."

"It's who we are. It's not out of malice or because we dislike each other."

"Speak for yourself," she muttered.

I scowled until she relented.

"Fine. You're okay." She rolled her eyes at my smile but was ready with more half-hearted arguments. "It's bound to fall apart."

"Then I'll help you move when it does."

"Ian..."

I was so close.

"I have a baby room ready, but we can trash it for what she already has if you don't like it." Wide eyes lifted to mine. "But I matched it pretty well to the stuff you got."

"You have a baby room?" she almost whispered.

"Yeah. As soon as she was born, I set it up in case she ever stayed at my place." She swallowed and, like a lawyer, I got ready to deliver my winning closing argument. "It's about being practical, Carina. I have a guest room for you as well as Audrey's room. There's tons more space everywhere, and you can decorate however you want. No more cramming stuff between other pieces of furniture. And we've proven we can inhabit a single space without killing each other."

She licked her lips and swallowed, and I swear, I heard the Jeopardy song playing somewhere as I held my breath and waited for her answer.

"Fine," she said on a huff.

Victory surged through my veins and flooded my body with adrenaline. Holy shit, she agreed. Without thought, I lifted her in my arms and hugged her tight, standing, and swaying side to side. "I win. I actually won."

She pushed off my shoulders and stood, doing her best to glare, but I saw the humor lurking behind those baby blues. "I may rescind so you don't get a big head."

"Too late, baby."

She heaved a sigh and rested her hands on her hips, looking down at the scattered papers. "Well, not to interrupt your self-celebration, but I'm going to clean this up and head to bed. We can discuss the details in the morning."

I helped her pick up and moved Audrey to the bedroom. Carina was in the kitchen, getting a glass of water when I grabbed my pillow and blanket. I was just getting ready to lay down when she stopped at the end.

"Oh, my god. Just come to my room. I can't stand to watch you sleep on that tiny thing one more night."

It wasn't that tiny, but I was a big guy. A big guy who wasn't going to argue with the offer to sleep next to the most beautiful woman I knew. I hopped up. "Hell, yes."

"Calm down," she warned. "Just to sleep."

Walking past, I waggled my brows. "If you insist." She slapped my back and narrowed her eyes. "Alright, alright. I'll be on my best behavior."

Standing across the bed from her as I stripped out of my clothes and she pulled her long hair up in a messy bun thing felt surreally natural—domestic. I had to stop and stare and take in that this was my life right now. It may only last a moment, but it was a moment I wanted to recreate again and again.

The more domestic moments we had, the more I realized how much I wanted it. My parents accused me of never wanting to settle down, but they were wrong. I did want a family of my own. One better than the one they gave me. I just never found anyone who made me want to try.

"What the hell, Ian?" Carina whisper-yelled.

"What?"

"Where are your clothes?"

"Umm, sorry, but I don't have pajamas. I figured I was being a gentleman by leaving my underwear on."

She tried not to, but her eyes kept bouncing down my body like she was in a battle with her mind over where her eyes should look. If she kept looking, I'd get an erection that would be impossible to hide behind these boxer briefs.

Her eyes slid down until they rested on my crotch. Heat built and burned its way to my cock. I knew making me hard wasn't what she wanted, so I broke the moment, rocking my hips Magic Mike style.

"Oh, my god." Her hand shot up to cover her eyes, and I laughed.

"That's the real reason you invited me in. You just wanted a show."

She glared between her fingers, and I linked my fingers behind my head, exaggerating my dance moves, even humming a song.

She shook her head but laughed. "God, get in bed, you perv."

She may have given me shit about what I slept in, but the way her breasts swayed under that thin cami and her thighs flexed in her short shorts as she got in bed was damn near indecent.

I quickly got under the covers before she could catch my semi. She flicked off the light and moved around about seven million times before settling on her back. She didn't even have to speak for me to know her mind was going a thousand different places. I closed my eyes and counted, making it to seventeen before she finally spoke.

"Are you sure about this?"

"I've never been more sure about anything in my life." The answer was heavier than I intended, and I made a joke to ease the tension radiating off her. "I'm bound to break something if we stay here."

She laughed, but it faded, and I could hear her thoughts again. Shifting to my side, I took in the shadow of her profile. Her nose perfectly sloped over pouty lips she was currently gnawing on.

"Carina, look at me," I commanded. After only a moment, she complied, turning on her side to face me. We were both at the edge of our pillows and less than a foot apart. "We'll make this work. Even if we're just friends the whole way. Like Batman and Robin."

"K, but I'm Batman."

147

I narrowed my eyes, and she pinched her lips, fighting back a smile. "Fine."

Her lips parted as she finally gave in to a full smile. With just the moonlight shining through the curtains, she glowed like a siren calling me to her. My breath stuttered in my chest as the smile slipped from her lips, and her eyes dropped to my mouth. Unable to help it, I licked my lips just imagining the taste of her on them.

"Can I...can I try something?"

Her words took me back to the night at the bar when we first met. She'd uttered the same words before kissing me, and I held my breath waiting, barely getting the answer out. "Of course."

She inched forward, closing the small distance between us. I tried to stay still but could only hold back so long and moved to meet her halfway. Our lips barely pressed against each other's, but my body quaked with desire. She pulled back, but only enough to take in a breath and latch on to my bottom lip, flicking it with her tongue.

I lost it.

My hand buried in her hair and held her to me, trying to meld myself to her. Her soft hand explored my ribs and tugged me closer. I wasn't going to deny this woman anything and inched over until my cock pressed against her body. She moaned, and I took the opportunity to slip my tongue into her mouth, making my own sounds of pleasure as her tongue tangled with mine.

Her nails dug softly into my skin, and I abandoned her hair to grip her thigh, tugging it up over my hip so I could rock my hard length against her hot core.

"Ian," she gasped. The desperate plea of my name on her lips shot down my spine, lighting me on fire.

I was just about to roll her over—take control of the situation

—when a soft baby grunt came from her side of the bed, and she froze.

Each of her muscles tightened before she softly pushed back and lowered her leg out of my grip. I didn't want to ruin what we had accomplished tonight. I didn't want her to think she couldn't give an inch without me taking a mile. I didn't want her to over-think this and come up with some off the wall conclusion that had her changing her mind about moving.

So, I brushed her hair behind her ear and pressed a gentle peck to her lips before re-situating back on my own pillow. "Don't overthink it, Carina. Just enjoy the comfort tonight, and I'll let you get away with hiding from it tomorrow."

Her jaw dropped, and I knew challenging my little hellcat on hiding would be enough to bring out her fight rather than flight.

"I'm not hiding."

I just cocked a brow and smirked, barely holding back my laugh when she growled and rolled to face the opposite wall.

Pushing my luck, I gripped her hip and tugged her back to me, wrapping my arm around her. She laid stiff for only a moment before finally relaxing.

When her breathing evened out, I kissed her shoulder and whispered my promise.

"I'll make you happy, Carina. You deserve it."

I thought she'd been asleep, but her hand moved to slide her fingers through mine and when she didn't say anything, I took my own advice.

I didn't overthink it. I just held her close and enjoyed the night.

18 CARINA

"This place is amazing." My eyes roamed from the hardwood floors, past the floor to ceiling windows, up to the exposed ceilings. "Are all the walls brick?"

"For the most part," he answered, setting down a box we'd just carried up. He looked around with me like he was seeing it for the first time. "It had been mid-renovation when I stumbled upon it, so I was able to have a say in what was kept and what wasn't."

I stacked my box next to his and tried not to drool over the wall of bookshelves. "I love it."

"Well, feel free to make any changes. It's yours now too."

Moving in with Ian still made me a little short of breath. I hadn't even really lived with Jake, and here I was, moving in with a guy I wasn't even dating. Breathing a laugh, I bit back the manic laugh that threatened to break free. It was all so surreal.

"Why don't I show you the rooms."

I followed his broad back down around a corner behind the ridiculously modern kitchen.

"All the bedrooms are down here. If you turn the corner at

the other side of the living room, there's an office you're welcome to use. But this first room is Audrey's." He gestured inside, and I choked on my breath.

"It's exactly the same."

"But bigger. I didn't have any clue what baby stuff to get, so I just copied what you had."

"Ian, this is amazing."

"I figured at some point she'd stay here."

"Yeah," I breathed. It was moments like this when it hit me how Ian and I had avoided talking about what our future looked like. We made Audrey the center of our universe and just took each play as it came. Which was the opposite of who I was. I liked everything planned perfectly, but with Ian, my fear of the feelings that constantly hummed beneath the surface of my veneer scared me more than any chaos could.

"This room is yours. Again, change whatever you like. We can throw out everything and bring your stuff in. Hell, we can throw out everything and start from scratch."

The room had the same wood floors and brick walls. The large windows made the large space seem even bigger, and the bright sun shining in made me want to twirl and fall back on the fluffy gray comforter. "This is perfect."

"Awesome. The bathroom is through that door over there and connects to Audrey's room."

"Perfect," I said again like a broken record.

"Why don't we head downstairs and grab some more boxes?"

"Okay. Aunt Vivian said she'd watch Audrey as long as we needed her."

"Great. Let's see how much we can get done today and then go from there."

Five hours later, everything on me ached, and I couldn't wait to collapse and nurse Audrey until we both passed out.

"We can get the rest of the stuff later. Your lease isn't up for a few more months, so we have time."

"Sounds perfect," I sighed, falling back on Ian's couch.

Ian picked Audrey up out of the car seat and sat right next to me. Audrey made herself comfortable on his chest, placing her tiny thumb between her rosebud lips. Her big blue eyes blinked a few times before growing heavy, like Ian's heartbeat lulled her back to sleep.

"This sunset may make the whole move worth it."

We sat on the couch facing the wall of windows, the orange and golden colors warming up the entire space.

"This sunset and no more tripping and almost breaking my neck."

"I can't believe you've been sleeping on my couch this whole time when you had this place sitting empty."

I'd been grateful not to be alone, but who wouldn't want to be in their own home with their own things in a bed big enough to hold them?

"Home isn't the place," he explained softly. "It's the people. So, I was happy to be with you guys."

I rolled my head against the back of the couch to look his way in time to watch him place a soft kiss to Audrey's head, and my heart ached.

"Why do you have such a big place?" I asked in the silence, the stars starting to peek out in the darkened sky.

He shrugged. "I guess I always wanted to fill it with a family of my own."

For the first time, with Ian saying something so serious to me, I didn't scoff or make light of it. His easy sense of humor and child-like attitude made it easy to pigeon hole him into this aloof playboy. And maybe that was what he had been, but this apartment screamed how wrong I'd been, thinking it was what he

152

always wanted to be. I'd distracted myself from Ian, focusing all my attention on our baby. I'd used his jokes as a wall to keep space around my heart. I told myself I needed someone serious by my side.

But right then, with his face glowing in the light, holding our little girl cradled safely against his chest, I felt the first crack in the wall begin, and I worried what really living together was going to do to my restraint. This wasn't him staying over to be with Audrey. This was me giving up a huge part of myself and making a new home with him.

It was terrifying, and I held on to that fear to patch the crack up the best I could.

"Well, it's beautiful," I choked out.

"Thank you."

"How about dinner?"

"I won't turn down some food. All that moving made me hungry. Where do you want to order from?"

"I can cook."

He turned to me with a raised eyebrow. "Damn, woman. You cook too? I've died and gone to heaven."

His eyes heated as they scanned as much of me as he could reach over Audrey's head, and I looked away, laughing to hide the heat simmering on my cheeks.

"Fair warning, my kitchen is a little lacking."

"I'll make do."

Those were my famous last words. I opened empty cupboard after empty cupboard, coming up with a single pot and a couple cooking utensils.

"Oh, my god, Ian. This is horrible."

He'd set Audrey in her rocker and leaned against the back of the couch. "I tried to warn you."

My shoulders shrugged over a heavy sigh, and I dug through

his pantry and fridge to come up with something. "I'll figure something out."

"Okay. While you're doing that, I'll unpack this box that says vibrators and sex toys."

I whipped around. "What?"

Ian almost doubled over at my reaction. "I was joking, but the fear there makes me think maybe I wasn't too far off the mark."

"I do not have sex toys." At least, I hadn't packed them all up and brought them over...yet.

"The lady doth protest too much, methinks."

"Ugh." I rolled my eyes, turning my back on his devious smile. "Incorrigible."

"Well, I did find a box of your CDs. Who keeps CDs anymore?"

"I know. I should get rid of them."

"Yes, you should. But first, we should listen." He began digging through my collection and whistled. "You've got a hell of a collection here. Cranberries. Blink-182. Backstreet Boys. Green Day. Digital Underground. Damn, woman."

"I like all kinds of music."

"What should we play first?"

"How about Digital Underground?"

"Coming right up."

Ian got the music going, and I fell into a rhythm I hadn't had in a little over a year. I swayed my hips and sang The Humpty Dance as I cut veggies and created my one-pot concoction.

I wasn't sure if Ian noticed me bouncing to the beat, but he never said anything as he worked on unpacking boxes. I wasn't sure I cared either. I loved listening to music and cooking. I used to do it all the time for Jake, but when we broke up, I buried myself and lived on take-out.

I had to admit; it was nice to loosen up and laugh as I mumbled through the words.

"I'm glad you're here, dancing queen."

I turned to meet his smiling gray eyes across the island and another crack fissured along my wall, letting honesty slip out.

"Me too."

19 CARINA

Surprisingly the move went well. The week since I'd agreed had been great. Almost too great. So great I felt like I was holding my breath, waiting for the other shoe to drop. Like Ian said, it made sense, and when moments of doubt lingered, I reminded myself of the practicality.

"Hey," Ian said from where he was packing up after the meeting in Erik's office. "Do you want to grab a box of your pots and pans on our way home. You've got better stuff than I do."

"Because I actually have stuff, Mr. One-pot-one-pan."

"It was all I needed for my Mac and cheese and bacon," he defended, laughing.

"Yeah, we can do that. That way I can maybe make dinner some nights."

The conversation was surreal. If you had asked me two months ago if Ian and I would be talking about going home together to cook meals after a meeting, I would have laughed until I cried.

"God, yes," Ian moaned, his eyes rolling back in his head.

"You can make me dinner any night you want. Who knew you were the best cook ever?"

"Wait…" Alex said from where she sat, breaking her conversation with Hanna. Her eyes bounced between us.

"You guys moved in together?" Hanna's voice rose to a pitch that put me on the defensive. Like she would have been less surprised if I said I was actually a man.

"Yeah," Ian answered slowly, a smile tipping his lips like he found their shock hilarious.

Maybe Alex's shock was fun because it quickly shifted to excitement. But Hanna's remained fully in horror.

"We're slowly moving all of her in. Her lease is up in a couple of months, so we figured there's no rush to move it all at once."

"B-but," Hanna stuttered, her eyes blinking as she tried to process. "You don't take anyone there. Hell, I've only been there a handful of times."

Ian shrugged, turning soft eyes to me. "Yeah, I save it for family."

Home. Family. Us. Ours.

These were words I wasn't sure I'd ever associate with him, but they soaked into my lonely soul and filled a gap that had been broken by Jake.

"Are you guys together?" Hanna asked, trying to mask her initial reaction.

"No."

Ian narrowed his eyes at my quick denial but didn't seem overly bothered. He knew me well enough that my answer didn't surprise him. "We're partners raising our baby. Now just in a place that can hold all of us and not risk my life with each step I take."

"Oh," Hanna finally said after a too-long silence.

"Well, I think it's amazing," Alex chimed in.

"Yeah...Amazing." Hanna said the words, but her eyes didn't match.

"What's amazing?" Erik asked, walking back in from talking to Laura, who was currently watching Audrey.

"Carina moved in with Ian," Alex announced.

Erik's eyes shot to Hanna for a brief moment before moving to Ian and giving a genuine smile. "Good for you, Ian. I don't know how you convinced her to do it or if she's locked in a tower, but I'm happy for you." He cupped his hand over his mouth and muttered to me, "Blink twice if you're being held against your will."

Ian flipped him off but laughed.

"Hey, Carina," Erik started. "I'd been meaning to ask you if you're going to the wedding?"

"What wedding?" Ian asked.

"Jake's—the other half of her company," Erik answered. "I've gotten to know him through his donations to my charity."

Ian's curious gaze flicked to mine at the news. I'd kind of forgotten, slash didn't want to acknowledge it.

"Jake, your ex?" Ian asked.

"Yup."

"Oh, you're going," he said like I'd thrown down the gauntlet.

I parted my lips to argue, to make an excuse, but he held up a hand. "Don't argue, Carina Russo. You're going to dress up and be the hottest woman. You'll eat cake, dance, and be the happiest person there."

My shoulders sagged, not wanting to fight him because I kind of liked showing up to my ex-fiancé's wedding and looking happier than ever before. I loved Jake, and I loved Jackson, but I also had a petty side that laughed with glee at the idea. "Fine."

Ian's fists went up, and he hissed, "Yesssss."

"Are you going to do this every time you get your way?"

"Probably."

"Just go with it," Erik suggested.

Everyone got up to go. Alex offered to go shopping to look for a dress for the wedding, and Hanna gave a forced smile before making excuses about a phone call. We were just about to go grab Audrey when Erik stopped Ian.

"Ian, before you go, I talked to Kyle in London just a bit ago, and he let me know they need you there for the final viewing of the building. I thought Alex and I could make a trip of it, but they need you."

"Shit." He looked to me with regret, and I gave him a reassuring smile.

"It's okay. We knew you'd have to go to London at some point."

"I know," he said, dragging his hand through his hair. "I just didn't want to leave so soon."

"When do you leave? For how long?"

He grimaced, and I knew it would be bad news before he even said it. "Tomorrow. For a week, maybe two."

Then it was me standing there, a weight on my chest, muttering, "Oh."

He gave me a regretful smile, but there was nothing to do but push on.

"Okay. I'll grab the pots and pans from the apartment, and you can start packing."

"Sounds like a plan."

By the time I made it home, it was already late, but I wanted to make dinner. Cooking would help take my mind off the fact that Ian was leaving tomorrow.

Turning up the music, I swayed my hips and stirred the sauce. I brought the wooden spoon to my lips and tasted the tangy, sweet tomato sauce, licking it clean before using it as a microphone belting out the lyrics to *That's Exactly How I Feel* by Lizzo.

I stopped mid-sentence when I heard a deeper voice also singing behind me. Turning slowly, I found Ian strutting out from the hallway to the beat with Audrey in his arms as he sang.

He set Audrey in her swing before strutting toward the kitchen.

"Don't stop now. I was hoping for a duet."

"Oh, my god," I laughed.

I wasn't sure I could sing because my jaw hung open, probably with drool leaking out. Ian only wore a pair of basketball shorts. His muscles flexing with each hip thrust and roll. His biceps bulged when he rested one hand behind his head, and the other pointed my way as he humped the air.

I wouldn't have been able to stop my eyes from traveling to the way his thick cock bounced against his shorts even if I'd taped them shut. He swiveled his hips, belting out the lyrics entrancing me with each move.

"Stop watching my dick bounce and dance with me."

"Ian," I screeched.

"At least jump around so I can watch your boobs bounce."

I wanted to feel affronted at his suggestion, but happiness bubbled up until it came out as a laugh and something in me urged me to give in.

Maybe it was the way he issued it with a raised eyebrow. Maybe because I wanted to have his eyes track over my body like mine were doing to his.

Once he was finally in the kitchen, he stole my wooden-spoon-microphone and screeched more lyrics.

"You're horrible."

"Like you can do better?" he challenged.

I narrowed my eyes and tugged back my microphone, singing off-key and loud. I swayed my hips, twerking my butt to the beat. His eyes heated and tracked my moves, and I continued to steal glances at his bouncing tripod.

We laughed and danced around each other, not touching, but having our own little dance-off. When I thought I'd got the laughing under control, he'd pelvic thrust toward me, forcing my eyes down again. Heat spread from my cheeks down my body, making my hands twitch to tug the shorts down so I could watch him without anything blocking my view.

As the seconds ticked by, we got closer and closer, our bodies coming together like magnets. When I was sure he was going to grab me and pull me in to turn this into a dirty-dancing dance-off, the song ended, and we both stood there breathless, with wide smiles, and sexual tension vibrating between us.

The moment broke when the sound of water bubbling over the pan had me jumping into action.

"Shit."

"Do you need help?" he asked, leaning against the counter. I made a point to ignore his knowing smile.

Now that I wasn't entranced with his swinging dick and hard abs, I got my dirty thoughts about us screwing on the kitchen floor out of my mind.

"No, I'm good," I answered, my voice too high-pitched.

I held my breath waiting for him to call me on my bullshit—waited for him to corner me against the counter and press close, maybe kiss down my neck.

But it never came, and I did my best to convince myself I was relieved. Instead, he stood tall and said, "Whatever you say, dancing queen. I'm going to go finish doing some laundry."

And hopefully, put on a shirt before I sexually assaulted my baby-daddy.

THE NEXT DAY I helped him pack and vetoed his Hawaiian shirt ideas. I also vetoed a quick drop off at the curb. Instead, opting for parking at the airport and walking him in. I held Audrey in the baby carrier, bouncing side to side as he got through check-in.

"Daddy will miss you, my sweet baby girl," Ian baby-talked between all the kisses to Audrey's dark head of hair. "You be good, but get all those stinky poops out before Daddy comes home, okay?"

"Yeah, right. You'll owe me after this."

He looked up from her head and smiled, his mouth only inches from mine. I stared at the full bottom lip and wondered if I could pretend to stumble and fall against his mouth. He'd stayed true to his word and not brought up the last night in my apartment, but it didn't mean I hadn't laid in his guest room and dreamed of reliving it over and over.

Someone bumped into him, unfortunately knocking him sideways. He recovered and gave me the smile I was always fighting to give in to. The one that said he knew I wanted him, and he could make me scream. All I had to do was ask.

That smile.

"Don't miss me too much."

I scoffed. "Hardly."

He breathed a laugh and rested his hand atop Audrey, brushing her downy hair. "Be good girls. I'll be back soon, and we can FaceTime. Call me if you need anything at all."

"Okay."

He took one step away but stopped and turned back to crowd me. Holding my wide stare, he leaned down and pressed a kiss to the corner of my mouth and muttered the words that had me smiling the rest of the day.

"You may not miss me, but I'll miss you."

20 CARINA

Day Two:

Ian: What are my girls doing tonight?
Carina: Having tummy time.
Ian: I love tummy time. I may have some tummy time myself later.
Carina: Well, it isn't our daughter's favorite. She may learn to roll over just to avoid it.
Ian: She better not roll over until I can see it.
Ian: FaceTime me. I need to tell her not to roll until Daddy is home.

Day Five:

Ian: Did you know all the museums are free here? We should bring Audrey when she's older.
Carina: I'll put it on her calendar.
Ian: Good. Now send me a picture so I can see my girls.

Day Seven:

Ian: What are my girls doing tonight?
Carina: Bath time.
Ian: Both of you? ;)
Ian: Quick, send me a picture.
Carina: No, you perv. Just Audrey.
Ian: Still send a picture.

Ian: She's getting so chubby. I love it.
Carina: She's getting heavy to hold.
Ian: Don't worry, I'll be home soon with my big, man muscles.
Ian: Quick question...
Carina: Shoot.
Ian: A local paper is wanting to do an interview and offering a discounted ad space. I was wondering if it was worth it to invest the time and money since their name wasn't recognizable at first mention.
Carina: Send me the name, and I'll look into it and get back to you.
Ian: Thank you.
Ian: Damn, I'm lucky I have the smartest girl on speed dial.

Day Nine:

Ian: Send me a pic.
Ian: Of BOTH my girls.

Ian: God, I miss you guys.
Carina: We miss you too.
Ian: We, eh?
Carina: Shut up, Ian.

Ian: You love it.
Carina: I'm rolling my eyes.
Ian: I'm imagining it now. Sooo sexy.
Carina: When do you get back?
Ian: Three more days.

THIS TRIP WAS MAKING me question my sanity because I had to be insane with how much my body flushed with happiness when I saw Ian's messages pop up on my phone each day. I had to be insane with how much I sat around waiting to hear from him and wondering what we'd talk about.

I had to be insane because three days felt like an eternity, and I wanted him home now. These past nine days have dragged on, making me realize how much I missed him. Me missing Ian. I never thought that was an emotion I'd feel when it came to him. Maybe it was because I was just lonely. I'd been out of work for almost six weeks now, only coming on for a few consulting jobs that didn't require much of my time or to leave Audrey.

But even that sounded like a false reason since I'd spent more time at my aunts' houses than I had all month. I didn't lack adult interaction.

I thought back to how hard I laughed dancing around the kitchen with Ian and the fluttering in my belly kicked up. When was the last time I'd laughed so hard? When was the last time I'd had that light floaty feeling of happiness?

The day I had Audrey stood at the forefront of my mind, but Ian was there too, holding my hand and sharing the moment with me.

Somehow over these past two months, despite how hard I tried to fight him off, he'd ingratiated himself in my life, and this

165

pang of missing him reinforces how close to the edge of falling I'd come.

That thought brought a new wave of adrenaline that felt a lot like fear. What if I was setting myself up for failure again? What if I was falling into what was easy and all of it meant nothing?

My phone vibrating pulled me out of my head, and when I saw Ian's name on the screen, I rushed to pick up.

"She's napping," I greeted, already smiling.

"Well, it's a good thing I called to talk to you."

His deep voice rumbled across the line and shot straight to my core. "Did you need to ask me something?"

"Can't a man just call his baby-mama and say hello?"

"I cringe every time you call me that."

"It's true though."

"All right, sperm donor," I deadpanned.

"At your service, whenever you need me."

I couldn't hold back my laugh no matter how much I tried to keep it in.

"What are you up to?"

"Watching a movie?"

"Porn? Please say porn?"

Another laugh. "No, but I did find your stash. Quite a collection there."

If I expected him to be embarrassed, I would have been disappointed. "Man, you dug in the back-back of my movie collection. That stuff is from my teen years. Now, I just use the internet."

"I shudder at your search history."

"Oh, you know exactly what I like."

His voice was soft and seductive, pulling me into memories of our date. Heat infused my cheeks, and I struggled to keep my breathing even. This conversation was taking a turn, and the fact that the thought of falling into phone sex with Ian didn't completely turn me off, had me forcing the topic change.

"I found Monty Python and the Holy Grail."

"Good choice. I haven't seen it in forever. Maybe we can watch it when I get home."

Home. Each time he called the place we lived together home, I melted and took a few more steps toward that cliff.

"Yeah," I answered breathlessly. "What are you doing up so late?"

"Dinner ran long."

"Who'd you meet with?"

"The main foreman and his daughter. Apparently, she's in town for a photoshoot, and he asked if she could come. I figured why not."

Because who would turn down dinner with a model? That was what I wanted to say; instead, I went with a much more eloquent answer. "Oh."

"Yeah, it went well."

"Good."

"I can't wait to get back home to my girls."

And just like that, the sinking feeling of imagining him with some model vanished.

"We can't wait to see you too."

"I miss you."

And unlike the time when I dropped him off at the airport, I didn't hesitate to say it back. "I miss you too."

"I'll call you tomorrow. Maybe we can FaceTime?"

"Yeah, Audrey will like that."

I didn't have to say it for both of us to hear that I would like it too.

And that thought brought me a little bit closer to the edge again, both terrifying and exhilarating me.

Ian

Day Ten:

Ian: Chinese or Mexican?
Carina: What?
Ian: Which do you want for dinner?
Carina: What????
Ian: ...
Ian: You took too long. I chose Mexican.

I slid my key into the lock and opened the door just as my phone vibrated in my pocket. Carina's head jerked up from where she stood in the middle of the room, a confused look scrunching her face. When she took me in standing there, her look changed to something else.

Something I had never seen before. At least, not unless it came with an eye roll.

She looked...happy.

No, not happy. But joyful.

I barely had time to drop my bags before she was across the room and in my arms. My hands went to her slim waist, and I was drowned in the masses of her long hair as she buried her head in my neck.

I would have been less surprised if Audrey came running across the room into my arms.

"You're home early."

Home. I'd never get tired of hearing her say that. The fact that I could feel her breath on my skin as she said it, lit me on fire.

"I missed my girls."

I'd just begun to fully embrace her when she let go and stepped back, clearing her throat and looking down at the floor before peeking up through her lashes. "Sorry. That was a bit much."

"Nah. I think it was just enough."

She stared for a bit longer before dropping her eyes again. The moment grew tense, and I didn't want to ruin the warm welcome with her overthinking it, so I didn't push and picked Audrey up from her rocker.

"Were you that bad that Mommy actually missed me?"

I held her close and breathed in her sweet baby scent I'd grown addicted to. Kissing her fat cheek, I relished the feeling of being whole with her in my arms.

"Say, no. You'd never be that bad," I baby-talked and smiled. "You're an angel."

Her big blue eyes blinked up at me before the most magical thing happened. Her little cheek twitched until she was giving me a gummy smile.

"Holy shit! She smiled," I said to Carina but didn't take my attention off Audrey. "Did you smile for me? Yes, you did. Yes, you did."

"I should record this and send it to Erik."

"Don't you dare. He'd post it on the company website."

Carina came over to stroke Audrey's cheek, and I soaked in her citrus and lavender scent as well. I had to fight from turning my head and burying it in her neck to breathe more of her in.

It'd been the longest week of my life being away from my girls. Even with all the messaging and FaceTime. Each time I talked to Carina, I expected her to call me out on including her with Audrey when I called them "my girls," but she never did. Not that it would have mattered. They both were, whether Carina would admit it or not.

"I was just about to put her down," Carina said.

"I'll do it. You grab the plates, and we can eat once she's asleep."

It was maybe ten minutes of rocking and bouncing before Audrey's eyes slid closed despite how hard she fought to keep them open. Part of me wanted to keep her in my arms, but I was looking forward to dinner with Carina. So, I sat her in her sleeper and headed to the dining room where Carina had everything set up.

"Let me guess you wanted Chinese?"

She glowered but smiled a radiant smile. "Actually, Mexican sounded good."

I stumbled back and put my hand to my chest. "Did hell just freeze over? Is this a dream?"

She laughed and slapped my shoulder. "Sit down and eat before I change my mind."

"Yes, ma'am."

I'd just taken my first bite when she asked, "How are you here?"

"Well, Miss Russo, there's this flying metal box they call an airplane. It's magical and amazing."

She laughed and rolled her eyes. I knew I was a goner for this woman when I even missed watching her daily eye rolls.

"Shut up."

"I rushed some meetings and took the soonest flight home. It was too long of a trip anyway."

She pushed some rice around her plate, and her hair fell, hiding her face. "Well, I'm glad you're here."

Reaching across the small space, I brushed her hair behind her ear and waited until she met my eyes. "Me too."

Christ, I loved that blush on her cheeks. It always made me wonder how far down it went. One of these days I'd find out.

"Maybe next time you and Audrey can come with me."

"Yeah, that would be really nice." She cleared her throat and changed the subject. "So, tell me about work."

We spent the rest of the meal talking shop, but I regaled her with stories of the interesting things I saw and people I met. I could have sat there all night watching her laugh and hearing her opinion on the marketing, but soon she was yawning.

"We should probably head to bed. Audrey will be up soon."

"Yeah, let me help you clean up."

She took the plates in, and I gathered the trash. She was just putting the last plate in the dishwasher when I walked in. Her round bottom looked extra ripe under her black leggings. Her waist had slimmed like Audrey had never been there at all. She was beautiful and I just...I just had to have a taste.

Setting the bags aside, I walked up behind her, not being subtle about what I was going after. I brushed her hair aside and lowered my nose to her neck, taking in the smell of her like I'd wanted to earlier. She tensed but didn't pull away, and I took the opportunity to kiss up her neck to her ear.

"God, I missed you."

"Ian..." she breathed my name like a plea. I didn't know if it was a plea to stop or a plea to go further, but I knew which one I was going to give her.

I gripped her full hips under my palms and pulled her back against my growing erection. "Just go with it, Carina."

I continued kissing her neck, moving from small kisses to full-on, making love to it with my tongue. All the while, my hand crept across her abdomen—that did still bear the signs of carrying our child—and descending into her pants.

She gasped and jerked back when my finger slipped through the lips of her pussy and fingered her clit. My cock was impossibly hard and desperate for her. It'd been entirely too long. Thrusting against the curves of her ass, I dipped into her opening and pulled wetness back up to her bud, rubbing harder.

"I want to be inside you, Carina."

Her throat moved under my mouth with a swallow, and she shook her head. "It's too soon."

I was about to argue that it'd been almost a year when she clarified.

"I can't have sex until six weeks."

"Fine," I said before nipping her neck. "Then I'll settle for hearing you come."

I played with her clit, using my other hand to move up to her breasts, pulling the cup of her bra aside and thumbing her pebbled tip. She moaned and rocked into my hand. Her fists clenched tight on the counter, her head fallen back on my shoulder.

"Does that feel good, baby?"

"Yes. More."

I pinched the bundle of nerves between my fingers and rolled it back and forth.

"Ian," she almost screamed. Almost.

"Come on. You can do better than that."

"Make me," she issued the challenge over her shoulder.

"My pleasure."

I dipped into her wet pussy again and furiously rubbed across her clit, not stopping until her legs shook, and she squeezed my palm between her clenching thighs. Not until I felt her opening throbbing against my fingers. Not until she screamed my name.

Slowing my movements, I peppered kisses down her shoulder and up her neck until she finally controlled her breathing. I was slowly removing my hand from her pants when she jerked away and immediately fell to her knees in front of me.

"Uh, C—Carina." I stuttered, shocked at her position.

"Shut up, Ian."

Her hands efficiently unbuckled my pants and tugged them down my hips until my cock sprang free.

"Fuck, I forgot how big you are."

She was so close to the head of my cock, I could feel the words against my skin, and I shuddered. My legs almost gave out when her tongue slicked across the tip, collecting the drop of precum.

"Show me how much you like it."

She smirked and held my gaze as she sank down my length and slid back up, achingly slow.

I buried my hand in her hair and gave her my own smirk in return. "Come on, Carina, you can do better than that."

She repaid my comment by dragging her teeth along my cock and nipping at the end gently. But then she did more than better. She did fan-fucking-tastic. She had my eyes rolling to the back of my head, and my legs damn near giving out.

She used one hand to play with my balls and the other to stroke what her mouth couldn't cover, which wasn't much because she was giving it her all to get every inch of me in her mouth. One of these days I'd teach her how to take me into her throat. The thought of her laying on the bed and my cock buried so deep it bulged against her throat, mixed with the sight of her full lips wrapped around my dick was too much.

"I'm gonna come. Are you going to swallow? You going to let me spill my cum in that pretty mouth?"

Without stopping, she cocked a brow, and I growled, gripping her hair tight and fucking her mouth with quick short thrusts until everything zeroed in on the pleasure consuming me. I didn't want to close my eyes but couldn't help it. The orgasm was too strong. It'd been way too long since I'd come any other way than my own hand.

She sucked and swallowed, but not fast enough to not have some leak out the corner of her mouth.

"Fuck, that is sexy," I barely breathed, taking my thumb and wiping away what escaped.

She popped off my cock and took my thumb in her mouth.

"Yes," I moaned.

Her tongue swirled around my finger, and I couldn't take it. I jerked her up and pinned her to the counter, claiming her mouth with mine. Loving the taste of my cum on her tongue.

But as the kiss slowed, I could feel the doubt creeping in. Each muscle slowly stiffened under my hands, and I needed to do damage control. Carina was giving in to her desire a little more each time the tension between us snapped, and I found backing off before she could build a giant wall against me worked better than trying to break it down.

"Don't overthink it, Carina," I whispered against her trembling lips. "Everything is still fine."

"But, Ian. I—"

I pressed my fingers to her lips. "Don't. Over. Think. It." When she nodded, I pulled my hand back and fastened my pants. "Now, let's go to bed and let me hold you."

"Ian—"

"Ah, ah, ah." I halted her argument. "Just so I can help you through the night with Audrey. You've been on solo duty all week."

After only a moment's hesitation, she gave in.

We got ready, and she tried to sleep on the edge of the bed, but I pulled her close so I could spoon her, keeping my hands in safe territory.

"I'll be right here if Audrey wakes up. Get some sleep."

It didn't take long for her breathing to even out and for the first time since she'd been born, Audrey slept through the night, letting Mommy and Daddy stay pressed together until dawn.

21 IAN

"Are you sure you don't want me to go with you?"

Carina didn't turn to face me, but I could see the tension in her shoulders as she slipped her earrings in. "We don't have anyone to watch Audrey, and I don't want to bring her around that many people."

"We could find a stranger on the street."

She gave me a deadpanned look in the mirror. "Very funny. Besides, I won't stay too long. Just enough for everyone to stare and make comments about the poor ex."

"Nonsense. More like the sexy as fuck ex."

I lived for the way she tried to hide her smiles when I complimented her. She looked down, and the long tendrils framing her face fell forward, begging me to tuck them back.

Before I could, she faced her reflection and pulled her shoulders back like she was preparing for battle. "I won't be long."

When she turned, I was there waiting, forcing her to take a step back and bump into the dresser. "You look beautiful."

We were so close I could feel the small puffs of breath escaping her red-painted lips. "Thank you."

I made a fist to keep from grabbing her and tugging her close. It had been a week since I'd touched her, tasted her, felt her and each day got a little harder than the last. I knew she felt it too. How could she not when it was like a living, breathing giant in the room with us.

It became just a matter of time for when one of us snapped—and I knew that when we did, I couldn't go back. I couldn't let her hide from it anymore, even if it only ended in a serious conversation about where we stood. This limbo wasn't good on either of us.

"I should go," she whispered, stepping around me.

I followed her out of the room, grabbing Audrey on the way. "Remember the rules, young lady. No drinking and driving, call every thirty minutes, so I know you're safe, and no drugs."

"Very funny, Dad."

"Oh, you want me to be your daddy? I can get into that. Maybe some spanking."

"How can you say that while holding your daughter?" she laughed.

"Easy. Little Miss Audrey doesn't know what Daddy is saying and doesn't care as long as it comes in a happy voice. Do you, baby?"

She shook her head at my baby-talk and grabbed her purse. "You two behave."

"I guess we'll have to cancel the house party then."

"We'll see you later," I said, waving Audrey's little fist.

As soon as Carina left, I swept into action. I was a man with a plan and didn't have time to waste.

Watching Carina prepare to attend this wedding had been painful. She would never have asked me to go, but I knew she dreaded going alone. Thankfully, I was a proactive kind of guy, so I'd already messaged my parents to see if they would be able to watch Audrey.

As soon as they'd given me the go-ahead, I packed a bag for Audrey while Carina was showering. I quickly changed into my suit, choosing a silver tie to match Carina's dress and headed out the door.

"Thank you so much for this," I greeted my mom.

"Of course," she said, taking Audrey. She smiled down, and Audrey rewarded her with a gummy smile.

"We just got back last night," my dad said behind my mom. "A little heads up would have been nice."

"It's kind of a spur of the moment idea."

"That's typical," my dad grumbled.

I hadn't seen my parents since right after Audrey had been born. They'd visited the hospital and then left for another country, and maybe some of that resentment had been brewing because hearing my father's displeasure was too much.

"I know this may shock you, but I'm trying to be there for someone. It may be spur of the moment, but I saw Carina needed me, and I'm going to be there planned or not."

"Did she ask you to come last minute?"

"No, but being there for someone doesn't always require to be asked. Not that you'd understand."

"Ian," my mom protested.

"No. No, Ian. You both may be okay with checking boxes and not showing up, but I'm not. I want to build my family with Carina. I want to be there for both of them no matter what. Nothing I have going on with me will come between that."

"You never wanted for anything," my dad defended.

"Except my family. How many Christmases did I spend alone? How many missed birthdays. It was like you didn't care."

"Ian, we didn't mean to," my mom said softly, her eyes filling with water.

"That's not what this is about right now, and it's not something I'm trying to make you feel guilt over. But I have my own family to think of now, and I can't have Audrey growing up feeling like a burden, who feels like the only way she can see you is when you feel she's worth it. I want you in her life, but not at the cost of her happiness."

My father stood with his jaw clenched, but not looking at me. It was the closest thing to regret I'd ever seen from him.

"Of course we want to be in Audrey's life," my mother said. "And maybe...maybe we can cut back on some trips. Be there for her—for both of you." She looked to Dad for confirmation and even cleared her throat when it took too long. "Right, Santo?"

"Right."

It wasn't much, but it was enough for now. I didn't have complete faith in a change, but at least they knew where I stood and that I was done accepting less.

And it was enough right then because Carina needed me, and I intended to be there.

CARINA

I SAT in the car as long as possible. I'd left the house almost an hour ago, and I just sat there, breathing through the worst-case scenarios rolling through my head.

In the silence, with no one to admit it to, I wished for Ian. I wished I wasn't alone. I wished for him to be there to hold my hand and walk by my side, whispering in my ear that I was the sexiest woman at the wedding.

But I was stubborn and didn't ask, convincing myself I could do it on my own. My stubbornness was really getting in the way of a lot of things. My stubborn fear that by letting Ian in I'd only get hurt again. My stubborn pride refusing to talk about all the times he set my body on fire. My stubborn mind holding me back from giving my body what I wanted.

I was tired of it.

Really, I was just tired of fighting it.

Not that Ian would let me keep pretending nothing had happened.

"Ugh," I groaned. "Get over yourself, Carina."

Talking to myself in the car was the last straw. There were only five mere minutes until the wedding started, and I needed to get in there.

Stepping off the elevator into the opulent lobby, I looked side to side figuring out where to go.

"It's about damn time, woman. I thought I'd showed up at the wrong wedding."

My heart thundered in my chest at the deep voice behind me. It couldn't be? Maybe my crazy mind had conjured a mirage of him to make myself feel better. I prepared myself to find nothing when I turned—prepared to laugh at myself for hearing things.

But when I spun on my heel, the most beautiful man I'd ever seen stood with his hands in his pockets, waiting for me. He looked stunning in his dark suit. His white, snowy shirt stark against his tan skin and black suit. I took slow steps forward like if I moved too fast, he'd vanish.

"You okay?"

His gray eyes sparkled like silver, matching his tie, and I wanted to sink into him. "You're here."

"Sure am. I left Audrey to spend a night at the Bergamo mansion with Grandma and Grandpa. Seemed like you could use a sexy date."

His assured smile and wink made me laugh, and I almost choked on it. I was sure laughing, and happiness would have been the furthest thing from my mind.

"You'll do...I guess."

"You guess? Baby, I'm grade A prime meat, the perfect arm candy to prove you're the happiest woman here."

I stood less than a foot from him and let his presence wash over me. Something eased in my chest. More than just not being here alone.

A lingering pressure from being alone, for not having someone show up just for me in life, lightened.

Ian had shown up for me and that had me swallowing around tears.

A countdown ticked in the back of my mind, but we had a wedding to get to. Now wasn't the time to acknowledge the fact that I was inching closer to something big I wouldn't come back from. Something like giving in to this need for Ian.

"Shall we?" I asked, holding out my hand.

"We shall."

His large palm slipped in mine, and for the first time all day, I could breathe. People stared when we walked in, but none of it mattered.

Instead, I was immersed in blue and white flowers, candles and dim lighting with soft music and love pouring out of every person. Especially the happy couple I'd just watched pronounce their vows to each other. It'd been a beautiful ceremony with many happy tears. Not from the masculine couple on the altar. No, they were way too manly and only allowed choked voices and long pauses to collect themselves.

Hell, I'd even shed a tear myself. Ian had been gentleman enough to not call me on it. Instead, he'd remained by my side. He never asked me how I was doing or if I was okay, which I knew half the guests at the wedding were dying to know.

Poor Carina. It must be hard watching her ex-fiancé get married.

No, Ian hadn't given me pity looks or even tried to boost me up. He stood by me like a sentinel.

Now, we sat at a table with Erik and Alexandra, awaiting the happy couple's arrival at the reception. They'd been shocked to find Ian by my side, but Erik smiled and patted Ian on the back, muttering, "Good choice," as we sat down.

"So," Alex started. "How's living together?"

"Great," I answered.

"The worst," Ian said at the same time.

"What?" I jerked my head to the side to scowl only to find him smiling.

"I'm kidding," he reassured, resting his hand on my knee, sending a flurry of butterflies to my stomach. "She's the best roommate I've ever had."

"Hey, now," Erik protested.

"What? She has boobs, and you never cooked for me."

"Ian!" I admonished.

He cocked a brow, and I knew zero apology would come from him. "I'm not going to sit here and pretend you don't have an amazing rack. It's true, and you should be proud of it."

I tried to hold it back, but a laugh broke free.

"So proud," he continued, a devious glint sparking like a flash of silver in his eyes, "maybe you should walk around topless."

"Jesus, Ian."

"It's just a suggestion."

Erik ended that train of conversation, thank God. "Have you had a better roommate?" he asked me.

"Almost all of them," I deadpanned.

"Hey!" Ian protested, and I quickly smiled his way to let him know I was joking. "Would it help if I walked around topless? Oooo—let's do topless Tuesday. Audrey would love it. She hates clothes."

Alex and I were both laughing behind our hands, and Erik was shaking his head at his best friend.

Topless Tuesday talk was put on hold when the happy

couple was announced and came parading in, holding hands in dark tuxes and matching radiant smiles. Jackson held Jake's stare as he kissed his hand before pulling him into his arms for their first dance.

I watched with an ache in my heart that I had grown to accept. I was so unbelievably happy for them. Rationally, I knew that Jake and I would have been unhappy together and that things worked out perfectly with Audrey in my life. But rationality doesn't care about your heart. Rationality doesn't stop the pinch each time you see what hurt you. It can only dim it. But having their happy ending literally surrounding me, rationality didn't stand a chance.

Taking a deep breath, I looked out the corner of my eye to the left, taking in Ian's profile. He must have noticed me staring because his hand crept across the small gap between our chairs and wrapped his large, calloused hand around mine. Meeting his eyes, I gave a forced smile before watching the couple dance around the floor, not removing my hand from his.

"I think," Ian said right against my ear, sending chills down my spine, "Billy Idol's *White Wedding* should be our first dance when we get married."

"What?" I whisper-yelled, jerking to face him. I expected to find his signature smirk letting me know he was joking, and instead, found expecting eyes like he was waiting for me to agree, and my jaw dropped.

"Come on. It'd be a hit and shock everyone. I've already shown you my sweet moves."

His hips swiveled in his chair, mimicking the hip thrusts he did around the house. I huffed a laugh but was too shocked by his statement to do more than that.

"Ian, we are not getting married."

And then the smirk appeared. "I know, but it took your mind off them."

Blinking, it took me a minute to process his words. I looked around the room to find the dancefloor empty and the couple sitting at their table. He'd distracted me. He'd noticed my discomfort and distracted me. It was such a typical Ian move, yet it came with a warmth seeping deep into my bones and had a fire burning up the back of my throat. "Thank you," I whispered.

"Anytime." He patted my hand and turned back to the table. "Now let's eat. I'm starving."

Like the rest of the wedding, the meal was delicious. The night moved quickly. The cutting of the cake, toasts, and speeches given, before the dancing finally commenced.

Ian and I were standing at the bar when Jake and Jackson finally came by.

"Hey, gorgeous," Jackson greeted, wrapping his big arms around me.

"Hey, handsome. Beautiful wedding."

Jackson had been the catalyst to the end of mine and Jake's relationship, but in the time he'd been part of that relationship, I'd grown close to him. I hadn't loved him like Jake, but I'd still loved him. Now, we were just three close friends who shared a painful past but didn't let it define our future.

"That would all be Joanne's doing," he said, talking about Jake's mom.

"Carina." Jake pulled me into his arms and held me for a while. "Thank you for being here," he said against my neck.

I had to swallow the lump in my throat. "I wouldn't miss it for the world."

A throat clearing behind me broke us apart, and I turned to find Ian awaiting introductions, all humor and jokes missing from his eyes.

"Jake, you know Ian. And Ian, this is Jackson."

Handshakes and congratulations were exchanged. Ian was

stiff, and as soon as his hand left Jackson's, it went to my waist, pulling me close to his side.

"Make sure you save a dance for me," Jackson said.

"We'll see if I let this wild woman out of my arms," Ian joked, but a hard edge cloaked the light words.

A part of me wanted to be embarrassed about how possessive he was acting when we weren't even a couple, but in that moment, it felt good to have someone to be possessive over me. Even if it wasn't real.

"Well, I'll leave you to it," Jake said. His eyes flicked between the two of us before giving me a knowing smile. Except he didn't know. Because Ian and I weren't a couple.

Ian led me to the table only to set our glasses down before pulling me out on the dancefloor.

He twirled me out, my silver silk dress flowing around my legs, before pulling me back into his chest.

"I may have to do that again so that I can see the peep show again."

I scoffed. "That was hardly a peep show. At most, a thigh."

"The most delicious thigh I've ever seen."

Biting my lip, I held back a sigh, heat blooming on my cheeks at his compliment. My dress was a floor-length wrap that—when moved the right way—exposed a slit that reached my upper thigh.

"You look beautiful," he said smoothly, holding me so close to him, I could feel the words rumble in his chest.

"You don't look too bad yourself. Your silver tie matches your eyes perfectly."

"I was just trying to match you. I wanted it to be like prom night all over again. Sorry, I forgot the corsage," he joked.

We settled into a comfortable silence and moved around the other couples on the dancefloor. We were in a long stretch of slow songs and the way his thighs brushed against mine, the way his shoulders flexed deliciously under my touch, they could have played slow songs all night.

Something about the comfort of his arms around me, or the way he saw the hurt that still lingered, had me confessing. "It's my fault, you know," I said, staring into his chest. "It's my fault that he left me."

When he laughed, I looked up to find one eyebrow arched high. "How's that?" he asked.

Slicking my tongue across my lips, I took a deep breath, about to admit what only the three of us knew. "I invited Jackson into our bed." Ian gave barely any reaction beyond that arrogant, all-knowing eyebrow lowering. "I could feel the distance between Jake and me. Or maybe it was harder to lie to myself about the fact that we were just friends, staying together because it was comfortable. But it was *my* crazy plan to have him join us in the hopes of masking it all with sex."

"You had a threesome?" Now both his eyebrows shot high.

"For a while."

"So, this wasn't a one-time thing. A wild night?"

"No," I said slowly, waiting for the judgment.

Like the Cheshire Cat, his lips curled up, and his silver eyes turned charcoal. "You dirty girl."

I was so shocked by his reaction, a bark of laughter escaped, and I looked around to see if anyone noticed. But it was still just us like we were in our own bubble.

The smile slipped, and his eyes turned serious, his hands tightening on my waist. "It's not your fault, Carina. He made those decisions when he could have said no."

I hadn't had anyone to really talk about the breakup with. Not the real reason or the part I played in our demise, and until now—with Ian staring down at me, looking more serious than I'd ever seen him—I hadn't realized how much I needed someone to say those words to me. His hands tightened around my waist, slowly creeping closer to my ass. They were so large they almost spanned from the curve of my bottom to my shoulder blades. Leaning down to make sure I couldn't look away, his chest brushed mine and my nipples pebbled from the contact.

"And just so you know," he growled, his tone full of possession. "I would never, *ever,* share you. You would belong to me and only me. I'd take care of you, fill you up, so there was no room for anyone else in our bed."

Everything faded as I stared into his eyes, my chest heaving over my panting breaths. I tried to swallow the desire burning through my veins at his words. Had there ever been anyone that had looked at me so wholly, I knew they couldn't see anyone else? Heat bled through my chest, down my abdomen and sinking into my core where it throbbed. I rubbed my legs side to side, and the ache felt impossible to ignore. It consumed me.

I twisted out of his arms and latched onto his hand, dragging him behind me to grab my purse and head out the doors to the lobby. I didn't say goodbye or acknowledge anyone staring. My pulse pounded with a need I couldn't pretend didn't exist anymore.

Ian caught on to my plan and muttered, "Oh, fuck yes."

Then he was the one leading me, dragging me past people lingering in the sitting areas staring at the couple damn near running through the hotel.

He pushed through a door, and I saw the men's bathroom sign before he dragged me inside. He checked the stalls and locked the door.

I was in the middle of the large bathroom when he turned to face me. He prowled across the room, his dark suit doing nothing to mask the power and command underneath.

When he reached me, he didn't hesitate, he gripped my ass and hoisted me up, turning and walking to set me down on the counter.

As soon as I was steady, he attacked my mouth. Our lips clashed, and our tongues fought for dominance. I buried my hands in his hair and held him to me, not even wanting to come up for air. But I had to pull back to gasp when his fingers slid into my panties and tore through the thin lace at my hips.

Ian, the consummate jokester, towered over me with the promise of domination, and I was ready to submit. He tugged the underwear free and shoved them in his pocket as he sank to his knees, shoving mine apart.

The skirt of my dress was pushed to my hips, and cold air caressed my wet folds. I almost jerked off the counter when a rough finger slid from my clit to circle my opening.

"Such a pretty pussy. So wet." I held my breath as his head lowered, and he dragged an illicit tongue from below my opening up to circle my bundle of nerves.

"Is all this wetness for me? Do I make your cunt wet and beg for more?"

"Yes," I breathed.

His smirk was the last thing I saw because as soon as his mouth latched on to my pussy, my eyes rolled back in my head, and I did nothing but feel.

Feel the way he sucked on each fold. Feel the way his tongue pushed in and out of me as his thumb circled my clit. Feel the way he bit at the tender flesh as two fingers slid into me slowly. Feel the way they curled as he sucked me to one of the best orgasms I'd ever had. I was biting my palm, barely holding back my screams when he eased me back to earth.

He peppered kisses everywhere he could reach from his crouched position.

"Carina."

Just my name and I knew I'd used my last life. There was no more pretending this wasn't happening. And right then, in the men's bathroom of my ex-fiancé's wedding, I didn't want to.

"Please tell me that's not it. Please tell me I can fuck this pussy."

"Yes," I panted, my lungs still working overtime with his words caressing my soaked folds.

"Good." He pressed one last kiss to my mound before he stood and tugged me off the counter, supporting me when my legs wobbled. "Let's get a hotel room because I'm not going to make it back to the apartment. I need you now, and I need a bed for all the dirty things I'm going to do to you."

Losing my ninth life had never felt so good.

22 IAN

I DRAGGED Carina behind me toward the elevator, and everything screamed faster, faster. I needed to get her in my arms before she changed her mind again. I wondered if the man at the front desk knew the illicit things I was going to do to this woman if he knew why I had snatched the key card out of his hand when he'd finally given it to me.

It wasn't like it was hard to guess with my hair a mess from Carina's fingers, the fact that we had no luggage, and both of our flushed faces had kiss swollen lips. I didn't care. I would have thrown her down right then and there in the middle of the lobby if it meant having her. If it meant letting everyone know that she was mine. And she was mine. If nothing else got cleared up tonight, it was that she wasn't running from this anymore.

But that could wait until after.

The elevator dinged and opened to a blessedly empty car. The gods were shining down on me today. As soon as the door closed, I had her pinned to the wall with my mouth glued to hers.

"Ian, people could get on," she protested between kisses.

"Yeah, they could. And then they'd get to see me taking the most beautiful woman. They could watch me make you come."

Her only response was a whimper. Probably because my hand had moved up her skirt and was teasing her pussy. She squirmed and thrust, trying to get my hand where she wanted, and I kept tugging back.

"You're so wet—such a mess."

Another whimper. I'd just pressed a finger through her slit when the door slid open to an older couple on the other side.

Carina jerked her clothes back in place and pushed me away, her face flushed with embarrassment. Me? I exited the elevator with no remorse, even winking at the couple when I walked past. The man laughed and shook his head.

Once we reached our door, I pressed my front to her back, growling into her neck, "I can't wait to finally see how far down that blush goes. It's been taunting me for months.".

Pressing my cock against her ass, I swiped the key and shoved the door open. I had no clue what the room looked like. I didn't care. All I knew was that I was going to be inside this woman as soon as possible and if a bed happened to be waiting for me, then so be it. But any flat surface would do.

I'd managed to get the small zipper of her dress undone on my way to the bed and jerked the silky material from her body, letting it pool at her feet. She was kissing down my neck, biting, sucking, licking every inch as she undid my tie and ripped through my shirt. Buttons went flying, and I guessed it was only fair since I'd torn her panties. Her hand was busy on my belt when I stopped her, knowing if she got my cock free, this would be over too soon.

I gripped her wrist, and wide blue eyes looked up.

"I need to make you come again before I fuck you. I want to make you a wet mess so my cock can slide inside that tight pussy with one push. Would you like that, Carina? To fill you up with my fat cock."

Her mouth opened and closed like a fish out of water, and I had to hold back laughing out loud at a speechless Carina. I did allow a deep chuckle to slip free and shoved her back on the bed. She sat up, supporting herself on her hands, leveling a pissed off look my way. But the tongue lashing I was about to get from shoving her died on her lips when I lowered myself to my knees and worked my mouth up her leg.

Her thighs were strong from all the running she did, and I loved the way the muscles jerked and twitched under my ministrations.

"What do you want, baby?"

"I want you to stop playing."

"Oh, I'm just getting started."

She growled, her head dropping back in frustration, and I took the chance to dive in.

"Oh," she cried with the first swipe of my tongue.

She whimpered and moaned while I tasted every inch of her cunt. She supported herself back on her hands and thrust her hips against my face, watching my tongue fuck her.

My cock was straining against my pants and about to burst through the zipper. Everything in me throbbed, urging me to come, but I needed to be inside her. Done playing with her, bringing her to the edge and back, I shoved two fingers inside and latched onto her clit, sucking hard while my tongue flicked across the tender bud.

Her thighs tightened around my ears and muted the sounds of her orgasm.

I didn't even let her pussy stop spasming before I pulled out and quickly shed my pants. Grabbing my wallet, I extracted my strip of condoms.

"Three?" she asked.

"I've been carrying these around since I saw you again. Usually, I only have one. But I knew that once I had you, I was going to need way more than that."

"Once you had me? Not if?"

"I'm a confident man," I explained, pushing her up the bed as I climbed between her thighs.

"An arrogant man," she deadpanned.

"Call it what you want, but either way, I'm the man about to be inside you." I gripped my dick and slid it through her folds across her clit, both of us moaning. "I'm the man about to make you scream my name." Another slide. "The man who will fuck you over and over until you can't take it anymore. Then I might fuck you again."

"All talk," she breathed.

I huffed a laugh and pulled my hips back just enough to lodge my length against her opening. Just as I was about to push in, she tensed, and I stopped.

"Just...go slow this first time."

"This first time," I agreed. "Next time I'll take you how I want."

Part of me expected her to protest my domineering statement, but instead, her eyes darkened with desire and need.

Holding her stare, I slid in, taking my time to pull out and ease back in further on each pass. It didn't take long because she was so wet from all the other orgasms I'd given her. When I was finally seated fully inside her, I held still, burying my face in her breasts and relishing the moment. It'd been so long since I'd felt this woman around me, and I just needed a moment of gratitude.

Her hips moved, and I smirked, knowing she was just as desperate as me to move.

Kissing across her clavicle, I slid my hand up her arm until it rested on the pillow above her head, where I linked our fingers together and pinned her there. Holding her stare, I slowly slid out and back in, loving every pleasurable desire crossing her features.

"You're fucking beautiful."

The blush came back, and I got to watch it spread down her neck and down to her beautiful breasts. Kissing across the curves and back up to her mouth, I thrust in hard and ate the cries from her lips. I went slow to give her time to tell me if anything hurt, but when she didn't stop me, my pace picked up.

Her fingers squeezed mine, holding on tight like she was afraid to be washed away by the waves of pleasure consuming us. Sweat dripped down my temples and coated both our skin.

"I missed being inside you."

"Please, Ian."

"What do you need, baby?"

"More."

Linking my other hand with hers, I brought them both above her head and lifted to my knees. "Tell me if it's too much."

With her lip firmly clenched under her teeth, she nodded, giving me the go-ahead to let loose the fire that had been raging inside me since the first moment I ever saw her.

Since the first moment, she asked me if she could try something and kissed me, changing everything in its wake.

I thrust harder and harder, making sure to hit her clit on each slide. Her breasts swayed from the force I was fucking her with. Her legs wrapped tight around my hips, her heels digging into my ass. Her fingers clenched tight around mine, and I knew she was close, could feel the way her core clenched tighter around me.

"God, Carina. Your tits. I could watch them bounce all day. I could be inside you all day. Buried so deep you don't know where I end, and you begin."

"Ian, yes."

"Can I do that? Can I fill you up with my cock whenever I want?"

"Yes. Please, please."

Her mouth hung open around her gasping breaths, and it only took a few more thrusts before she was crying out, filling the room with her moans of pleasure, the orgasm ripping through her.

Her pussy throbbing around me, her hands pinned in mine, under my total control, her breasts swaying from me fucking her. It all consumed me and swallowed me whole, pulling me down with her until I had to fall and bury my head in her neck to groan out my own orgasm. It lasted forever until I was sure my cum would spill from the condom. I couldn't remember the last time I came so hard.

By the time the ringing had cleared from my ears, I felt her lips against my hair, the side of my face, anywhere she could reach. Releasing her hands, I slowly dragged my fingers down her arms, loving the way she trembled under my touch. Coming up for air after one last kiss to her neck, I looked down at her. She was glistening with sweat, her hair a dark, wild mass against the white pillows, her lips swollen and rosy.

She was perfect.

And when she smiled, my chest ached. My heart thundered so hard the rush of blood made me lightheaded, and I knew—right then, I knew—I loved this woman.

Swallowing the words down, I kissed her.

My mind was already conjuring plans on how to keep her under me, how to keep her from running like she did every other time we fooled around. If I told her I loved her, she might run from me further than just inside herself, and I couldn't risk that.

Her lips moved under mine, and I tangled my tongue with hers until I could safely pull away without releasing my truth.

I took care of the condom, and when I came back to pull her into my arms, I could already see her hesitation in the way she wouldn't meet my eyes. But she also didn't pull away. She curled into my arms and rested her head on my bicep.

I had to take my wins where I could.

"Carina, I can't let you keep hiding from this."

"I know."

Needing to see her face, I buried my hand in her hair and tugged until she looked up at me. "I..." I hesitated, thinking over my words to not scare her. "I care for you. And not just as the mother of our child. I care for you so much, and if you give us a chance, I could make you happy."

"What if it doesn't work?"

The worry in her eyes killed me. I wanted her to be as confident as me that we could make this family work—that she could trust me. But I knew trust didn't come easy for Carina, so I'd just have to prove it to her, no matter how long it took. Right now, though, she needed reassurance that this wasn't going to implode on us. She needed to feel safe—like she had an exit plan.

"Then the same rules apply as when we moved in together. I will help you move out. We will make it amicable because we need to always be friends for Audrey. So, let's give us a try and promise to end it before it gets bad."

"Okay," she whispered, the simple word filling every inch of my body to exploding.

Her smile matched mine and I couldn't see how this could go wrong when this moment felt epic—life-changing—unbreakable.

I kissed her hard before pulling away, needing to change the subject before my feelings came pouring out, making a mess.

One step at a time.

"I'm thinking the next time I'm inside you, I'll fuck you from behind."

"Okay," she agreed, another small smile tipping her swollen lips.

"I could get used to an agreeable Carina."

23 CARINA

"I should get going," I said, popping the lid back on my empty salad container.

"Already?" Ian almost whined. "You just got here."

"Thirty minutes ago."

"I know, but since you went back to work, I never see you."

"Dramatic much?" I asked, laughing. I knew he was overreacting to make me laugh. He always tried to make me laugh.

"I'm not going to apologize for wanting you."

"It's not like you ever have before."

"Nope," he said with pride.

"You're a needy boyfriend."

Ian shivered in his office chair, his eyes sliding closed. "You know what that word does to me, dirty girl."

His eyes slid open, a devious smirk slowly tipping his lips.

"Oh, my god," I said laughing, throwing my napkin at him. "You're incorrigible."

He caught the napkin and threw it in his trashcan, a victorious smile stretching across his beautiful face. He hadn't shaved in the past few days, and the stubble had me squeezing my thighs together, remembering what it felt like on my skin this morning when I woke with his head between my legs.

Shaking off the feeling, I stood. "But really, I have to go. I have a meeting, and then I have to get Audrey from Aunt Virginia."

"Where's your meeting at?"

"Voyeur."

"Voyeur?"

"It's kind of like a sex club that isn't a sex club. More like a porn club."

"A sex club?" he asked, shooting up in his seat. "I don't think so, missy. Unless you're meeting nuns, then nope."

I crossed my arms and stood over him, giving him my best I-will-crush-your-sorry-man-ass glare. I knew he wasn't serious about controlling my work, because he knew if he tried, I'd storm out and never look back. But he did care, and that little jealousy had warmth blooming in my chest.

"At least tell me the owner is old and decrepit."

"Do you remember the two men we met at the wedding? They were older, one with blonde hair and the other with salt and pepper hair."

"Ugh," Ian groaned, flopping his arms wide and his head back. "Just go fall in love with the sugar daddies."

His dramatics stopped, and a smile broke free when he heard me laughing.

"Relax," I soothed, stepping close and running my fingers through his hair. He sat up again and tugged me onto his lap. "Maybe I can get us a free pass for a night."

He cocked his brow, considering his options. "Okay. I guess that makes it better. They can be both our sugar daddies."

His hand rested on my thigh and stroked up my skirt before moving back down to my knee. Leaning close, I nipped at his ear and whispered, "We can watch our dirtiest fantasies."

"Dirty girl," he growled, sliding his hand up further.

"What would you choose?" I breathed against his neck.

"Right now," he said, his thumb sliding over my panties. "I want to bend you over my desk and slide deep inside you."

"I have to go," I protested weakly. "We don't have time."

"Then, I better make you come quick."

He moved fast, standing us both up and pressing my chest down to the desk. The clink of his belt buckle had adrenaline flooding my body, heating me up, preparing me for him.

"Better be quiet. Wouldn't want all those employees to know that the bold Carina Russo is getting pinned to a desk and fucked like a slut on her lunch break."

The words had fire burning in my core. I'd forgotten how much I loved dirty talk, and Ian was all too eager to try it all out and test my boundaries.

He made me remember how much I loved having my boundaries tested.

I heard the crinkle of the wrapper a moment before Ian pulled my panties to the side and pushed in all at once. He'd kept to his word to go easy the first few times, but since then we began screwing like animals—hard, rutting against each other like we'd never get another chance.

"You could make life so much easier if you just stopped wearing panties,' he growled against my neck.

"I like you working for it," I moaned.

He laughed softly before standing up and gripping my hips and thrusting into me like a freight train. I tried to hold myself steady and plant my hands on the desk, but I knocked over a stack of papers, and an organizer went crashing to the floor. Finally giving up, I rested my chest to the hard surface and brought my hand to my mouth to stifle my cries.

"Fuck. Your pretty pussy is going to make me come," he groaned.

"Do it," I whimpered.

A few more pumps and my orgasm had me seeing white spots as all the air left my lungs. I almost missed the way he pushed deeper inside me and stayed there as he came.

After getting our breathing back in order, he pulled out and slapped my ass.

"Ian," I gasped. "That was loud."

I stood to face him, tucking his cock back in his pants, an unapologetic smile on his face.

"Good. Let them know I was buried deep inside your tight little pussy. I want them to know you're mine."

I should've been mad. His company was my client, but I liked this possessive side of him. I remembered how much I'd wanted Jake to be jealous of any man hitting on me. I wanted him to have even a hint of jealousy when Jackson was screwing me, and it never came.

So, to see it so plainly laid out in front of me by Ian made it hard to reprimand him. Instead, I stepped close and pressed up on my toes to kiss his bottom lip. "So." Kiss. "Fucking." Kiss. "Incorrigible."

He held me close and took my lips in one last possessive kiss before pulling back to rest his forehead against mine.

"What do you usually do for Thanksgiving?"

I'd kind of forgotten Thanksgiving was this week. These past few months had been crazy, and the past week I'd spent in Ian's bed had been a blur of pleasure and happiness.

"I usually go to my dad's for lunch and then head home to watch movies and fall into a food coma."

"Come to Erik's with me for dinner. They're my family away from family, and I go every year."

I pulled back enough to look in his eyes. "What about your family?"

His eyes dropped. "They're traveling. They usually are

around the holidays, but hopefully, this will be the last one this year."

I wanted to soothe the little boy I saw in that moment who missed holidays with his parents, but I knew Ian would just make a joke and brush it off. He usually avoided talking about them. So instead, I pressed one last kiss and gave him my best smile.

"Then, I'll be there."

The hurt marring his face vanished and back was the man who was slowly claiming my heart, one easy smile at a time. Jarred by that thought, I stepped back and collected my bag, heading to the door.

Before I opened the door, I turned, finding him right behind me. "But you need to come to my Thanksgiving for lunch."

"Deal," he agreed, kissing my nose. "And maybe I can eat you for dessert," he muttered into my ear. "I've never had pussy for Thanksgiving."

I cocked a brow and gave a dubious stare. "You've never spent Thanksgiving with another woman?"

"Nope. Not in any of my thirty-three years."

He held up the Girl Scout pledge hand sign and had me laughing, the joy of knowing I'd be the first to meet his other family flooding me.

"What am I going to do with you?"

"You could always have dick for dessert? Like a sixty-nine treat."

His finger stroked my cheek, where I knew I was blushing. "Sounds like a plan."

"Now, don't go falling in love with anyone today. If you have any daddy fantasies, I'm happy to oblige."

"Such a noble volunteer."

"I aim to please."

Looking up into his slate eyes and warm smile, I hesitated to leave. Our relationship was still new—only a few days old, and I hated to walk away just yet. "How busy are you this afternoon?"

"Umm, not very. A few phone calls and contracts to look over."

"Would you want to play hooky and come to Voyeur with me?"

His eyes lit up. "Hell, yes."

"They're not open for performances right now," I said, bursting his bubble. "But you can check it out."

"I guess." He heaved an overdramatic sigh but quickly perked up and pecked my lips. "Let me grab my stuff."

As soon as I opened the door his eyes flicked beyond my shoulder. "Oh, hey, Hanna."

"Hey, sorry to interrupt."

"Nothing to interrupt now," Jared said, flipping through papers by Laura's desk. "Now if you would have come ten minutes before when Ian was trying and failing at having quiet office sex, then you would have been interrupting something."

My eyes almost bugged out of my head, and heat consumed me. Ian, on the other hand, had no shame. He bobbed his eyebrows at me and flipped Jared off at the same time.

"You're just jealous."

Jared laughed and disappeared in his office again, leaving Hanna still standing beside me, her red cheeks rivaling mine.

"Ignore him," Ian said. "What's up?"

Hanna swung a depressed look my way before visibly pulling back her shoulders. It was a move I was very familiar with. She was hurt but trying to hide it. I had a moment of feeling bad for Hanna. I always felt a connection to a woman in a male-dominated office, and to have a crush on one of your bosses didn't make it any easier. I liked Hanna. She was quiet at times, but funny if not a little socially awkward.

However, the fact that she was crushing on my boyfriend dimmed the empathy for her situation.

"I was just coming up to run some numbers by you."

Ian winced. "Can we do it tomorrow? I was going to leave the office early."

"Yeah. Yeah. Of course. Are you feeling okay?"

"In perfect health," he answered, puffing his chest up like a goof. "I'm just skipping out to spend some time with my girl."

"Oh, yeah. Of course. I'll catch you tomorrow."

"You sure?"

"Yeah. Have fun." With a forced smile, she left, heading to Erik's office.

"Ready?" I asked.

"For a sex club? As I'll ever be."

We drove together to Voyeur and pulled into an overly full lot. "They must be doing some training. Usually, there aren't as many people during the day."

"Hopefully they don't mind you brought me along."

"I'm not worried. Daniel and Kent are pretty relaxed."

When we walked in, the club was quiet, and I checked my phone to make sure I didn't get the time wrong.

"Maybe they're all back in Daniel's office?" Usually, for the meetings, they moved all the club chairs into a circle and conducted them there.

I'd taken two more steps into the dim interior when all the lights flashed on and a crowd of people popped up from behind the bar.

"Surprise!" they shouted in unison.

Adrenaline flooded my veins, leaving tingles in its wake. "Holy shit," I gasped, my hand to my chest. "What the hell?"

"It's a surprise baby shower," Jake explained.

I blinked a few times taking in the group of people behind the bar, including Jake and Jackson. "What the hell are you two doing here?"

"Well, hello to you too," Jackson joked.

"You know what I mean. Why aren't you on your honeymoon?"

"Flights are cheaper on Wednesdays," Jackson answered as Jake rolled his eyes beside him.

"We never got to throw you a shower before the baby, so we figured better late than never," Kent explained, stepping out behind the bar.

Warm goo filled my chest as everyone came over to give hugs. Kent and Daniel co-owned the club together, and I helped them set up their bar. Kent was also one of my first independent clients who I was helping set up multiple hotels.

"A little party from your family here," Daniel said, wrapping me in a tight hug.

"Even I was allowed to come," Olivia said behind him.

Daniel grumbled about his niece being in his sex club.

"Carina would want her here," Kent said, slapping Daniel's back.

I raised my brow at his explanation because I did love Olivia. I'd gotten to know her while she interned with Kent at his hotel, but I knew Kent liked to keep Olivia close when he could.

I was also pretty sure that Daniel had no idea his business partner was boning his niece, who was almost twenty years younger.

But it wasn't my place to say anything or judge, so I pulled Olivia into my arms. "I am glad to have you here. We need to balance all this testosterone."

"Is this the famous Ian I've heard about? The baby-daddy?" she asked.

"In the flesh," Ian answered, offering Olivia his hand.

"Not bad, Carina," she said from the side of her mouth.

Next up was Oaklyn, Olivia's friend and a former employee of Voyeur. As well as a few other employees.

Ian smiled and shook hands with everyone as cake was brought out, and drinks were served. He only grumbled and placed a possessive hand on my hip when Jackson pulled me in for a tight hug, rocking me back and forth.

"It was last minute, but we couldn't forget our favorite baby-mama," Jackson said.

"Thank you. I feel like I had a million before Audrey came."

"Well, there's no harm in one more. Especially since we're the coolest."

Ian wrapped his arm around my waist and pulled me close to his side. "Especially since her boyfriend gets to attend this one."

Jake's brows shot up as he looked between us.

"Boyfriend, eh?" Kent asked.

"Yeah," Ian answered over his shoulder before looking down at me. "I changed my Facebook status and everything. It's pretty official."

I rolled my eyes and earned a slap on my ass. "Watch it," I warned.

Ian leaned down to my ear. "I'd love to watch my hand on your ass. Is there a room for that?"

"There's a room for everything."

"God, yes," he groaned. "New favorite place."

We moved the chairs around to sit in a circle, and I opened my gifts. I gushed over every baby outfit, hairbow, and tiny shoe. Of course, there were more diapers and wipes, but I almost cried over the spa package Olivia and Oaklyn, had given me.

"Callum chipped in too," Oaklyn explained, talking about her professor boyfriend.

"It's perfect."

"I'll give you a massage any time you want, hellcat," Ian promised, his eyebrows waggling.

"Let me guess," I deadpanned. "A chest massage?"

"Hey, you said it. Not me."

"So predictable."

So perfectly predictable.

I didn't know what drove me to invite Ian to Voyeur today, but I knew I was happier than I ever thought possible with him by my side.

He was becoming a fixture.

One I was coming to never want to be without.

24 CARINA

"It was good to have a little more testosterone this year at Thanksgiving," my dad said, shaking Ian's hand goodbye.

"Had to balance out the extra female at the table," Ian joked, gesturing to Audrey who was asleep in her car seat already.

My dad wasn't always the lone male at Thanksgiving. Jake and his mother usually joined us, even after the breakup. Our families had always been close, spending most holidays together. But Jake was on his honeymoon and Joanne was on what she called a mothermoon.

I had to admit, not having Jake there with Ian and Audrey was kind of nice. I was able to relax more and enjoy my little family's first holiday together.

"So, what can I expect," I asked, once we were on our way to his Thanksgiving. My family's lunch was always more formal with a catered meal, but I knew that wasn't always the norm.

"Much more casual than yours. Louder," he said with a smile that let me know he loved every loud noise. "Momma Brandt cooks everything despite everyone asking to help. The men drink beer and watch football, as the kids run around hopped up on any candy they managed to sneak in before dinner."

"Sounds like the Thanksgivings you see on TV."

"Exactly like that."

"It sounds perfect."

We pulled in the driveway, and I had to wipe my sweaty palms on my leggings. What if I didn't fit in? What if they didn't like me? I'd met Ian's parents, but this felt like I was meeting his real family for the first time.

We didn't knock. Ian just opened the door and called out a loud, "Honey, I'm home."

A short woman with dark short hair came around the corner with her arms open. The apron had me guessing this was Momma Brandt.

"Ian, my favorite son," she gushed, pulling him down for a hug.

"Thanks, Mom," Erik said, coming over to give Ian a manly, backslap hug.

"Ian brought me a baby," she practically swooned, looking down at a now awake Audrey. Her wide eyes blinked, taking in the crowded room. Momma Brandt looked about ready to burst, and I couldn't help but smile. When someone looked at your child with that kind of love, you automatically approved of them. "But first, let me gather my manners." She shook her head at herself and turned to me. "Hello, dear."

"Momma Brandt, this is Carina. Carina this is Amelie."

I considered offering her my hand to shake, but something told me this woman didn't do handshakes. She stepped forward and embraced me, pulling me down to squeeze me tight and rock back and forth. I'd never had a hug from a mother, but something told me this woman did it the best.

"I'm so happy you're here, Carina." She stepped back but

held onto my hands. "And I promise it's not just because of that adorable squishy baby."

"It'd be okay if it was. She's pretty adorable." We both laughed and then she finally gave in and held her arms out for Audrey, who Ian had just taken out of her car seat.

Amelie gushed over her orange dress and thick thigh high stockings that exposed the rolls on her chunky little legs.

"Carina, this is my husband, Luka, and I understand you know my daughter, Hanna." A tall man stood with his arm around Ian, after some more manly hugs. He gave me a firm handshake before looking down at Audrey. Hanna lifted her wine glass from where she stood by Erik and Alexandra in greeting.

Three kids came barreling through the room, followed by four other people I discovered were Erik's aunts, uncles, and cousins.

"Hanna, can you take their coats, please?" Amelie asked.

"Nonsense," Ian said, winking Hanna's way. "I know where it all goes. I'm hardly a guest here."

I swallowed down the jealousy at Ian's wink to Hanna and the smile she gave in return.

"Erik, when are you going to give me grandbabies?"

Erik gave a deadpanned stare like this wasn't the first time his mother had asked. "I'm assuming Alexandra would want to finish college first."

Alex gave a rueful smile and tucked her hair behind her ear, looking down. Sometimes I forgot how young she was. Kids probably weren't on her twenty-year-old mind.

"Don't worry, Amelie," Ian said, pressing a kiss to the crown of her head as he walked by with our coats. "You're basically her surrogate grandma."

Amelie smiled down at Audrey, brushing their noses and talking baby-talk, getting a gummy smile in return. Her shoulders shrugged on a heavy sigh. "I guess I should hand her back so I can finish dinner."

"Do you need help with anything?" I offered. Ian said she did it all, but I had to try, at least.

"Absolutely not. Ian, get your girl a drink and go relax."

"Yes, ma'am."

I was bouncing Audrey in my arms, taking in the photos on the wall when Ian brought me a bottle of water. One picture had me pulling up short and leaning in to get a closer look. "Hanna's a twin?"

"Yeah."

Something in Ian's tone had me turning to look at him, but he wasn't looking at me. His eyes were trained to the photo of the two younger-looking Hannas. His clenched jaw and haunted eyes had my mind racing. Had something happened between him and the other twin? Was I jealous of the wrong woman? Maybe he was so close to Hanna because she reminded him of who he truly wanted?

"Is she here?" I asked, my voice tight.

After a long blink, he finally answered. "No."

"Oh." My mind reeled trying to understand the devastated look covering Ian's face. I felt like I was missing something. "Why not? Does she live too far away?"

His eyes were dark and blank when he finally looked at me, and I should have known the answer before he even said it. No one in this kind of family let distance keep them away. "She died."

"Oh, shit," I breathed. God, I felt like an asshole. I was jealous of someone who wasn't even alive. "I'm sorry, Ian," I said, offering comfort with my hand in his. He linked our fingers together and squeezed.

"It's not something we really talk about."

I opened my mouth to ask more when Amelie called from down the hall. "Dinner's ready."

With one last squeeze, he led me to the long table. A folding table was added to the end to accommodate all the guests. Another table stood off to the side for the kids.

We all crammed into our spots, passing food around the table, making jokes and poking fun. It was loud and controlled chaos. It was wonderful. Although, I slapped Ian's hand more than once when he kept stealing my food.

"It tastes so much better from your plate," he explained.

I rolled my eyes and stole a scoop of his mashed potatoes in return.

Once the meal was over, Amelie finally broke down and let a few of us help clean up. I was walking back from the restroom when I stopped at the entryway of the living room. Ian sat back on the couch a sleeping Audrey sprawled on his broad chest. While that sight always stole my breath, it was the woman sitting next to him that had me stopping in my tracks.

A heavy rock settled in my stomach as I took them in crammed right next to each other, her side completely pressed to his.

Everyone had filled up the living room, playing games and watching football, so it wasn't like there was anywhere else for her to sit. But did she have to lean into him to stroke Audrey's cheek? Did she have to look up at him like the sun set on him? Did she have to laugh lightly and squeeze his leg when he told a joke?

The worst part was that those weren't even the biggest questions flooding my head. No, the one roaring the loudest, flooding every cell in me with doubt and hurt, was why wasn't Ian stopping her? He even patted her hand resting on his knee. He smiled down at her with his casual smirk I wanted to claim as just mine.

I closed my eyes, counting to ten and barely swallowing down the need to shout across the room for her to stop touching him.

Bile rising in my throat and the squeezing pressure on my chest reminded me of the first time I realized Jake and Jackson were closer than I thought. The feeling consumed me and tried to pull me down into a panicked spiral. I couldn't stand there and watch them anymore because the more I saw, the easier it was for my mind to convince me that history was repeating itself.

I stepped into the kitchen, leaning against the counter and rolling my neck to ease the muscles pulling tight. I never wanted to feel this again, and I sure as hell didn't want to stand by and let it happen, allowing it to grow and get worse in my silence.

No, I wasn't going to allow someone to step in this time. I sucked in a deep breath, stretching my lungs to the max, forcing the muscles to relax and grabbed a bottle of beer. Pulling my shoulders back, I walked—strutted—into the living room to my man. The tension eased when I stood in front of Ian, and his eyes tracked from my hips to linger on my breasts before finally meeting my eyes with undeniable heat.

Ignoring everyone around us, even blocking out Hanna, I held the beer up, letting my eyes track over him too. "Trade?"

I decided not to feel bad that I used my sultry sex voice to ask if Ian wanted to trade our baby for beer in a room full of people. I had a point to make, and a crowd wouldn't stop me. For the most part, everyone ignored us, but I could feel Hanna's eyes glued to our every move.

I should feel bad for flaunting our relationship in front of her, but then I remembered her hand on his leg, and just like that, any remaining guilt disappeared.

"You sure?" Ian asked. "Do you need help?"

I smirked, knowing he was offering a make-out session somewhere, but while I wanted to mark my territory, I didn't know how I felt about making out in a room at a house I was a guest at.

"I've got it. You relax."

Before I took Audrey, I leaned over him and planted a soft kiss, loving the way he lifted his head to chase my lips. He growled and nipped at my smiling retreating lips.

"Dessert," he whispered.

Smiling, I hefted Audrey in my arms, finally taking a moment to peek over at Hanna who was staring down into her wine glass, her thumb tapping against the side.

Point. Proven.

The entire time I rocked Audrey to sleep, I couldn't stop smiling. I'd taken control and not sat idly by, and it felt good. I felt strong.

I was still smiling when I walked into the kitchen a little later. I was just turning around from grabbing a water from the fridge when Hanna walked in. She smiled without it reaching her eyes.

"I'm shocked to see Ian so domesticated and bringing someone to Thanksgiving," she said before I could walk out.

Part of me screamed to just shrug and walk away. Her tone promised nothing good. But pride had me turning to face her.

"Why do you say that?"

She shrugged, her face turning red and her eyes avoiding mine. "He's just always flitted around from woman to woman—never serious about anyone. I have no doubt he's going to be the best father, but he always claimed he'd never settled down. He said no woman was enough for him and never would be."

Somehow, I managed a forced smile. "Well, people change. We have a baby together, and we're devoted to making it work."

Her eyes flicked around the room, avoiding mine. She swallowed a few times and licked her lips before she gave the most condescending smile. "Okay."

Fire started low in my stomach and rose up my chest, but before it could break free, she turned to leave.

"Bitch," I growled under my breath.

I'd just closed my eyes to take a deep breath when Alex walked in. "Who pissed in your cheerios?"

"Huh?"

The brunette scanned me with her crystal blue eyes. "You look like you're about to murder someone."

A laugh broke free, because in that moment, I kind of felt like I could do some damage. I probably should have smiled and said everything was fine, but I needed to talk about Hanna. The fact that Alexandra probably knew her better might give me some better insight into the situation.

"Do Ian and Hanna have a previous relationship?"

"Umm, no. But I'm sure Hanna wishes there was something. Erik said she's crushed on him since she was a kid."

That's a long time to want someone. "That makes our last interaction make sense, I guess."

"What happened?"

"She definitely insinuated Ian wasn't going to stay with me because he was too much of a player."

Her brows shot to her hairline. "What?"

"Yeah. I've never known Hanna to be quite so forward and..."

"Bitchy," Alexandra filled in where I couldn't.

"Exactly. I've known her for a year, and she's been so nice. Hell, we've had lunch and inside jokes about being some of the few women in our line of work. I wouldn't have said we were friends, but I also wouldn't have expected what just happened."

"Look, it's not my place to say anything, but Hanna doesn't feel comfortable around many guys, so I think she latched on to her comfort with Ian. If it makes you feel better, I'm not sure Ian even notices anything other than having brotherly affection to her."

"I'd like to say it does, but I think my own issues block me from feeling relief."

"Past hurts never fail to weigh us down."

"Ain't that the truth."

Alex tapped her wine glass to my water bottle and gave a sad smile. "Maybe try talking to Ian. He can be oblivious sometimes, so maybe pointing it out will change things."

Maybe.

I couldn't help but think maybe it would put me in the same position I'd been with Jake, of him choosing between past and present. Jake chose his past, and I wasn't sure I could handle it if Ian did too.

Hanna's words stuck with me the rest of the night, and I struggled to convince myself they weren't the truth.

She was wrong.

She was just jealous.

Ian was committed to me.

I was enough for him.

I repeated the affirmations to myself, but even with his head buried between my thighs later that night, having me for dessert, doubts crept in.

Was I enough?

25 IAN

"Maybe we shouldn't go," Carina suggested, holding Audrey close.

"No," I responded, taking and passing her off to Alexandra. "I have reservations, and we have capable babysitters. We're going."

"If she loses a lung, we'll call you," Erik said.

"You're not funny," she deadpanned.

Audrey had formed a little cough last night, and it had Carina waking up each time she heard the pathetic little noise. But she ate fine and seemed alert. *Nothing to worry about,* I'd reminded her before we left the apartment.

Alexandra bumped her shoulder to Erik's in a reprimand. "I promise we won't take our eyes off her. You guys are only a phone call away if anything happens."

I pointed a finger between Alex and Erik. "No screwing on the job." Then leaned down to press a kiss to Audrey's forehead. "You let Daddy know if you see anything inappropriate."

Erik rolled his eyes but smiled Carina's way to let her know all was fine.

Worried that Carina wouldn't be able to enjoy the night, I

worked extra hard to keep her mind off Audrey and focused on us. Audrey was the center of our universe, but tonight, Carina was the center of mine.

I'd taken her to dinner at a steak house that was built in an old police precinct, wanting to give her the best. The dim lighting and table tucked away in a corner gave us the feel of seclusion and set the mood for romance. Taking advantage, I slid my hand up her skirt at the end of the meal.

"Naughty girl," I growled when I found out she wasn't wearing panties. I'd just swiped my finger between her folds, damn near groaning at the wet heat, when the waitress came back with our bill.

"How was dinner?" she asked.

"Delicious," I answered, bringing my finger to my mouth to taste Carina's sweet pussy.

My cock had been at half-mast all night with Carina in her tight black dress, but after that, I was hard as a rock, ready to explode.

She tried to jump me in the car once the valet brought it around, but I somehow found the strength to hold her back. I had plans for her tonight, and if I let her distract me, we'd end up fucking in the car for hours. "Not yet, Carina."

She grumbled adorably but sat back and waited. When we parked, I moved around to open her door and offer my hand, loving the way she easily slid her palm against mine. We'd come so far from the hesitation and regretful touches. Now, she reached for me without thought, linking her fingers in mine.

"Where are we going?"

I gestured over my shoulder to the giant Ferris wheel. "Have you been on it yet?"

"No." A smile stretched her cheeks like an excited kid on Christmas. "I've wanted to, but never had a chance."

"Good." I couldn't wait to get her up high above—alone.

When we reached the top, we looked around at the sparkling lights of the city, taking in the iconic bridge and lit up towers, sparkling off the river below.

"It's beautiful," she breathed.

I closed the gap between us on the bench. "You're beautiful."

The cart was completely encased in glass, but the lights were dimmed to not interfere with the view. I rested my hand on her knee before moving to her thigh, pulling it up onto the seat between us.

"What are you doing?"

"Finishing what I started at dinner. Just to take the edge off."

I walked my fingers up her thigh until I was right outside her pussy, feeling the heat begging me to play.

"Ian, what if people see?"

"They'll just see a couple cuddling, taking in the sights. They won't be able to see the way my fingers fuck into your tight cunt until you come."

Without any warm-up beyond the torture of the last hour, I shoved two fingers roughly inside her. We both moaned, the sounds filling the cart.

Her eyes slid closed, and her head rolled back when I curled my fingers inside her. Not allowing her to hide her reaction from me, I buried my free hand in her hair and tugged her up. "No. Look at me. I want to watch you try and control your cries when you come all over my fingers."

"Ian," she whimpered, my thumb now rubbing at her clit.

"We don't have long, Carina," I warned against her lips. "I won't stop until you make a mess on my hand. Not even if he opens the doors when we stop. He'll have to stand there and watch your orgasm."

I wasn't trying to drag it out and tease her, although part of me wanted to. I moved my fingers with a purpose to make her come as fast as possible.

"Would you like that?" I whispered against her lips. "To have someone watch you as you fall apart in my arms, my hand buried deep between your thighs."

Her hand shot out and held on to my shoulder, struggling to keep her eyes on mine. I liked watching the colors change the closer she got to coming. They were light like the ocean, but when she was turned on like this, on the brink of losing control, they were as dark as the midnight sky.

Her nails dug in through the material of my shirt, and she lost the battle. Her eyes slammed shut, and her teeth dug into her lush bottom lip as her pussy squeezed around my fingers. I ached to fill her with my cock, but that would have to wait. I'd hate to get arrested on our first night out as parents.

Her eyes slid open again just in time to watch me lick every spicy-sweet drop from my fingers. Taking deep breaths, I had to fight from falling to my knees and eating her until she came again. Thankfully, we reached the bottom, and our time was up, removing temptation—for now.

We walked out, hand-in-hand like nothing happened. When she turned to head back to the car, I tugged her in the opposite direction.

"Where are we going now?"

"I have another surprise."

"Okay, but if I don't get your cock in me soon, I may die."

"We can't have that now. I'm not into necrophilia."

I pulled her into me and nibbled at her lips, taking my time to taste her and feel every inch of her mouth on mine. Before I lost control, I pulled back with a groan.

"We're on a timeline. Otherwise, I'd take you right here and now for everyone to see."

"Promises, promises."

She yelped when I smacked her ass, followed by her musical laugh.

She kept giving me curious looks as we approached the baseball stadium and a janitor let us in. I led her up into the stands behind home base, giving us a perfect view of the stadium under minimal lighting.

"How the hell is this happening?" she asked, laughing at my side.

We sank into the seats, and I linked my fingers with hers. "I knew a guy in college who works here now."

"You know all kinds of people. Are you trying to impress me with your contacts?"

"Would it work if I tried?"

"Nope."

"I figured." I shrugged and looked back out at the field. "Erik and I used to go out to the fields all the time. We liked sitting in the middle of an empty stadium like all this space helped us think. We'd lay behind second and drink beers and talk about how we'd become the next Bill Gates."

"Those are some lofty goals."

"We may have also smoked a little pot too." She laughed and slid her fingers between mine, sending chills up my arm. "Empty baseball stadiums are one of my favorite places."

This was my private place, and I'd never taken anyone here before. Not that I could get into the Red's stadium very often, but I'd never taken anyone to any of the fields I frequented.

But when I planned this date for Carina, I wanted to share it with her. I wanted her to be a part of this.

"You played baseball too, right? Not just frequent the fields to smoke pot," she said, laughing.

I almost forgot that I'd told her. That time before Audrey seemed like a lifetime ago. "I sure did."

"Were you good?"

"I got picked up for college. My parents wanted me to go pro, but without Erik playing with me, it lost its appeal."

"Was he not good enough?"

I snorted. "He was way better than me, but he tore his shoulder in high school and decided not to push it. I guess neither of us loved it enough to go for pro."

"But your parents wanted you to? Even if you didn't love it?"

"Yeah." I laughed, remembering telling them I was through. "It was my junior year when I finally quit. My dad was furious and said I couldn't commit to anything and if I didn't stick with something, I'd be a waste."

She didn't say anything, but her hand squeezed mine in support.

"Erik and I had just sold our first application and had a slew more in our back pockets. I didn't need the scholarship anymore from baseball. I had more money than any twenty-one-year-old knew what to do with."

"That's amazing. They had to see how amazing that was."

I tipped my head to the side and smiled at her innocent view of everything. "Not really. They honestly didn't really care about it. They claimed a backroom application made in a college dorm was a waste of time."

She leaned forward and pressed her lips to mine, pulling back just enough to let me see the sincerity in her eyes. "Well, you showed them."

"I did, didn't I?"

"But," she said, cocking her brow, her lips tipping just slightly, "I will definitely need to see you in tight pants, playing ball."

"Oh, yeah?"

She licked her lips, her eyes gleaming. "Yeah."

"Maybe someday I'll play for you."

Being done with her in another seat, I reached over, gripping her hips to pull her on top of me. Her knees went on either side of my hips, her skirt riding up, and her hair falling around us like a curtain.

"God," I groaned, pushing her skirt up the rest of the way around her waist. "Look at that pretty pussy."

Both of my thumbs slid along each of her folds, loving how wet they still were.

"Ian," she whimpered, thrusting against my hands. "I need you."

I jerked her hard right over my length, sitting up to reach her mouth. "Then take me."

Her hands fumbled with the belt buckle and zipper, but she managed to free my cock. A few strokes already had me at my breaking point, and I needed to get inside her before I made a fool of myself.

"Someone could be watching," I taunted. Her breath caught, but she didn't stop. "Do you want them to watch you take this fat cock up your tight little pussy."

Instead of answering, she lifted up and held the head at her opening before slowly sliding down. Her back and forth, never fully sliding down all the way, had me grinding my teeth until I'd had enough. I gripped her hips tight and slammed her down, loving the way she cried out.

Her hands gripped my shoulders and rocked back and forth, her warm heat driving me mad.

"Look at you," I groaned, pushing her back so she could see my dick stretching her opening. "Look at all the cream on me— making a mess of me." I slid her back down slowly, watching myself disappear inside her. "Would you lick it off? Would you suck me clean?"

Her hands buried in my hair, tugging hard. "Anything. Now shut up and fuck me."

"Such a bossy little thing." I nipped at her chin. "I may let you sass me daily, but like this, when I'm buried deep inside you,

you're mine. And if I want to sit here with you full of my cock and not move, that's what we'll do."

"Ian, please," she whimpered.

"Begging sounds so good from your pouty lips."

She rocked, trying to gain more friction. Her warm heat like an inferno.

"Carina," I said, holding her steady. "I'm not wearing a condom."

Her movements stopped, but she didn't pull off. "I'm on the pill."

"I've heard that before," I said with a smirk.

She shoved my shoulder. "I'm not on any antibiotics either."

"Are you sure?"

"Yes, Ian."

"Not that I don't want to have more babies with you," I muttered without thinking. That had her pulling back, almost dislodging me.

"What?"

I buried my head in her chest and kissed all over her cleavage, pulling her back on me. I needed to distract her because that wasn't a conversation to have in a baseball stadium when you're balls deep in a skittish woman.

"Focus on the feeling, Carina. Focus on how good it feels with nothing between us."

She moaned and rocked her hips harder. "I love how you feel inside me."

"I've never been inside another woman without a condom."

As if the admission was the flip to her switch, she lost it. She rocked harder, bouncing up and down, her tits swaying under her dress. I swiped my thumb across her clit and pulled her down so I could feast at her lips.

"Ian," she cried. "Ian. Ian."

I could listen to that chant until I died. "Come all over me, baby. Milk my cock."

Goosebumps broke out across her skin, and then she was crying out, trying to bury her head in my neck to mask her pleasure. Her tight pussy squeezed me impossibly tight, dragging my orgasm right behind her.

When we were nothing but a panting mess, I did what I did best and made a joke, stroking down to her bare ass. "Whoever is on duty tonight got a hell of a view of this tight ass."

She jerked up and tried to tug her skirt down over her bottom, unsuccessfully since my length was still lodged inside her.

"It's not funny," she reprimanded.

"It's pretty funny," I said, dragging the material back up so I could palm each cheek, squeezing her ripe bottom.

With one last kiss, I lifted her off me and helped her adjust her clothes.

"Now, I kind of wish I had panties," she muttered.

"Why's that?" I knew why, I just wanted to hear her say it.

She blushed beautifully and stuttered. "Well, I—I'm kind of—I'm—"

"Are you a mess with my cum leaking down your thighs?"

"You're incorrigible," she laughed, a smile tugging at her lips.

"You love it."

Needing to feel it for myself, I moved my hand under her skirt and collected the sticky mess dripping down her leg. Just feeling my cum leaking out of her had me hard and ready to go again. But our time was running out. So, I pulled my wet fingers out and brought them to her lips, painting each curve.

Her tongue snaked out to trace the path before sucking my fingers into her mouth.

"Goddamn, woman," I growled, adjusting my cock.

"I'm going to fucking own you when we get home."

"You already do."

"Fuck," I whispered, clenching my fists to keep from ripping her dress off of her. "You're lucky we have to go, or I'd have you bent over and let whoever came by watch."

"Promises, promises," she laughed, backing away to go.

"One of these days..."

She linked her hands with mine, a satisfied smile on her lips.

The walk to the car was fraught with tension; both of us eager to continue our night. When we'd almost made it to the car, she grabbed my arm, stopping me on the sidewalk, her face filled with a different kind of tension.

"Hey, I wanted to mention something and kind of hope it doesn't piss you off."

"Okaaaay?" My mind reeled with all the things it could be.

My nerves that I'd screwed up somehow grew with each second she bit at her lips and stared at the ground. We'd been sparking with sexual energy moments before, and now it felt as if we sat on the edge of a precipice with the chance to crash and burn.

I was about to come out of my skin when she finally asked, "How much do you and Hanna hang out?"

If she threw an advanced math problem at me and asked me to solve it, I wouldn't have been more surprised. "What? Why?" She just stared, waiting for my answer. "I see her at Erik's sometimes, less since Alex is around. Otherwise, work. An occasional lunch."

She swallowed like those few times were hard to hear, and I still didn't understand where this was going. "I think she's uncomfortable with us being together."

"What? No. She's happy for me."

"Not really. I mean she's happy you have Audrey, but not us," she explained gesturing between us.

I shook my head. "She's happy for us. You just aren't around enough to see it."

"Ian, she's in love with you."

I couldn't help it—I laughed. My head fell back, and big bellows of laughter escaped into the night sky.

When I looked down again, she had stepped back from me with her jaw clenched tight. "It makes me uncomfortable that you're around her so much."

Trying to keep up with what she was saying, I sobered and shook my head. "What? Do you not want me to be alone with her?" I asked like a joke because surely this was nonsense. Hanna wasn't in love with me. She was like a kid sister to me.

But it wasn't a joke because Carina kept staring, not saying anything. She stepped back again, and I didn't like the distance she was creating. I didn't like the idea of having to censor myself around my family—of distancing myself from someone who didn't have feelings for me, just because Carina believed she did. Hell, she'd only been around her a handful of times.

"I'm not going to stop being around her," I said rationally. "I work with her. She's like a sister to me. My family."

Carina took an aggressive step forward, her eyes sparking—no longer calm. "I'm your family. *We* are your family." She swallowed and collected herself. "You need to make it clear that you're taken and there's no chance of you and her."

Was Carina doing this to drive a wedge between us? Was she scared about my comment about wanting more babies with her—about what we just shared and was trying to push me away? The thought burrowed under my skin, pricking at my own irritation. She barely acknowledged our relationship, held me at a distance for so long, and here she stood making demands.

"Am I taken, Carina? Or are we doing this until you want to pretend we didn't?"

"That's not how this is," she said, her voice cracking.

"Then, how is it?"

She swallowed and squeezed and relaxed her hands. The more time I spent around Carina, the more I got to know her tells, and her hands were giving away her nerves. "I—I...care for you."

"What a benevolent declaration," I deadpanned.

Her shoulders rose and fell on a deep breath, and all irritation was sapped from my body when she lifted wet eyes to mine. "I can't be cheated on again, Ian."

Everything in me softened, and I pulled her into my chest. I was being a dick. We both came into this relationship with our own baggage, and we both were bringing it to this argument.

She sniffed, and I held her tighter, stroking my hand up and down her back, pressing a kiss to the crown of her head. "I'll say something, okay?"

"Yeah?"

"Yes. If it makes you feel more comfortable, then that's what I'll do."

"Thank you."

Maybe Carina saw something I hadn't because whenever I looked at Hanna, I saw the kid who always hung around Erik and me. I saw the fragile woman who'd suffered too much and needed some kindness her way. But maybe all the hugs and laughs and the way she sat next to me every chance she got meant more to her. I dreaded bringing it up.

"Just let me do it my way. Hanna is sensitive. She's been through more than most." That was an understatement.

"Okay." She nodded her head and lifted her wet eyes to mine.

"You need to trust me," I ordered.

Only a moment of hesitation before she finally agreed. "Okay. I do."

"Good." I leaned down and kissed the tip of her nose. "Now, let's go home and have makeup sex."

26 IAN

Everyone collected their files at the end of another meeting and piled out back to their offices. I tried to smile at Hanna, but she'd barely looked at me for the past week. I can't help but wonder if Carina was wrong about Hanna and that maybe I don't need to bother saying anything to her. She obviously wasn't in love with me. She'd been avoiding me since Thanksgiving.

Carina's fears were obviously conjuring things that weren't there.

"Hey, Little Brandt," I called to Hanna. Maybe if I was more direct, I'd get a better feel for her mood. "You want to grab lunch?"

"Can't. I'll already be here late, so I'm working through lunch."

She gave a forced smile, her usually vibrant green eyes duller. Was something else bothering her? My protective big brother alarm was going off, and my first instinct was to soothe her. I'd always been there for Hanna. And Sophie when she'd been alive too. The Brandts were my family, and despite Carina's concerns,

I wasn't going to abandon Hanna when she was so obviously hurting.

I pulled her into a hug, and it only took a moment before her slim arms wrapped around me. Looking down, I was relieved to find the first genuine smile I'd seen all week. The same smile she'd given me when she was eight. Hanna was definitely not in love with me.

"Yeah," I said, commiserating with the late night ahead of me. "I should get some work done too. Next time."

"Okay. Definitely next time."

She gave me another smile and was about to turn away when I stopped her. "You know you can talk to me about anything, right?"

It was a coward's approach, but if Hanna did have anything going on, she could come to me, and I could avoid bringing up a potentially beyond awkward topic. Carina had asked me to talk to her, but if there was nothing to talk about, she'd understand, right?

A voice told me she wouldn't, but I shoved it down, giving Hanna the opening to talk to me about any misplaced feelings.

Hanna's eyes softened. "Thanks, Ian. You're always there for me."

"Always will be, kid."

With a nod, she headed back to her office the floor below, and I headed to mine with a weight lifted off my chest.

I'd been working non-stop when my cellphone vibrated across my desk.

"Bergamo," I answered.

"Ian?"

Carina's soft voice had me sitting back from the computer and smiling. I'd never tire of hearing her say my name.

"Hey, babe. What's up?"

"You coming home tonight?"

I looked at the time. "Shit. I didn't realize it was so late. I'm trying to finalize this contract. I can finish it tomorrow though."

"It's okay. Finish it tonight and that way you're home tomorrow night. No need to stay late two days in a row."

"You sure?"

"Of course. Is Erik staying late too?"

"Nah. It's just me, myself, and I shutting down the building."

"Poor baby."

"I know. Promise to soothe me later with a blow job."

She snorted her laugh, and I could imagine her rolling her eyes perfectly. "You wish."

"I do wish. I'll see if I can earn it when I get home."

"I can't wait."

"Bye, babe. Tell Audrey goodnight for me."

"Bye."

I hung up and let the happiness of my life wash over me. I had a beautiful, smart, caring girlfriend and probably the best baby that was ever created. All waiting for me at home and I couldn't wait.

I threw myself into my work so I could get home sooner. I was finishing up a few final details when Hanna knocked on my open door. She had her purse, and coat cinched tight.

"Heading out?"

"Yeah. In a bit. I just wanted to see if you happened to still be here."

I rolled back my chair and held my arms wide. "In the flesh."

Hanna stepped into my office, setting her purse down and taking a deep breath.

"You said I could talk to you," she started, fidgeting with the tie around her coat, not meeting my eyes. "Well, there is something I've wanted to say for a while and the more time that passes, the more my chance of saying it slips away."

Oh, shit.

Warning bells rang like sirens in my head. They all sounded a lot like Carina telling me *I told you so*. She was right, and I was fucking dumb.

I stood from my chair, needing to move and approach this with care. This was Hanna. I couldn't brush it off from behind my desk.

I made it around, standing only a few feet from her. "Hanna, you don't—"

"I love you," she said, halting me in my tracks. She looked up at me, her eyes wet, and my heart broke. "I've loved you for so long, and I didn't think I could ever love anyone. I didn't think I'd ever feel anything like this. Not after what happened. Not after losing Sophie."

Each word dropped like a landmine between us. Each word twisted like a vice around my lungs, squeezing them tighter and tighter until I was sure I couldn't suck in another breath.

"Hanna," I breathed. "Shit—Carina..."

My body ached with thoughts of how this conversation would end. There was no good way out of it, and it terrified me to hurt her.

"I—I know," she admitted before swallowing hard. Her cheeks burned red hot, and I hated everything about this situation. "But you need to know how I feel. Know that there's someone else who loves you—who's always loved you."

"God, Hanna. You know I love you—"

Her trembling hands moved with purpose, undoing the sash around her coat before tugging it open to reveal barely-there black lingerie.

Shooting my eyes to the ceiling, I took the last step toward her, and tried to close the coat, only succeeding in pulling her closer. Her bare skin brushed my hands and I cringed because this was Hanna—the girl who'd been like my baby sister almost all my life.

"I l-love you, Ian." I could hear the tears in her voice, and it pierced at my heart. She pressed close, trapping my hands between us, her hands sliding around my neck and pulling me down to kiss me.

Her lips landed at the corner of my mouth, and I broke my hands free, gripping her hips to push her back.

Movement over Hanna's shoulder had me freezing, allowing Hanna to step closer and rub against me, pressing an open-mouthed kiss to my neck.

"Carina..."

Her wide eyes filling with tears unlocked my muscles, and I pushed Hanna back, but it was too late.

She stood there with a paper bag of food in her hands. The other pressed to her chest like she was trying to hold her heart together. Time stood still, slowing down so I could memorialize the biggest mistake of my life. So I could always look back and remember the time I fucked up and lost the best thing I'd ever had.

Her chest heaved like she was barely holding back sobs, her mouth open over her broken breaths. But then, her eyes slid closed, two tracks of tears sliding down her cheeks and it was like that was it for her—a switch was flipped.

"Oh, my god," Hanna gasped, jerking her coat closed. "I-I'm s-so sorry, Carina. I'm so sorry."

Carina's mouth slammed shut, her jaw clenched, and when she opened her eyes again, they were filled with fire. She pulled her shoulders back, dropping the bag before turning and bolting.

"Ian, I'm so sorry." Hanna's tear-filled voice broke through the shock. "I didn't think. It was impulsive, and stupid and I'm so sorry."

I looked down at the girl who I would always care for—who I'd always look out for, and who I hated to leave like this.

But the love of my life had just run out, and I couldn't let her get far without her knowing it wasn't what it looked like. I couldn't let her lock her heart away before I could fall to my knees and apologize for not believing her—for not taking her concerns seriously.

"I have to go."

I ran out of my office, but the elevator was already closed and going down. The door to the stairs slammed against the wall, echoing down the twenty flights. Somehow, I managed to make it to the bottom without breaking anything, but I didn't manage to get there in time. All the elevators were headed back up, and Carina was nowhere in sight.

"Fuck," I shouted, burying my hands in my hair. "Think, Ian."

I needed to get home. Everything she had was at my place. She'd have to go there first before running. God, I hoped she didn't run.

My skin vibrated like a live wire, adrenaline making me twitchy as I waited for the elevator. When the doors started opening on my floor, I didn't even let them fully open before running to my office. I held on to my doorframe and swung inside, coming up short at finding Jared leaning against my desk, arms crossed.

"I had to drop off some papers," he explained, nodding to the new files on my desk.

"I don't know what you saw, but it's not what you think," I shot off, moving past him to grab my jacket and keys.

"I'm not touching that with a ten-foot pole," he said, holding his hands up. "But you better hope Erik never finds out his little sister left your office crying in a half-done-up coat with her lingerie showing."

"Shut up, Jared," I growled, shoving past him. I didn't have time to explain myself and didn't owe him one either.

I needed to get to Carina.

CARINA

STANDING OUTSIDE OUR APARTMENT DOOR, I swiped at the tears that wouldn't quit and took a deep breath. There was no way I was hiding that something was wrong. I just needed to convince my Aunt Vivian that I was okay enough for her to leave. I couldn't talk to anyone yet. I needed to get inside, pack up me, and Audrey and get out before Ian came home.

"Carina, baby. What's wrong?" my aunt asked as soon as I stepped in.

"I—I can't talk about it. Please," I choked out. "I just ne—need some space."

"Sweetie, I'm worried," she said, pulling me into her arms.

"I know, and I understand, but I just need some time. Thank you so much for coming to watch Audrey for me."

She scanned my face, her frown sinking lower, but seeing my stubbornness and knowing she wouldn't get anything from me tonight. "You know I'm here for whatever you need."

The lump in my throat prevented me from responding, so I nodded instead.

"Audrey's asleep in her rocker."

"Thank you."

She pulled me in for a hug, and more tears slipped free. Vivian wiped them away and pressed a kiss to my forehead and left.

Standing in the middle of the apartment, I looked around at the happy little life we'd created. It took everything in me to not scream and tear it all down—destroy every inch of the lie.

God, walking in there and seeing her in his arms, her lips against his neck, his hands on her hips barely clad in anything, hearing them say they loved each other, all of it had my head pounding. It swirled like chaos until I wasn't sure what was real and what was false. Half of me was picturing things so much worse than what was in front of me, conjuring the worst, wondering how long they'd been fooling around behind my back. My mind screaming that this was what I would always have. I would always come last. There would always be another better than me.

The stupid, hopeful part of me prayed for a rational explanation, wondered if I imagined Ian pulling away. Maybe he hadn't been cheating. Maybe it was just a mistake.

That side of myself got crushed to oblivion under the negative doubt.

I was still standing in the middle of the apartment when Ian stormed in, the door slamming against the wall.

He looked at me with frantic eyes and almost sagged to the floor in relief at finding me there.

"Oh, thank God. You're still here."

"I'm getting ready to pack, and we're leaving."

He shut the door and walked toward me slowly with his hands held up like he was approaching a rabid animal. "It's not what it looked like."

Anger at his lame excuse flooded me. For a moment, I almost laughed at how different I was in the face of Ian's betrayal than I'd been with Jake's. When I'd confronted Jake, it had hurt, but we'd separated with understanding. With Ian, it was a soul-deep pain. I wanted him to feel right along with me. I wanted him to hurt more than me. There was no understanding, just rage. "How fucking original, Ian," I growled at him.

"I know. It sounds cliché, but it's true. She came in and confessed her feelings, and when I tried to explain myself to her, she just pushed on. I had no idea what she planned to do. I was shocked. I pushed her away, Carina. Nothing happened. I promise."

He stepped closer still, and I stood my ground, not giving in to running into his arms so he could soothe me and tell me it would all be okay.

"I'm sorry, Carina. I didn't know what to do."

"How about talking to her like you promised me you would." My voice cracked on the last word. Finding Hanna there almost naked in his arms was only half the betrayal. He'd told me he'd talk to her, but he was just placating the crazy woman and her baggage. "You were supposed to let her down easy before it got to her stripping for you."

"There's no letting her down softly without doing damage."

"You just talk to her, Ian."

"It's not that easy," he said through a clenched jaw.

I closed the distance between us, stepping into his personal space. "That's the thing," I whispered. "It *is* that fucking easy."

He winced and growled his frustration, spinning away before turning back to face me, resignation marring his beautiful face. "Hanna and Sophie were sold into sex slavery for months before Erik could find them. Hanna was the only one to make it back home alive."

I stumbled back, his confession splashing over me like a bucket of ice water, sapping the fight from my body.

Holy shit.

Sold.

Sex slavery.

Hanna.

The words floated around, but they couldn't form a coherent understanding. That was something that you heard about but never had to face in reality. I pictured Hanna, a strong, bold woman in the boardroom, and struggled to mesh her with what he just confessed.

But then I saw her in Ian's arms, declaring her love and

throwing herself at him. I saw the woman who cornered me in the kitchen trying to make me feel insecure and small.

I understood how Ian struggled to talk to her—how maybe she was more fragile than most, but it didn't excuse what had happened. It didn't take away the damage and pain.

He should have listened to me. He should have supported me and done what he'd promised.

"I'm sorry that happened, but you should have trusted me when I told you. I *needed* you to trust me when I told you what I knew. Not laugh in my face."

"I know," Ian choked out, his eyes glassy. "I'm so sorry, Carina."

I knew he was, but I couldn't keep looking at him right then. I couldn't say it was fine and move about the apartment like normal.

I wiped my eyes and tried to stand tall. "I need space."

"Do you want to move back into the guest room?"

"No, Ian. I need to be alone. I don't want to be in this apartment. I don't want to be around you."

I hated his wince—hated knowing I was hurting him, but in that moment, all that mattered was getting through this.

"What about Audrey?"

"I'll take her with me."

"Carina—"

"Please, Ian," I begged. "I just need a little space to think. I'll call you tomorrow."

He searched my face and swallowed a few times before finally nodding. "Okay."

Ian sat with Audrey while I packed a bag for both of us. He kissed her goodbye and winced when I pulled back from any contact with him. I couldn't feel his touch—I'd crumble.

It didn't take long to settle into my old apartment. Most of my stuff was still there since Ian already had furniture. At the time we'd held on to the space to finish out my lease. I had no idea that I'd need it to come back to when it all fell apart.

Gripping my phone in my hand, I thought about calling someone, asking them to come be by my side. But when I scrolled through my contacts, I realized I didn't have any girlfriends to help me through this. The past two years had consisted of me throwing myself into work and keeping everyone at a distance.

Then I'd relied on Ian—he was everything I'd needed.

Now, I sat here in a mostly empty apartment, back where I started.

Alone.

27 CARINA

Aunt Vivian gave me a skeptical look the next morning when I dropped Audrey off before work. Thankfully, she didn't ask any prying questions about my swollen, puffy eyes. She knew me well enough to let me process, and I'd explain in time.

I thought work would be a good distraction from the mess my life was currently in. That tactic had worked when Jake and I broke up. I'd buried myself in contracts and clients, and it had blocked out the hurt. Now, I sat with my hands frozen over my keyboard, staring blankly at my computer screen that had long faded to black.

I just couldn't get my mind to stop reeling.

Would I always be in this situation? The girl that got cheated on.

No, Ian hadn't cheated. I believed him when he said Hanna had pursued him and he'd put a stop to it. But would I be the girl who was always an extra, the one who didn't come first. Ian had been so concerned about Hanna's feelings that he completely dismissed mine, deceiving me into believing he'd talk to her.

The biggest, most daunting question was if Ian and I could get past this.

Did I want to?

Yes.

That answer came through loud and clear. I loved him. I loved our family. But maybe I was the only one. Maybe he didn't love me in return. Maybe he was only in it for Audrey.

"Carina."

My name jerked me out of my thoughts, and I looked over to find Jake standing at my door, brows drawn together.

"Hey. What's up?" I tried to give an aloof tone, but it was too high-pitched, and Jake knew me too well.

"I called your name a couple times."

"Sorry," I laughed at myself, but it came out choked. "I was just lost in thought."

"You okay?"

Maybe it was the concern and sincerity behind his question. Maybe because it was Jake and he was the closest thing I had to a best friend. I didn't know, but the next words out of my mouth shocked us both. "Did you love me?"

He blinked a few times, his mouth opening and closing like a fish before he ran a hand over his face and closed the door, walking deeper into my office.

"Carina, I still love you. Jackson and I both love you. You know that, right? That what we shared together wasn't a lie?"

His deep voice rang with passion, and I knew he meant every word. Deep down, past the hurt, I knew we all had cared deeply for each other. But this thing with Ian was wearing me down and putting cracks in things I thought were whole.

I swallowed the lump in my throat before answering. "I do, and I know why it didn't work out. I'm just...having a moment."

"You're allowed those, and you don't take enough for yourself." He leaned his hip against the edge of my desk and stared down with his assessing look. I tried to lift my chin higher and pull my shoulders back, afraid of what he might find behind the exterior. "Is this about Ian?"

And just like that, the thin shell I'd been using to support myself cracked, and Jake became a blurry figure. Once the dam had one small fracture, it shattered, and all came pouring out.

Jake reached me just as the first sob broke free. I tried to cover my face, ashamed to be crying so openly in my ex-fiancé's arms. I could only imagine if my dad came in right now. He'd proclaim he told me so—that women were too weak and cried in the office over trivial things.

But Jake didn't say anything, he held me close and let me bury my head against his chest and let loose everything I'd been holding in the past twenty-four hours. He rubbed his hand over my hair and whispered that it was all okay. My whole body shook with each cry that wracked through me, and it seemed to go on forever, sapping my energy until there was nothing left.

Finally expelling every last tear I had, I was down to a few sniffs, trying to wipe at my cheeks like nothing happened.

Jake continued to rub my back and hold me close. This was the reason I forgave him for what he did to us. This was the reason I decided our friendship was more important than our mistakes. Because no matter what, he was there for me without judgment. He was my best friend.

"I'm sorry," I said with my soggy voice. "My hormones are still kind of crazy."

Jake held my face in his hands and gave the same comforting smile he'd given me when I broke up with my boyfriend in high school. "No need to apologize. You don't always have to be the strongest one in the room."

"I know, but I want to be."

He pressed a kiss to my forehead. "Do you want to talk about it?"

"No...not really."

"Okay." He stepped back but kept his hands on my upper arms as if I would crumble at any moment. "If you change your mind, I'm a phone call away. And if you need to laugh, I'll put Jackson on."

Just the thought of Jackson trying to cheer me up brought a small laugh out. "Okay. Thank you, Jake."

"Anytime. Why don't you head home and spend the day with that beautiful baby? She'll cheer you up."

"You know what? I think I will."

SPENDING the day with Audrey was exactly what I needed. Her little giggles and chunky legs that were always kicking made me feel lighter. Made the ache distant and less.

At least until she was asleep, and my phone vibrated with a message from Ian.

Ian: I said I'd give you space and I am, but I haven't heard from you all day. Is everything okay? Is Audrey doing okay? How's her cough?

Audrey's cough from last week still lingered, it would fade and then come back, and my chest squeezed at his concern, reminding me he really was a good man. Just a good man, I couldn't see yet.

Me: Everything is fine. We're staying at my dad's for now.

It was a lie, but I couldn't have him showing up at the apartment just yet. I still needed space to think everything through.

Me: I'm sorry I didn't message sooner. I just… I need time.

Me: I'll call tomorrow, and we'll figure something out with Audrey so you can see her.

I quickly snapped a pic of her sleeping and sent it to him before putting my phone on airplane mode, leaving it on the coffee table. Ian always knew what to say to me, and I didn't want to be tempted to do something I wasn't ready for.

My heart jerked in my chest when a knock at the door came ten minutes later.

Shit. He'd promised he would give me space—he promised he wouldn't push it.

I stood on shaky limbs and made my way to the door like a bomb waited for me on the other side. Each step had my muscles pulling tighter and tighter until I was sure I'd snap. Leaning in quietly to hold up the ruse I wasn't there in case it was him. I checked through the peephole and found a dark head of hair and an easy smile.

Just not Ian's.

This one had salt in his hair and wrinkles around his eyes.

I opened the door to a smiling Kent. "Surprise."

Not that I wasn't happy to see him, but Kent had never been to my place before. We'd all formed a friendship, but it rarely went outside of meetings and drinks afterward.

At my hesitant stare, he explained. "Jake told Daniel and Daniel told me. I come bearing gifts," he said joyously, holding up a bottle of expensive bourbon.

"I can't drink," I said with a deadpanned stare.

His brows furrowed and he looked to the bottle before back at me, confused. "Can't you like…pump and dump or something?" he asked, gesturing to my chest with the bottle.

His concern that I couldn't drink, and his solution had a laugh breaking free I didn't know I was capable of. It hurt my face to form a smile and my chest to shake with anything other than tears.

But it also felt really good.

For the first time, I saw a glimmer of light at the end of the tunnel—that maybe it would be okay eventually. I was damaged, but not broken.

Shaking my head, I stepped aside and let him in. He held up a grocery bag in his other hand once the door was closed. "Good thing I brought ice cream. Now, let's watch chick flicks and cry together. Olivia told me it's the female heartbreak survival kit."

Another laugh, and it hurt less this time.

He brought out a few more laughs through the night, each one coming easier than the last. It was nice not to feel alone like I had the night before. It was a nice reminder that I had more friends than I realized.

It was all nice...but it wasn't Ian.

28 IAN

With a deep breath, I prepared myself to do what I should have done last week. What I should have done as soon as Carina brought it up with me.

I rapped my knuckles on Hanna's open door and tried to appear like my heart wasn't thundering in my chest. Her wince of regret upon finding me standing there made me realize one of us needed to hold it together.

"Please don't, Ian." She kept her gaze locked on the paper on her desk, her jaw clenched.

The big brother part of me didn't want to cause her any more pain than she'd been through and urged me to step back and abide by her wishes, but even if Carina wasn't my driving force for being there, we needed to talk.

"Hanna, you're my family. We need to talk about this."

"Here's a better idea: we never talk about this."

"While I see the appeal, it won't work. The holidays are coming up, and we should clear the air of all the awkward silences around each other."

She sighed, sitting back in her seat, finally giving me an irritated glare. Good. That was much better than the embarrassed shame when I first walked in. "Then let there be awkward silences."

"See, here's the problem." I closed the door behind me and made myself comfortable in one of her office chairs. "Erik would notice, and then he'd figure out what happened, and then he'd kill me because, while I want to believe he loves me more, we all know you're his number one. He'd find out I'd hurt you and promptly murder me. And I have a little girl to raise. So, death would really put a damper on that."

She tried to look anywhere but at me, swallowing a few times, hesitating, but I waited her out. We couldn't avoid this—I wouldn't.

"I'm sorry," she finally muttered. "It was a mistake."

"Don't apologize. I told you, you could talk to me about anything."

When she nodded and dug her teeth into her bottom lip, I knew she was done talking, and I needed to make her understand. We couldn't leave it like this.

"Listen, Hanna," I began, leaning forward to rest my elbows on my knees. "We're family, and a little proclamation of love won't break us. Because here's the thing, what we share isn't that deep romantic love you deserve. It isn't the romance, flowers, dates, kisses in the rain kind of love." A single tear slipped down her cheek, and she quickly brushed it away. I wanted to go to her and hold her, make it better for her, but I couldn't. She needed to hear this and, more importantly, believe it. "What you feel for me is comfort. I'm the only single male you allow yourself to be you around. And while I'm an exceptional specimen," I winked, earning me a small laugh, "I'm not for you. He's out there once you let yourself look."

"You know I can't," she said, shaking her head.

"No, Hanna. I know you *can*." She lifted her emerald eyes to mine as more tears slipped free. "I understand it's hard, but one day you'll be going about your day and not even realize it happened—you're on a romantic date telling someone you love them—really love them. And I can't wait to watch it and be the one to tell you I told you so."

Another small laugh. "Ian…"

"I love you, Hanna, but not like the love you deserve."

Another nod and some more sniffs before she stood to make her way around the desk. I stood too and met her halfway, pulling her small frame into my body and holding her close. She shed a few more tears, but eventually pulled back and smiled.

"But, hey," I began, my eyes narrowed in warning. "Don't ever wear lingerie like that again. You're a young lady, and I'd have to gouge the eyes out of any guy who saw such innocence. You should try a muumuu. Men love muumuus."

She stepped back and slapped my chest. "Ha. Ha. Such sage advice."

"I'm Yoda over here. Basically, the Gandhi of relationships."

"Speaking of relationships," she began, tucking her hair behind her ear. "Did I ruin things between you and Carina?"

I wanted an immediate denial to fall from my lips, but I wasn't sure. I'd messaged her a little bit ago, and she'd asked for more space. Fear had climbed up my throat, but I'd forced it down, believing she didn't want to make the space permanent.

"We'll be okay." Bending my knees, I made sure Hanna was taking in my words. "We'll *all* be okay." She nodded, and I took a deep breath. She wasn't going to be happy with what I said next, but it needed to happen. "I need you to apologize to Carina."

Her eyes shot up, wide. "Ian—"she protested.

I hardened my expression. "You have to, Hanna. She deserves it, at the least, but also, I need you to do it, so we can fix this. You're both my family, and I need you to be able to be in the same room at some point, and that starts with a pretty damn big apology."

She swallowed and nodded again. "Okay."

"Thank you, Little Brandt."

We had one last hug and agreed it was best never to mention anything about it to Erik and then I was on my way home.

My empty home.

God, I missed my girls. It'd only been a day, but I hated coming home to an empty house. I miss the baby coos that greeted me, and Carina dancing around the kitchen. I looked down at my phone, taking in sleeping Audrey, barely fighting back the urge to call them.

She said she was at her dad's, but I knew better. She was back at her apartment. She'd want to be alone, not somewhere she'd have to explain herself. I almost turned right to head to her place rather than left to go to mine, but I didn't.

Instead, I promised myself that tomorrow...tomorrow I'd go get my girls.

Carina

KENT STAYED for two movies and almost half the bottle of bourbon.

He'd called an Uber and told me to call him if I needed anyone's ass kicked.

It'd been nice having company. It'd been exactly what I needed because while I'd enjoyed my time with Kent, each second that passed, I realized how much I wanted it to be Ian laughing by my side.

I was still beyond hurt, but even through the ache, I wanted him. I wanted to talk to him. I wanted to work through whatever had happened. I wasn't ready to give up on us just yet.

By the time Kent left, a weight had lifted off my battered heart. I wanted to call Ian, but when I looked at the time it was so late, and Audrey was cranky. I promised myself I'd call him in the morning when I was less beat.

Audrey's cough was a little worse than earlier, and when I tried to feed her, she was having none of it. She'd been disgruntled and whimpering on and off until she finally passed out.

I didn't know how much time had passed before her cries jerked me out of a deep sleep. Her face was red as she let loose. The only time she'd stop crying was when she was coughing. When I picked her up to comfort her, she was warm. Quickly, I pulled the blanket from around her and took her temperature.

Adrenaline coursed through my veins when it read one-hundred-and-one-point-nine. After a quick google search, I stripped her down and held her close as I called the on-call nurse. She informed that I could give her Tylenol and see if it brought her temperature down. If not, to bring her in immediately.

Audrey was pissed about the medicine, and I wasn't sure how much of it actually made it in her mouth. I used a warm washcloth to help with her fever and tried to feed her, but she wouldn't eat. When she'd finally cried herself to sleep again on my chest, I let a few tears fall. I hated seeing my baby in pain and not knowing what to do to help. She slept and coughed every once in a while as I sat still and wished Ian were there to help.

It wasn't long before Audrey stirred again, woken up by another coughing fit. Her skin burned hotter than ever, and when I took her temperature again, it read one-hundred-and-four.

Panic stole my breath and pulled my skin too tight. Blood rushed too hard to my head, and I was sure I was going to pass out.

With shaking hands, I put her in her car seat and grabbed the diaper bag, rushing down the stairs to head to the ER, constantly talking and soothing her the whole time. Not that she could hear me over her cries.

When I pulled into the ER, they took my information and surprisingly had an empty room, so we got checked in immediately. They'd run a slew of tests and Audrey slept as we waited for the results.

With the lights dim, and Audrey's wheezing cough the only sound in the room, all the adrenaline rushed from my body and the tears I'd been holding back came. I couldn't remember the last time I'd cried as much as I had in the past two days.

I was tired—drained and exhausted—and I didn't want to do this alone.

It was three in the morning, and I knew he might not pick up, but I had to try.

"Hello?"

Ian's sleep roughened voice only made the tears come harder.

"Carina? Baby, what's wrong?"

"Ian." I barely got his name out.

"Please talk to me. Please. Where are you?"

I could hear the panic in his voice, and I took a deep breath, trying to calm down.

"Audrey's cough was really bad, and she woke up with a fever. I tried to get it down, but it just got higher. And she was so upset."

"Carina, where are you?"

"Cincinnati Children's Hospital. They're waiting for test results. I just...I need you."

"I'm on my way. Hang in there, baby. I'll be there as fast as I can."

"Okay. Thank you, Ian."

Just knowing he was on his way calmed me more than I thought possible. And when he finally made it, walking through the door, I didn't hesitate to throw myself in his arms, feeling like I could breathe for the first time.

"Thank you. Thank you," I whispered over and over again.

He leaned back and cradled my face in his palms, wiping tears away from my cheeks. "I'm here now. Okay. We've got this. You're not alone."

I couldn't get words past the lump in my throat, so I settled on nodding. He walked over to where Audrey slept in her little baby bed, just staring, so he didn't wake her up.

"Is she okay?"

"Yeah. We're just waiting for the doctor to come in and tell us what's wrong."

He pulled me into his arms again and held me up when I was sure I'd crumble.

"Ian," I mumbled into his chest. "I thought I could do this alone, but I can't. I need you with me to do this. I have no idea what I'm doing, and I'm not strong enough to do it without you."

"What are you talking about?" he asked above me, stroking my hair. "You're Carina freaking Russo, ruler of them all. You don't need me. I'm just here to look pretty."

Somehow, I managed a choked laugh and held on tighter, finding strength in his arms. "Thank you, Ian. You always make me laugh."

"I'll remind you of that the next time you roll your eyes at my jokes." He tugged my hair until I was looking up into his silver eyes. "I wouldn't be anywhere else."

He pressed a soft kiss to the crown of my head and shifted us to sit in the two chairs against the wall. We didn't say anything while we waited. Just sat there, holding hands, being each other's lifelines.

When the doctor came back in, he let us know she had Respiratory Syncytial Virus. He said her oxygen levels were low and she was dehydrated. A nurse came in to give her an IV of fluid, which took seven tries. I held her hand in mine and Ian held me, both of us being strong for our little girl.

By the time we had everything hooked up and monitoring her, the sun was coming up.

"Why don't you get some sleep," Ian suggested, rubbing my back.

"No. I want to be awake if she needs me."

"You'll be right here the whole time. Just rest your eyes. I'll take care of you both for now."

Tears glossed my eyes again and I managed a jerky nod, before leaning in to press a gentle kiss to his cheek. "Thank you."

"I wouldn't be anywhere else but with you."

29 IAN

By the time we walk into our apartment two days later, I could have collapsed in gratitude, falling to my floor and promising to never leave it again. Staying in hospitals was the worst. Staying in a hospital because the center of your world is sick, is epically horrible.

"Oh, thank God," Carina sighed, setting the car seat down by the couch and collapsing back.

I'd tried to get her to leave to shower and sleep in a real bed, but she refused to leave Audrey's side. It was the longest two days of my life watching her hooked up to machines. But in the end, it was worth it because now we were back home. Audrey had a little cough and some congestion but was eating and overall a much happier baby.

It was good to see both my girls smiling again.

"I'm going to feed her and then put her to sleep."

"Sounds good. I'll order some dinner. Burgers?"

"Ew. No. That Italian place on the corner would be great."

Huffing a laugh, I pulled out the menu and ordered. Who knew I'd find such pleasure in Carina correcting my choices.

When the food was ordered, I walked back to the living room, finding Audrey latched on like she hadn't ever eaten a day in her life.

"I don't think I'll ever not find that the most beautiful thing."

Carina smiled up at me and then back down to Audrey, stroking her fat baby cheek.

"I mean, don't get me wrong. I seriously miss kissing and playing with your breasts, but I guess I can share."

She rolled her eyes, and it sank into my chest, expanding my heart like she'd told me she loved me. It was her way of caring. If she really didn't care about you, she wouldn't react, but each eye roll was its own confession.

We hadn't talked about us when we were in the hospital. There were still so many unspoken decisions to be made, but for the first time since I watched her walk out my door, I felt like things were truly going to be okay. It hadn't been the time to dive into the words that needed to be said—the apologies needed to be heard. No, we'd been each other's rocks—our life rafts with each passing day in the hospital. It was like a truce had been made, but now that we were home, that truce would only last so long.

Once she'd finished feeding, I offered to change Audrey and put her to bed. Carina must have been tired because she let me without a fight. I was sure she'd stay glued to our baby's side for the next year, at least, to make sure she was okay.

When I came out of the guest room where I assumed Carina would be sleeping for a while, the bags of food were on the table, but Carina was nowhere to be found.

"Carina?"

I checked the kitchen, but it was empty. I finally found her laid out on our bed, asleep on top of the covers with her shoes still on. I could've stared at her forever, remembering the fear I had a few days ago that I'd never see her in our bed again.

Moving quietly, I slipped her shoes off and grabbed a blanket from the closet, pulling it over her. Then I climbed in beside her.

I must have dozed because it was dark by the time I woke and Carina was fully tucked into my chest, the hot puffs of her breath hitting my neck. Unable to help myself, I brushed my fingers through her hair and shifted back enough to press a kiss to her forehead.

"Ian?" she murmured, her voice thick with sleep.

"Shh. It's just me. Go ahead and sleep."

"Is Audrey awake?"

"No, she's still out."

"Did you eat?"

"Not yet, baby. I wanted to wait for you."

Her body stiffened before slowly easing back. "I'm sorry, I didn't mean to fall asleep in your bed."

Your bed.

The clarification that she didn't see this as her bed anymore popped my bubble of illusion that we could move on so easily.

She eased out of bed and finger-combed her hair, avoiding my gaze. Finally looking back over her shoulder, she gave a forced smile. "Let's go ahead and eat while we can."

"K. I'll go get it set up."

"I'm going to grab a quick shower and meet you out there."

I had the food reheated by the time she strolled out in an old T-shirt and black leggings; her face completely clean of make-up. She was stunning.

I was grabbing plates, almost dropping them, when heat pressed to my back before her arms wrapped around my waist.

"Thank you, Ian. Thank you for being there when I needed you."

I only hesitated a moment before turning in her arms, needing to see her face. "I'll always be there. Even if you don't want me to be, I will always be waiting to be what you need."

Her blue eyes shined with tears that didn't fall, her lips rolling between her teeth, but she didn't pull away.

"Carina, I'm so sorry."

She did step back then, dropping her eyes to the floor. "I know."

"No, you don't." I stepped into her personal space, lifting her chin so she could see how serious I was. "You think I'm sorry it happened, but you're wrong. I'm sorry for how much I hurt you. I'm sorry that it was all my fault for not making your concerns more important than my comfort. I'm sorry I questioned your reasoning because I should always stand by your side."

When one tear slid free, I cradled her face in my palms and wiped it away with my thumbs.

"Mostly, Carina, I'm sorry I made you feel like another person was more important than you. Because I love you. I love you more than I thought possible and I'm terrified I broke any chance of you loving me back when I didn't give you one-hundred-percent of my trust. I'm more sorry than you'll ever know."

"Ian," she breathed, her voice shaky.

"You don't have to say anything back, just please say that you won't leave."

"I won't leave."

Three simple words that had my body on the verge of floating away. "Thank you, baby."

I leaned down to kiss her, but she pulled back, and I froze.

"I'm not leaving, but we still need time to work through this. I just need that time with you by my side."

"Okay. I can do that."

"Thank you for understanding, Ian."

"Anything for you."

With a small smile, she stepped back, but I had one more thing to say.

"I talked to Hanna. I know it's too little, too late, but I did talk to her to clear the air. Being completely honest with you, I can't cut her out of my life. She means too much to me, and I mean that in the most familial way possible, but you and Audrey are my world, and for that, I can compromise. Just tell me what to do."

She swallowed hard, and I held my breath, waiting for her to tell me it wasn't enough.

"Just be honest with me and don't let her flirt with you."

My first reaction was to deny that Hanna ever flirted, but I think about it from Carina's point of view and understand. "I can do that."

"Okay. Then, let's have some dinner."

CARINA

THAT NIGHT, I decided to sleep in the guest bedroom. I'd had to force myself to stay under the covers and not tiptoe across the hallway and slip into Ian's bed, demanding he tell me he loves me again and again.

Ian Bergamo loved me.

I closed my eyes against the morning light, picturing his face when he said those three perfect words.

They'd washed over me and made me want to collapse in his arms and tell him it was all okay, but I didn't want to rush it. I didn't want to let my emotions be rash, and control my decisions, blinding me to everything else going on. So, I'd held back, giving myself a moment to think it all through, to remember the pain he'd caused and know for sure his love could outweigh any doubts.

I'd made it all of twenty minutes before my mind had screamed at me to stop being so stubborn and to get on with the makeup sex. He'd smiled at me over our dinner, making me laugh over ridiculous jokes and comments.

Somehow, despite my body's urging, I managed to crawl into my own bed. But the new day brought new plans that didn't consist of me staying in this bed alone another second.

The sunlight washed over me, taking away the doubts from last night.

Ian Bergamo loved me, and I needed him to know how much I loved him too.

Flinging the covers back, I go to grab Audrey and prepare for the day, only to find it empty except for a note.

OUT FOR A SPA DAY, *be back soon.*

LOVE, *Audrey and the best man ever*

I LAUGHED at Ian's note, wondering how he snuck in here to grab her without me knowing. Stepping from the room, I listened in the hall, trying to decide where they were.

A deep voice singing *You Are My Sunshine* came from Ian's bathroom. Each step bringing me closer to him had my heart thumping harder. It'd been eight hours since I'd seen him, and excitement flooded my body like it'd been eight months. At this rate, I'd be confessing my love as soon as my lips parted. It filled me to bursting, and I wasn't sure how to hold it anymore. I wasn't sure how I'd held it in so far.

Steam billowed out from between the crack in the door and I peeked in to find Ian cradling Audrey against his broad chest. I took my time, getting my fill of his perfect form through the foggy glass. His strong legs and perfect ass that swayed side to side as he bounced our little girl. His thick length that was impressive even when soft. His ridiculously broad chest that always tested the seams of his shirts. His smile that never failed to make me feel every good thing a woman should feel.

He was perfection, and he was mine. I just needed to reach out and take it.

"Nice song," I called, stepping fully into the bathroom.

His head jerked in my direction, and his lips stretched into a perfect smile. "Look who's here, Peanut."

Audrey snuggled further into his chest, bringing her tiny thumb to her lips.

"The doctor said steamy showers were good for her, so I figure we'd take one."

"Lucky girl," I said, stepping up to the glass, scanning his body from head to toe.

"Why, Miss Russo, I'm feeling a little objectified," he mock-gasped.

When my eyes made it back to his beautiful gray eyes, that had entranced me from the start, I couldn't hold it back anymore. "I love you."

The playful smile dropped, and he blinked a few times like I wasn't real and would vanish at any moment. "What?"

"I love you, Ian. When I thought I could never love again, you made me love you. I love you so much."

His lips twitched into a smile like his mind was catching up to his body and wasn't sure to believe me yet, but eventually, he was beaming.

Before I could react, he was opening the glass door. "Damn, woman. Get your sexy self in here and kiss me."

"Ian," I screamed when he tugged me in, clothes and all, and kissed me. He had to bend his knees so he could keep Audrey propped on his chest and devoured my lips. His tongue brushed mine, but he quickly pulled back with a growl, resting his forehead to mine.

"I love you. Fuck, I love you so much."

"I love you too."

As if Audrey could sense the moment and wanted to be part of it, she let out a little baby coo, pulling out attention to her.

"Don't worry, baby girl. I love you too." He kissed her dark head of hair before turning molten eyes to mine. "But spa day is over. Daddy is going to dry you off, rock you to the fastest sleep you've ever taken, and then I'm going to come back to Mommy and make love to her against this shower wall."

My legs rubbed together in anticipation.

"Better hurry," I whispered.

He stepped out and wrapped Audrey in a towel, slipping on a pair of pants and pointing at me before walking out. "You get naked and don't touch that pussy until I get back."

"That's not fun."

"It will be. Promise. I have plans."

"I love you."

"I'm going to make you scream that."

"Good."

"I love you too."

Audrey must have got the message because he was back by the time I was done washing up. He stepped in the shower, stroking his length, prowling toward me until I was pressed against the wall.

"Now, where were we?"

"I believe you were going to fuck me until I confessed my love. But I'm not sure you can."

A low chuckle vibrated from his chest. "Challenge accepted, Miss Russo."

A challenge he completed again and again.

EPILOGUE

CARINA

"If you guys don't mind, I'm going to go bang my fiancée in the office now."

I jerked wide eyes to Ian. "Oh, my god, Ian."

Erik and Jared just shook their heads, laughing.

"I'm not your fiancée."

Not that I didn't necessarily want to be, but we weren't there yet. Also, I wanted an epic wedding—Meghan Markle style, and between the opening of the London office and getting the new department set up for Wellington and Russo, I could barely do mediocre.

"I know," Ian agreed readily, a devious smile tilting his full lips. "But I figured I could distract you with that and get away with banging you. Also, maybe if I say it enough, it will come true."

"Jesus," Jared muttered.

"So, desk sex it is."

"Just keep it down, kids," Erik warned. "I think poor Laura has been traumatized by the sounds coming from your office."

My face flushed and I glared at Ian for constantly cornering me into office sex. It wasn't hard, but still.

"Laura?" Jared almost shouted. "I'm the one between your two offices. *I'm* the one traumatized. You're both loud."

His eyes bounced between Erik and Ian, and neither man looked bothered.

"On that note..." I said, shouldering my bag and heading to the door.

"I'll be taking a long lunch break," Ian explained behind me.

When I stepped out of the office, I came to a halt, finding Hanna standing by Ian's door. She briefly met my eyes and then looked down at her hands clasped so tightly her knuckles were turning white.

"Oh, umm," Ian stuttered behind me. "Can this wait, Hanna?"

Her eyes flicked to mine, and I did nothing to hide my anger. "I was actually hoping to talk to Carina."

"That's uh...up to Carina."

I could feel Ian's discomfort from behind me, but I also felt his support. If I wanted Hanna gone, he would make it happen. I loved him all the more for it, but the tension had lasted long enough in the silence.

"We can talk."

"You can use my office. I have to run some things by Jared."

Hanna nodded and swallowed. We stepped into the office, and I closed the door. She looked at me as if I was a tiger waiting to pounce, and maybe I was. I wasn't going to lie; I was hesitant to assume what this conversation would be about. I'd thought I understood Hanna, but she'd proven me wrong at every turn, so I stood with my arms crossed, not giving an ounce of what I was thinking away.

"I'm so sorry," she said softly. When I didn't answer, she lifted remorseful eyes to mine, and still, I didn't yield. "I know Ian told you what happened to me, and I foolishly convinced myself that the comfort I felt for Ian was love. Not that I'm trying to make excuses because none of it matters. All that matters is that I was wrong—so fucking wrong—and that I'm sorry."

I softened my stance, dropping my arms to my sides, but still stood frozen. After a deep, shaky breath, she continued.

"Ian is my family, but you're his. I know I don't have a right to ask, but I was hoping you could eventually forgive me so we could at least be cordial."

If I knew one thing, it was that comfort made us do crazy things. Like stay engaged to your best friend and suggest a threesome to make it work. We all make mistakes, and looking at Hanna trying to be bold enough to apologize for hers had me deciding I could be woman enough to forgive her.

"What you did was shitty."

"I know," she said, holding her chin high even if it did tremble a bit.

"It was wrong."

"I know."

I took a step forward and pointed a finger in warning. "And if you ever pull shit like that again, I will rain hell down on you."

"That's fair."

Stepping back, I relaxed but still gave a hard stare. "So, don't fuck it up and keep your hands to yourself and I think we'll be okay."

For the first time, her shoulders relaxed. "Thank you, Carina."

"We're not friends," I clarified. "At least not right now."

"It's more than I deserve."

"It is."

We stood a moment longer taking each other in before Hanna broke the silence.

"Okay. I just wanted to apologize. I'll leave you to it." She stepped around me, but I stopped her just as her hand turned the handle.

"Hanna." She turned over her shoulder. "The financial spreadsheet you created was amazing. I hope you don't mind if I use it for the boys at Wellington and Russo."

One side of her mouth ticked up. "Thank you. And go ahead. Just make sure they know a woman schooled them on how to do it best."

"Of course."

We all made mistakes, and I wasn't sure Hanna and I would ever be close. But we had an understanding and us women needed to at least have each other's backs in the office. I just hoped one day I could trust her enough to have my back outside of it too because strong lady friendships were where it was at.

As soon as Hanna left, Ian stepped in, eyes wide. "Everything okay?"

"It will be," I said, stepping into his arms.

"Good." He pressed a kiss to the crown of my head. "Now, about that office sex. What are you thinking? Bent over the desk or on top with your legs around my waist?"

I leaned back, and we both spoke at the same time.

"Bent over," he said.

"On top."

Doing what I always do with Ian, I shook my head and rolled my eyes.

"Go lock the door, Bergamo."

"Yes, ma'am."

HANNA

Six months later

"THAT WAS FANTASTIC, CARINA," Daniel said beside me.

I loved the sound of his voice. Every time he spoke over dinner, I had to remind myself not to get lost in the deep timbre of his voice or force myself not to stare at the way his lips moved over the words.

"Thank you," Carina answered.

"Hey, I helped," Ian protested.

"Ian, made the salad."

"Good job, man. We're all so proud of your cooking achievements," Erik said, earning a finger from Ian.

Ian and Carina had invited everyone over for dinner like they did a couple times a month. Carina loved to cook for everyone, and Ian loved to make Carina happy.

Taking in the happy couple holding hands on the tabletop, it was crazy to think how far we'd come in the past six months. Carina and I had bonded over our mutual goal to dominate the mostly male office, and that had slowly shifted to lunches and eventually a kind of friendship.

I envied her boldness and confidence. It reminded me so much of Sophie that it both drew me in and hurt my heart all at once.

One night I'd drank more than my share of wine and admitted how similar she was to my twin. Somehow, I ended up sharing stories of Sophie and I growing up and part of what we endured when we were taken. Carina had cried with me and fed me ice cream when the worst of it was over.

I'd confided how desperate I was to move on and become a sexual woman outside of my trauma but hadn't found a way yet. She'd held my hand and understood the best she could without false platitudes, and it had been everything I needed.

"When are you going to ask this girl to marry you?" Erik asked Ian.

"When are you going to ask Alex to marry you?"

Alex rolled her eyes, having heard this same back and forth before. We all knew they were waiting for Alex to graduate. I still cringed a little when I thought of the age difference between her and my brother.

Unconsciously, my eyes shot to Daniel. Then again, maybe a large age gap wasn't such a big deal. Daniel was an older man. Not that he looked much older than my brother.

He had fine lines around his blue eyes and full mouth, proving he enjoyed life and laughed a lot. It was alluring. That kind of positivity and vibrance pulled me in through dinner. And when he happened to turn and catch me staring at him, giving me a wicked smile, my whole body burned.

"I'll get the dishes, baby," Ian crooned, pointedly looking at Daniel and Erik to help him.

They grumbled but obliged.

Carina caught me watching Daniel's retreating back—his butt to be more specific. It was perfectly plump and firm under his black jeans.

"You know, Hanna," she said with a slow smile. "You should come to Voyeur one night. It may be a good way to get your toes in the water without any pressure."

Voyeur—the sex club Daniel owned. It wasn't actually a sex club, but more a place to watch people perform sexual acts. I could even do it from a private room from what she explained.

My eyes bulged at her suggestion; at the same time, my heart thundered with excitement. "Oh, umm..."

"I want to go to Voyeur," Alexandra said, perking up.

"We can make it a girls trip," Carina suggested.

"Oh...don't you need a membership?"

"I'll talk to Daniel about it."

"Talk to Daniel about what?" the man himself asked, strolling into the dining room.

"Can you get Hanna a night pass for Voyeur?"

265

All bodily functions stalled. My heart stopped beating, my lungs stopped inflating, and my neurons stopped firing.

At least, until Daniel's eyes slowly shifted to mine. Then it all rushed back into action, going into overdrive. Blood filled with adrenaline flooded my body until I was sure I'd pass out. His light blue eyes darkened as they took me in. I may have even whimpered when he licked his lips, thinking his response through.

Fuck me. Was this what real desire felt like?

It was consuming and life-altering. It made what I felt for Ian a joke in comparison.

"What?" Erik almost shouted from right behind Daniel. "Abso-fucking-lutely not."

"Stop being a prude, Erik," Alex reprimanded.

Daniel delivered a devastating wink before possibly opening the key to my future. "I'll see what we can do, but it shouldn't be a problem. Don't worry, Erik. I'll make sure she's safe with me."

But melting under his heated stare, I wanted to be anything but safe when I was with him.

Don't miss a thing and add Teacher, Daniel and Hanna's story, to your Goodreads TBR. Coming in 2020.

Dying to know more about Carina and her ex-fiancé and where she met Ian for the first time, grab your copy of LOVERS. This threesome is sure to have you holding your breath until the very end.

See where the Voyeur series all began in the forbidden, student-teacher romance, VOYEUR.

If you're looking for a little more angst in your books you can check out my new adult, second chance romance, SHAME. Find out how Anna and Kevin discover each other and learn to understand their unique sexuality.

Don't miss out on any of my upcoming books, giveaways, and important news by signing up for my newsletter... Fiona Cole Newsletter.

You can also join my Facebook reader group, Fiona Cole's Lovers, for exclusive sneak peeks and teasers.

ACKNOWLEDGMENTS

My family: I don't know what I would do without my husband. He loves and supports any crazy idea I may have and pushes me when I'm ready to give up and say never mind. I love you. Thank you for being there for the girls while I'm chasing this crazy dream. And thank you to my girls who are always more than understanding when I'm on my computer again. Madi: maybe you be stronger than I ever was. Emma: try not to kill anyone. I love you both more than anything ever.

Karla. Dream Team, baby. I could write a novel for how grateful I am for having you in my life. But why would I do that when I can send you at least seven voice messages every morning? Haha! You make my books better. You make ME a better person. Thank you for listening to me always.

Serena. Jeez ... where do I start? Thank you for always talking me up. Thank you for reminding me of all the things I'm forgetting. Thank you for being bossy and wonderful and for being the best damn PA a girl could ask for. Thank you for being my friend.

Najla Qamber. The best damn cover designer there ever was. This was the hardest one yet, but you of course came through and found me the best of the best. I couldn't imagine ever working with anyone else. Thank you for all your talent.

Linda. Thank you for holding my hand and petting my hair when I'm on the verge of crawling in a hole. I couldn't do this without you or your enthusiasm. I appreciate everything you do and can't wait to drink wine together some day.

Kelly. I can't thank you enough for word vomiting all the information there ever was about audiobooks. It sparked a friendship I can't imagine not having in my life. You're so funny and smart and talented beyond belief. Thank you for your wonderful editing and proofreading. I can't wait to finally meet you.

Michelle. Thank you for always being able to beta read. You're comments are invaluable and boost my confidence sky high. Thank you for helping me with my cover and talking books. You may not realize the power of your words, but you inspire me to find the spark of joy in my story every time. Thank you for that and so much more.

Julie. Thank you for always giving me that hard feedback. My books are a million times better because of it. Even if I'm plotting your death in the moment. Haha. Thank you for your friendship and always being there when I need to talk it through.

Kandi. Thank you for always being there when I have a million questions. You're one of the smartest women I know and I'm beyond grateful to call you a friend. Let's plan to hit the dance floor again some day.

All the amazing authors. I have more strong women in my corner than I can count and I'm grateful for every one. Thank you for inspiring me and supporting me. Your talents and amazing words push me to be a better writer and your fabulous stories calm me when I need a minute to sit back and relax.

Review team. You ladies are wonderful, fun, kind, and beyond supportive. Thank you for every share, every review, and everything in between.

Lovers. You guys are my safe place. You guys give me the best book recommendations and make me laugh. You're more than I could ever ask for. I can't tell you how many times I've scrolled through your comments and have been brought to tears. Thank you for being such an awesome group.

Bloggers. To every single one from personal pages to the bookstagrammers. You all work so hard and take beautiful pictures and write such amazingly kind words in reviews. I don't have enough words to let you know how much you all mean to me. I couldn't do this without you.

Readers. You guys rock my socks off. Thank you for taking a chance on my words. Thank you for taking the time to read something I've created. You're the best.

ABOUT THE AUTHOR

Fiona Cole is a military wife and a stay at home mom with degrees in biology and chemistry. As much as she loved science, she decided to postpone her career to stay at home with her two little girls, and immersed herself in the world of books until finally deciding to write her own.

Fiona loves hearing from her readers, so be sure to follow her on social media.

Email: authorfionacole@gmail.com
Newsletter: http://eepurl.com/bEvHtL
Reader Group: Fiona Cole's Lovers
https://www.facebook.com/groups/254919681647995/

www.authorfionacole.com